THE SOLDIERS OF PRESQUE ISLE

To Frank,
Thank you for your service to the country!

Your Friend,
Chris Chagnon

BOOK THREE OF

THE CHANDLERVILLE CHRONICLES

CHRISTOPHER CHAGNON

ISBN 978-1537530765

Cover design by Kim Barton
www.tymecaptured.com

Book design and production by Christopher Chagnon
www.christopherchagnon.com

Published by:
Cool Shots Inc.
5641 County Road 489
Onaway, MI 49765

Editing by Paige Trisko and Rob Nuhn

THE CHANDLERVILLE CHRONICLES TRILOGY

DEDICATION

This book is dedicated to the brave men of the 3rd Battalion, 8th Infantry, 4th Infantry Division, and the 221st Signal Company (Pictorial), who served in Vietnam, and fought the Battle of Hill 724, November 11, 1967.

My friends, Charlie Chapman, John Veihl and Dean Wilderspin who gave their lives during the Vietnam War. All of us who knew you have never been the same since you were taken.

PFC Charles Dane Chapman
25th Infantry Div., 2nd Battalion, 27 Inf.
Killed In Action: October 31, 1967-Binh Duong Prov., S. Vietnam

PFC Woodrow John Veihl
1st Infantry Div., 1st Battalion, 18th Inf.
Killed In Action: May 19, 1968-Gia Dihn Prov., S. Vietnam

LCpl Dean Allyn Wilderspin
1st Marine Div., 1st Battalion, 7th Marines
Killed In Action: January 6, 1970-Quang Nam Prov., S. Vietnam

ACKNOWLEDGMENTS

The preparation and research for this novel has taken over a year to complete. During that time I had lengthy conversations with many Vietnam veterans who graciously gave me their time so I could complete the work. Over that period I was lucky to find Lieutenant Paul Berkowitz, of the 221st Signal Company (Pictorial), who served in Vietnam from 1968 to 1970. Paul was instrumental by introducing me to Sergeant Mike Breshears, combat photographer with the 221st Signal Company (Pictorial) who photographed the battle of Hill 724, November 11, 1967. Mike was gravely wounded during the battle. Throughout the many long hours of our chats he shared his experience of the days leading up to, and the day when the fight took place. He has been a blessing to me. He put me in contact with Lieutenant Levie Isaacks, and Sergeant Bob Walkowiak, of B Company, 3rd of the 8th Infantry, who fought courageously that day. These three men are true, decorated heroes. The events of the days preceding and including the historical fight for Hill 724 are depicted in this work as told by them.

I wish to thank all of those who served in Vietnam, especially Gary "Spark" Palen, Tom

Peacock, Mickey Chapman, Frank McFadden, Terry Fitzpatrick, John Herring and Bob Schell for sharing their Vietnam experiences with me.

Finally, I thank Mike "Fitz" Fitzpatrick, my life long friend and Vietnam War hero. May 31, 1967, with only three days left to serve in Vietnam, he was tragically wounded. During a firefight a Viet Cong sniper shot him in the face. He nearly died from his wounds, and to this day is paying the price for choosing to stay with his unit so he could be with them during his last few days in country. Along with Mike Breshears, he has been my mentor and content advisor on this project.

CHAPTER ONE

A mid-morning sun quelled behind a string of low, fast moving clouds casting soft shadows on the corn and sorghum fields near the city limits of Brookings, South Dakota. The pastoral scene reminded me of a painting by Albert Bierstadt. From my hospital bed I had a good view of the countryside where I had hunted pheasants and grey partridges over the many years of my exile.

"The doctors said I will be dead before winter comes, but I feel lucky, I should have died years earlier."

"There must be something they can do? Maybe you should go to a more suitable hospital, see a team of specialists?" The fifty-one year old priest, Father Rohn, said. Father Rohn sat at my bedside. "Are you sure you want to proceed? I hope you do."

I wanted to tell my story for a long time, but I wasn't able to, the time was never right in my mind. "Most all of those who have known me know only part of me. What, with all I've had to hide over the years. I'm running out of time, now." I felt enervated and thirsty. "Would you hand me that?" I pointed to a Styrofoam cup filled with ice chips. I slurped the scant water through a straw from the base of the ice. "I'm not supposed to have too much water, the old pump doesn't want to get rid of it. At least I don't have to get up to take a piss." I lifted the catheter hose which trailed upward under the bed sheet and into my pecker. I tugged the oxygen line leading to my nostrils. "See? I've got hoses going in and out of me, like trains in a rail yard. They think of everything."

He laughed, but his round smile turned serious. "Have you called me here today to ask for last rights, to give your confession?"

I studied the priest, his broad shoulders formed into an athletic shape beginning at his narrow waist. He was ruggedly handsome and muscular, unlike any priest I'd ever seen. He had a full head of hair that had remained blonde, despite being in his mid-life years. I'm sure the women of his parish found it difficult to concentrate on his sermons when he preached.

"You might say that. You should know that I haven't been a religious man, but I watched a lot of men pray at their last breath. I haven't been to church for decades. I quit going to funerals because I attended too many. They're all the same, a dead person, and a congregation of folks wishing they had been more attentive to the deceased. Hell, all I can remember is, bless me Father for I have sinned, damned plenty!" I gave the priest an apologetic wink. "I'm sure my language will become spicier as we go, so hang on." He dismissed my swearing with another laugh.

"I must admit, I'm quite puzzled that you have called me here when there's a Chaplin in the hospital, and plenty of churches closer than mine over in Madison," the father said.

My lungs were feeling tight and full, I was wheezing badly. I coughed into a tissue to expel the citrine phlegm specked with blood. "There is good reason why I called you here, Father. If I can get through it, you will see why."

He crossed his legs to get ready for the long story I was about to tell. I asked him not to ask anything of me until I was finished. He said he would do his best to accommodate a dying man.

So I began.

"My name is, C. J. Wild. I was Yank Main, the soldier, and before that I was Christophe Cosette, a young boy from northern Michigan."

"C.J. Wild, the outdoor writer and photographer?" he asked, surprised.

"Yes, that's me. Christophe Cosette lived a normal life he cherished for seventeen years, until August, the summer of 1967. That's when Richard 'Yank' Main, the soldier, replaced him. Yank Main took lives, because that was what he had to do as a soldier."

In order for him to completely understand my life, and why it would be important to him, I had to tell him my story beginning that fateful summer of 1967.

****
June 1967

My father owned the Cosette Funeral Home in Chandlerville. The small town relied on farming and logging for a living at the far west end of Presque Isle County within the farmlands and forests of northern Michigan. Any main road would lead past farmlands into heavy growth wilderness. Mullet, Burt, and Black Lakes, three of Michigan's largest inland lakes, were less than a twenty-minute drive out of town. Black Lake was five miles north of Chandlerville, at the end of Highway M-211.

Harley Rossium, the Q-tip headed barber, was relaxed in his barber's chair reading the obituaries on page three of *The Chandlerville News* when I stopped in to drop off some unclaimed plants from the last funeral. Often, the funeral flowers were buried with the deceased, but the plants had value and were doled out on a first come, first serve basis. He and his wife of fifty-five years, Harriet, had a standing order for any remaining plants.

"Don't see our names there, yet, Harriet," he said. Harriet was sweeping the scattered mounds of customers' hair into a dustpan near his chair. "Tell your dad he'll have to wait for us a while longer," she said. I laughed and said I would pass it on to him.

A warm spring breeze made Harriet's pansies dance in their clay flowerpots outside the barbershop. A tired electric motor hummed above them turning the red, white, and blue helical stripes of Rossium's barber pole as it had done for the past fifty years. "We made it through another winter, Harriet."

"Amen," Harriet replied.

"Ay, Chris.   My offer still stands to cut your hair for free, son," Harley said. He made this offer many times that year.

I placed the plants near his doorway, and streaked my fingers through my shoulder length hair. "Nah, I'm okay. I'll wait until I meet Delilah." I don't think they knew the fable about Delilah convincing Samson to cut his hair, which made him lose his strength.

The spring of 1967 had begun in Chandlerville. The town's remaining old folks, like Harley and Harriet, were relieved knowing they survived another winter, delighted they could fuss around in their gardens again, and continue on with their spitzer and euchre card games. During its four-month stay winter had taken the twenty-five lives it wanted. They succumbed to the damnedest illnesses and accidents. In a small town no one is a stranger, and my family knew everyone. The holding vaults at the local cemeteries were over-loaded with caskets waiting until the ground thawed so the dead could be buried. Now it was time.

February saw nine deaths in one week alone. I'll never forget because I went with Al LeBlanc, the retired 3rd Mate from the *SS Munson* who worked for the Cosette Funeral Home, to pick up the deceased. Felix Finke should have made it twenty-six. Don Keating, the mailman, found him by his mailbox half-buried in snow, blue skinned, and not breathing. He was brought to my father, Romeo Cosette, at the Cosette Funeral Home. Before my old man could slice his carotid artery to begin embalming, Finke let out a gasp. Old Man said that was the first time anyone had objected to his work. It probably would have been best for old Felix if he went with the dead. He was nothing but a mean old bastard after that, and never forgave the coroner, or the mailman for their assumptions.

Verdie, Denis, and me, called our father Old Man for disrespectful reasons. He was mean when he was drinking. It wasn't because we didn't love him, because we did. It was because he was drunk most of the time, and got belligerent. Maybe we loved him too much; we tolerated him, wishing and hoping he would return to the kind father he once was. I think he just spent too much time around dead people, and found solace in the bottles of beer he drank. Claire, my three-year-old sister, wasn't old enough to really comprehend what he was like. Mom held us together by her unfaltering faith, and daily attendance at St. Paul's mass.

Northern Michigan winters were brutal to live through. The snow often gathered in chest high drifts, and there could be weeks of below zero temperatures. But summer had arrived and the town's spirit was renewed, however, it wasn't going to be another normal summer for me, it would end with my life turned upside down.

The war in Vietnam was taking what it wanted in 1967, too. The draft was going to diminish my Chandlerville friends, plucking them away like an orchard hand harvesting perfect apples from a healthy tree. Though war was never officially declared, it was there right in our faces, like the stench of a rotten egg no one can find. I was seventeen, and didn't believe it was going to get me, at least for a year. My rheumatic heart condition prevented me from playing football;

surely it would make me exempt from being drafted.

I was going to be a senior at Chandlerville High School that fall, I was the school's yearbook photographer for another year. The only reason I was excited to go back to school was to resume taking photos. Lou Maxon, a local boy, who eventually built a successful advertising agency after graduating when he left for Detroit years before me, donated a splendid Nikon F camera system to my high school's yearbook department. His agency created the slogan, 'Heinz 57 Varieties' which made him a millionaire. Desi Arnaz and Lucille Ball spent their honeymoon at Maxon's grandiose lodge on his remote 1,000 acre Black Lake retreat. Ray Beauregard, the local photographer, taught me how to use the camera and how to process black and white film.

The word 'draft' was like a swear word used by everyone. Eligible young boys said it often, as often as shit or damn, which usually followed its mention. Preachers, and parents with sons, spoke it in prayer at church, and at the dinner table, usually followed by "Amen." I wanted the ensuing summer to be like all my others, impromptu adventures with my friends and sleeping in late, but the draft began to take them away.

Bob Frytag was soon one of those plucked apples. He was a blonde, almost white-haired, three-hundred-pound farm boy who just graduated from Chandlerville High School, Class of 1967. The Fighting Cardinals football team was going to miss him come fall. He was returning from an all-night party and saw me leaning against a fire hydrant in front of the Dairy Queen as the sun was rising. I was waiting for Mrs. Hanover who would take her two sons and me to Snow Kist Tree Farms, in Cheboygan. We found summer jobs pruning Christmas trees for a buck an hour a couple days earlier. She only charged me fifty-cents a day for a ride to and from work. I was miserably disillusioned by the constant thrashing of my sharp machete that occasionally gashed my thighs and forearm. I thought it wise to quit before it permanently darkened my opinion of Christmas.

The Bug's exhaust whistled a metallic whir, the brakes ground a metal-on-metal screech when Bob downshifted coming to a stop near the curb where I was cupping my ears.

"You doin' anything important this morning?" He sounded like he was lost and needed my help. Bob's thunderous ogre-like voice emanated from some mysterious region within his prodigious innards, as though a J.R.R. Tolkien character possessed him. His pale face held a collections of red welts left by the mosquitos and black flies from the party the night before. "Wanna take a cruise out to the lake?"

I looked at my watch, then looked up and Mrs. Hanover, who was turning onto Main Street in her Chevy station wagon. The early morning June sun was rising brightly at the tops of the storefronts on Main Street, unimpeded by any clouds. It was going to be a hot, sweltering day in northern Michigan. I considered the prospect of walking the rows of Christmas trees, slinging my machete in the unbearable heat, or finding downstate girls with whom I could possibly round the bases. I gave Mrs. Hanover a "don't stop for me, I quit," wave. I told big Bob, "What the hell, we might as well."

Bob knew of my propensity to attract chicks because of my reputation of being good at it. He said he had a "ton a' fun" at Shoepac Lake the night before with the rest of the senior class. But not before they partook in the annual ritual of painting the enormous rock shouldered on Highway M-33, outside of town. They chose a gaudy, cosmic looking yellow this year. It read, "Class of '67." He was regrettably hung-over after the alumnae's ritual of encircling a bonfire, drinking piss-warm beer and planning how they were to spend their summer. Car radios played throughout the night, draining their batteries until the cars wouldn't start. I could tell he had puked sometime between the last embers of the fire burning out, and his arrival where I stood. The odor of sappy Jack Pine bonfire smoke, and regurgitation met me when I opened the car door. I had my work cut out for me if I was going to succeed in securing a temporary summer girl for myself. It was a losing proposition for Bob.

I jumped in the Bug and we sputtered off for the Black Lake shoreline road in his rust-ragged Volkswagen.

I had great expectations for the summer of 1967, and it was beginning nicely. I was setting out on my first mission to find the girls of summer who were arriving at the lakes outside of Chandlerville. I had three splendid months to find them.

Stuffed in the front seats like two over-sized galumpkis in a Kerr canning jar, we saw two nicely put together girls strolling marvelously on the side of the road near the Chandlerville State Park entrance five miles out of town. Two mason-stoned pillars stood at the opening to the park at the end of Highway M-211. A bronze plaque mounted on a pillar was dated, 1921. I told Bob to stop. His confidence with girls was minute compared to his physical size so I told him to leave the talking to me.

The tall one said her name was Connie when she eased up close to the passenger door, unafraid, trying to control the laugh escaping across her tanned face. Her almond eyes closed slightly, flirtatiously, at the site of us sardined in the Bug. I was doing my best to fashion my bleached-blonde hair away from my eyes with my fingers so I could cast my most prodigious lustful gaze in return. It was working wonderfully.

Connie and, the other girl, Beth, said they were from Flint. Connie told us her father was a plant foreman at GM's Fisher Body plant, and her family owned a lake cottage not far from the park. I sensed an apologetic revelation from Beth when she lowered her head to say her father was of less noble accomplishment with an assembly line job at Chevy's AC plant where he made spark plugs. Or, perhaps, she was cowering because she feared I would discover she was besieged by an objectionable case of halitosis. She would have been perfect for Bob. Connie streamlined a pleasant grin when I told her my father was an undertaker, but Beth cringed.

Bob followed my instructions dutifully, thank God. The girls were Carmen-Ainsworth High School friends, and Connie felt no less of Beth for her father's position in life, and her odorous speech.

A Van Morrison song began to play on the Bug's radio, Brown-Eyed Girl. I feathered the station selector getting a clearer sound.

"Hey, turn it up," Connie said. "I love that song."

Bob increased the volume. Connie, unabashed by our presence, began a mystical dance move I wasn't familiar with, like she was in a trance. Alluring and confident, she snapped her fingers rhythmically, while her hips and arms carved through the air like a forest nymph chasing a butterfly. The downstate girls knew all the latest dances. I had designs on her right off, but I could see Beth wasn't interested in Neanderthal-looking Bob, with his welted face, and putrid countenance.

I knew I had to ditch big Bob, partly because his VW just wasn't suitable for romance, given the size of both of us. When I was confident of her interest in me, I stepped from the Bug and whispered to Connie, "You wanna' go out tomorrow?" I told her I'd bring Sean Fitzpatrick, who was without an offensive odor, was good-looking, and owned a groovy convertible. She whispered, "How about tonight? We're going to the show in town. Seven o'clock?"

Big Bob dropped me off in town, unaware of my ditching him in lieu of Sean and his convertible. I found Sean to tell him of my accomplishment. He too had graduated the day before, and attended the Shoepac party, but was in much better condition than big Bob. Of course he was delighted; we were a girl-slaying team.

Later, when daylight blended unnoticeably to evening, a small crowd assembled below the amber marquee lights at Stone's Theater, waiting for the next showing of The Graduate. There, we found the girls from Flint waiting for us. They eagerly slid into the convertible as though they had as much anticipation for what could be a 'far out' evening as us. Especially, when the case of Hamm's beer came to view in the back seat.

Connie made sure she was paired with me. We promptly peeled away for the romantic surroundings of the spiraling coniferous and whispering maple trees in the Grove at end of town, one of our favorite necking spots.

Beth was delighted I brought Sean, and his beer. I never saw the two of them for the most part of our visit to the park, while they slumped in infatuation in the front seat, with only the slushy sounds of their lips separating occasionally. Sean didn't seem to mind the offensiveness of Beth's breath that had become more acceptably masked by the Hamm's beer.

I punched a church key can opener into a couple of beers, and handed one to Connie. Damn! Let the summer begin. She drank it quickly, and asked for another before I could finish mine.

"Hell yes," I said.

Connie was wearing a short-sleeved, white cotton blouse she left unbuttoned at the top where it spread below her rounded chin. Her white, skin-tight jeans, filled to the brim with her voluptuous body didn't allow any hint of a wrinkle to form anywhere from zipper to cuff. Before our date was over, I made sure her anatomy was where it should be by inspecting every region of her womanhood. I wasn't sure which base I had reached, but I was sufficiently pleased for a first date with the summer girl from Flint.

She sighed sadly, and said it was time to return from whence we found them. We putted off casually to Main Street while the organ solo of Light My Fire blared from the dashboard speakers. The warm summer air streamed through her Sun-In hair making dreamy wisps furrowing behind her now familiar profile as we drove about town with the top down.

"Oh shit!" Connie cried.

"What's wrong?" I thought she was stung by a bee, or maybe had to pee.

"That's my dad, you better let us off here." Connie broke away from my right arm surrounding her shoulders. Her cheeks were flushed, and her lips were even a brighter crimson from the teeth and tongue treatment I had just given her down in the Grove.

"That was your dad at the Dairy Queen?" I asked.

"Yeah, I hope he didn't see us. We're supposed to be in the theater."

"You think he'll be pissed if he saw us?" I asked, feigning concern.

"He will be if he saw your hand up my shirt," she said, stuttering her laugh.

"Geezzas. Sorry?"

Sean Fitzpatrick swerved his black 1963 Plymouth Fury convertible sharply to the curb on Main Street, near the Metropole Bar, well out of view of the Dairy Queen. Connie and Beth prepared to get out. The bar door opened, my father, Old Man, stepped into the early evening that was much brighter than the smoky darkness of the bar. Squinting in my direction, he saw me giving Connie the 'I want to bang you' parting kiss before she exited the convertible. He saw right off what I had been up to. Connie's white clothing bore witness to where my soiled hands had been. My handprints were prominently displayed like a well-worn path on the fabric over her breasts and crotch.

"Oh boy," Sean said.

Old Man paused, shook his head, and slurred, "Up to your same ole' bullshit, ay? Chasing girls, and livin' the dream with yer dick stuck in sand for the summer." He wobbled off toward his brand new, blue Lincoln Continental parked across the street.

Sean, reduced himself behind the steering wheel, and squeaked a demurring laugh. I lowered my head in embarrassment while Connie's face paled with surprise. She and Beth scooted away toward the Dairy Queen.

"Maybe I'll see you tomorrow?" I said, like a kid asking for forgiveness in a convertible confessional.

"Maybe? I've got some explaining to do to my dad." I watched her walk off, and she seemed to have gotten over the unpleasant introduction of my father as quickly as it happened.

Sean and I drove away in the opposite direction to the turn-around at the end of Main

Street. The streetlights flickered and brightened in a harsh, jaundiced luminance. We drove back to the Dairy Queen for a last look at the summer girls.   They were standing opened palmed addressing a greying fellow who pointed emphatically to Connie's soiled clothing. A double dipped ice-cream cone dripped a vanilla slurry atop his hand.

"Let's get the hell outta' here, Sean." Sean stomped the gas pedal. We sped into the cooling summer night in search of a party that certainly was planned by someone, somewhere in the outer reaches of town.

Indeed, the summer of 1967 was beginning nicely. So I believed for a brief time.

CHAPTER TWO

Old Man began believing I wouldn't amount to much when he found out I got Hana Haupt pregnant. It was three years earlier when it happened, I was fourteen-years-old and she was sixteen. Old Man's mind was like a scrapbook containing bad memories of me, past and present. This wasn't the first time Old Man preached I would be nothing more than a beach bum with my willy stuck in the sand for the rest of my life. I guess he felt I was on a quest to gather a harem of girlfriends again like I did the past two summers. Was I going to end up in the same predicament like I did with Hana Haupt? Maybe illegitimately fathering a slew of kids whose mothers came from an array of different zip codes? He thought so.

That's probably why he was a prick to me in Connie's presence. He expected more out of me than I was willing to provide. He, the thousand residents of Chandlerville, and the entire county of Presque Isle knew about Hana and me. But who really gives a shit, other than Hana, her family and me? So I thought. I pretended it didn't happen, but I was only fooling myself. Hana was now a member of a dangerous cult that had been around the county for ages, the Bundschuh, led by her grandfather, Fuhrer, Siegfried Haupt. She and the violent members weren't going to forget about me anytime soon. I had disgraced her family and the close-knit members who took residence in Moltke, Metz, Posen, and Calcite City. All of them were of German descent, were farmers or loggers, and their ancestry dated back to 1863 when they came from the old country to settle Presque Isle County.

I had talked to Hana only once after she had the baby. It was late fall in 1964. I was helping my brother, Denis, set up a vault for a burial in the Millersburg cemetery. Denis went into town for a couple Cokes. Hana showed up at the gravesite in her grandfather's truck to warn me that there were some who wanted to harm me, perhaps do away with me. Then she told me she still loved me. I believed her on both accounts, and told her I loved her, too. We both knew nothing could ever come of it.

It wasn't long after our meeting when a truck slowed as it passed along Main Street while I was walking home. The driver gave me a long once-over stare from his emotionless face, like he was sizing me up, remembering what I looked like. It happened several times after that, too. I went a year looking over my shoulder, paranoid at the approach of every slowing vehicle. Eventually, I was able to lower my guard after winning a few fights and I got more confident knowing I could handle myself.

I was used to Old Man's hurtful remarks by then, too. I had to turn a deaf ear to get by. Sort of like ignoring an annoying bug flying around that can't be escaped from except by ignoring it. My older brothers and me had endured this kind of verbal lashing most of our lives when Old Man was drinking. When Verdie graduated from high school two years before, and got accepted to Ferris State College's art program, he didn't have to hear it anymore. That was the saddest day of my life when he happily drove off for a summer job on a road construction crew in Ohio. Mom had given him an alarm clock for a graduation present. She said it was the most practical thing she could think of for a graduation gift. Denis got a job on an ore freighter, the *SS Robinson*, after he dropped out of school before his senior year. That was my next saddest day. He only returned occasionally to see mom. I was stranded, left to fend for myself, to endure the implacable Old Man, still at home with my younger sister, Claire. She was three-years-old and precious and gifted, gifted in a way I wished she wasn't-she showed signs of being clairvoyant.

I loved rock and roll music, and wanted to be a musician, a drummer. Claire would dance frantically when I practiced "Wipe Out" on the kitchen tabletop. I got pretty good by practicing on the dashboard of Sean's convertible too. It was the magical sixties where everything from changing our personal appearance by growing long hair, to learning a new lexeme of words like, "groovy" and "far out" and "man", words that preceded or followed every statement spoken by those who were 'hip'. So I let my brown-blond hair grow long, and bleached it with a pint of hydrogen peroxide for an extra "wow" effect.

Anyway, I made the best of my situation by avoiding the presence of Old Man by staying away from the house while he was home, and not returning until late night when I knew he was in bed sleeping. There was one problem with returning home though; I had to avoid using the stairs leading to my upstairs bedroom. The creaking treads were like a tattle-tail schoolgirl who showed no mercy when she squealed on anyone cheating in class. So I would climb the low-limbed magnolia tree near the front porch, and drop down on the roof where my bedroom window was. I always made sure the window was unlatched. Then, after his sobering night's sleep, Old Man would rise early and leave for the funeral home. I slept peacefully until the later hours of the morning, unless Claire expectantly came into my room with her stuffed critter companion who had a nametag reading 'Vincent' on its chest. The tattered Vincent was of an indeterminable species. She called the brown clump, Tuhta, because she couldn't say Vincent.

Saturday came with a mid-morning breeze bringing the sugary scent of the fully flowered Magnolia tree outside my bedroom window. Claire burst into my room with Tuhta, and her dog-eared copy of CAT IN THE HAT. She wanted me to read it to her for the umpteenth time. "You want to hear about the cat in the hat, again?" I faked a frown.

"Tuhta wants cat hat, too," she revealed.

"Okay, let me have it." Claire handed me the book. I began to read, and Claire plopped on the floor next to my bed to listen. A car's horn chirped outside my window at the edge of our lawn on Lynn Street, it was Sean in his Fury convertible. I told Claire I would have to finish her story the next morning.

"You mean after you fall into the water?" She replied, showing a hint of a child's concern.

"No, Claire, I'm not going to fall into the water. Why do you say that?" I smiled.

"Tuhta said a bad man made you fall in the water." She seemed worried now.

"Come here, little pumpkin." I picked her up and tickled her. I must have squeezed her too hard, a muffled fart squeaked out. Her eyes widened with surprise. She followed with a hearty, giggly laugh.

"See you later, Twis." She couldn't say Chris, either. I was Twis, or Twistoff if she wanted to get more emphatic. She left my room with Tuhta and her book.

I waved the thin cotton sheet covering my body to the side, and moseyed to the window in a stretching yawn. "Ay," I spoke down at Sean.

"You gonna' sleep all day? Get yer ass in gear. Let's go and wash the car." He revved the engine impatiently until I told him I'd be down as soon as I got dressed.

Sean had the day off from his summer job as a mason's tender for Clarence Ashe, out at Ferguson's ranch, a sprawling complex of barns, outbuildings, and a new massive brick home they were doing the block and brick work on. Ferguson was putting in a swimming pool, too, the only one in the county. Sean's forearm muscles began to take on a Popeye appearance, development from the strain of lifting heavy cinder blocks all day. His job would last beyond the summer and longer, or until he got drafted, which ever came first. His older brother, Charlie, was drafted that spring, and was due to come home on furlough in a couple weeks. We were planning a perpetual party for him while he was home. All of us knew he was certain to go to Vietnam for a twelve-month tour.

"Where to after the carwash?" I expected a lake cruise.

"Gramps said he's been catching Brookies and Rainbows on the Rainy. I want to check it out, then we'll cruise Norwood Campgrounds, ay? I saw a cute ass blonde the other day at Fay's. She's got a cabin near the campground. I heard her mom call her, Ruth Ann." The campgrounds were a few miles to the north from where the Rainy spilled into Black Lake on its east shoreline.

Sean always carried a fishing pole in the trunk. I asked him why. He said he could feel the earth better when his bare feet were planted in river sand and gravel, and a fish pole in his hands. "That's where my brother Charlie and me belong." He and Charlie promised each other if anything ever happened to them to sprinkle their ashes in the Rainy and churn them with a canoe paddle so anytime family and friends wanted to visit them they could swim in the peaceful, placid stream, and be able to feel their presence in the bronze water. I promised I would make sure of it, too.

"We haven't been there yet. Let's boogie, do it, maybe cruise town a couple times before we go, ay?" I said. "Louie Louie" was playing on the radio. I pegged the volume, and began practicing my dashboard drums.

"Sure. You got any gas money? I got just enough to wash the car. I haven't got my check yet." I had four dollars wadded in my pants pocket after I won an arm wrestling match with Billy

Hartman, one of the few times I ever beat him. I handed three of them over. "Ay, you know Spark Fallon knows the lyrics, man, but he won't tell anyone." Sean addressed Louie Louie like he was being prevented from gaining any special wisdom he could proudly impart at a campfire beer party. The sultry song had been around for a few years, but being sheltered away in Chandlerville, knowledge from the outer world was hard to come by. Knowing the words to "Louie Louie" was an accomplishment akin to knowing a foreign language. The song's lyrics where so incomprehensible and esoteric if you knew them, you would be revered throughout the town. I didn't have the heart to tell him Spark had taught the lyrics to me a few years back for two bucks.

"Yeah, I heard that." I secretly felt he'd be required to run some sort of gambit to be worthy of knowing them, or cough up some dough like I did.

"Stingy bastard. I hear the words really turn on the chicks." He tried to turn the radio louder.

When the Fury was clean, we gassed up and drove through town.

There was a mundane ritual of driving back and forth through Chandlerville between the old courthouse at Washington Street, where Main Street made a lazy angle to the south, and Glazier Road at the far east end of town. If anything of importance was happening we could surely find out by cruising endlessly back and forth, checking in with the other cruisers. It was too early to discover anyone or anything interesting, so we made our way to Rainy River Bridge with the top down on the Fury.

A handful of fishermen had collected on the bridge, dangling their baits in the water ten feet below the rusted bridge rails. A few galvanized washtubs sat by their feet on the flakey concrete bridge walkway, holding freshly caught suckers and assorted pan fish. Sean drove across the bridge and parked at the side of the road. He dressed his pole with a Mepps Spinner rig, its treble hook buried inside a wisp of horsehair. "I'm goin' up the river a piece. See you in a while."

I kicked the sand and gravel near the road preparing for the ensuing boredom, "I'll be on the bridge." I wished I had brought my fishing gear.

The eleven o'clock sun danced on the river's chrome ripples when someone cast their bait making a 'splash' on the otherwise calm surface. I watched as Sean made his way along the bank for the better holes he knew laid further ahead on his grandparents, Wes and Esther Chapman's, river property a hundred yards upstream.

Watching Sean fish was a special moment, something akin to seeing a magician plying his magic in a river. Within a few strategic casts he landed a couple of stout Brookies. He slid his belt through their gills where they curled and swayed at his waist in the gentle current. Sean was so proficient with his casting he could drop a lure in an empty coffee can twenty yards away. He disappeared from my sight at a bend where four tree stump sized pilings remained from the old bridge that had been torn down in the twenties.

I slumped my waist against the bridge railing with my hands in my pocket, hoping someone I knew would come by, maybe Connie and Beth.

High above me an electric power line stretched from bank to bank. The drooping black cable held an assortment of fishing lures, and stringy gobs of dangling fish lines left from first-time fisher kids casting too high into the river only to find their lines draping over the cable. There were enough lures and bobbers hanging from the cable one could outfit a sports shop. I leaned over the railing and watched my drips of spit splat on the river's surface.

Time to inspect the other side of the railing to see if there were any new initials spray-painted on the crumbling concrete.

I climbed over and held on with my hands behind me, like I was going to dive in. A car's tires quietly thrummed to stop on the bridge. A car door opened, a familiar voice I detested spoke, "Ay, asshole, remember me?" It was Homer Pace, my nemesis. He was home on leave from the Marines, and gung-ho looking as hell. My heart sank. The last time I had any contact with him was at a high school dance a few years back when he picked a fight with me, and promised he was going to kick my ass, sooner or later.

'Later' was here. I turned against the rails to face him, "Ay, how could I forget a fine specimen like you, Pace?" I growled back at him. I was grown up now, taller than he, but he was Marine chiseled, and looked formidable in his yellow tee shirt displaying a globe and anchor he had stuffed neatly inside his grey sweatpants. His hair was the length of a golf course green; shaved tightly, smoothly revealing the sun-tortured pinkness of his scalp. His expressionless face was taut as a bow's string around his narrow eyes and mouth. The Parris Island sun had ruddied his skin rather than tanning it during his eight-week boot camp, bleaching his eyebrows to an albino white. "I see you found your place in life. Looks like you're ready to kill some of those commie bastards in 'Nam, and keep us safe here at home, ay?"

Pace stiffened to attention, gave me a contemptuous look, then slowly sallied to the railing where I was holding on. His mother's car sat idling on the bridge with the driver's door open. "I see you found your place, too, ya hippie fuck. Get a haircut, Sally"

I should have leaped back over the railing when I had a chance. I knew he was going to take a cut at me, and I was severely deprived of a position of defense. The river was ten feet below me, he was arm's length away when he threw his first punch. I dodged below his roundhouse swing, and countered with a right cross of my own grazing his chin. But that was all I could do to defend myself. He threw another punch that found my cheek, and sent me falling backward into the shallow water below. The cold river water collapsed around me when I reached bottom. I inadvertently swallowed a mouthful. Lucky for me it was deep enough to cushion my fall. I sprung from the riverbed to the surface to find Pace leaning over the railing, arrogantly sniggering, letting out an indistinguishable cackle he believed was a laugh. A hearty laugh was something he could never do naturally, he was just too abominable by nature.

Pace wagged his way back to the car, and drove off. I stood waist deep in the lily pads, drenched and defeated.

"What the hell you doin' down there?" Sean asked. He was wet from his waist down. The Rainy River water was pooling at his feet.

I rubbed my reddening cheek, and admitted, "I just had a run in with Homer Pace, and he won."

"That asshole's back in town, ay? You all right?"

I looked up at the fishers standing on the bridge, who seemed to be perturbed at me for chasing the fish off, "Sorry."

Once we got in the convertible, and Sean cruised northward toward Camp Norwood, our clothes began to dry with assistance of the wind and overhead sun. We didn't talk. He knew I was stewing over Pace getting the best of me, but he let me be. I decided it best to wait it out to even the score with Pace, but I didn't know what or how I was going to do it. My thoughts brought me to Claire, and her revelation.

CHAPTER THREE

The first week of summer vacation was marvelous, except for my humiliating run in with Homer Pace. I had met Connie, and we had a brief, exciting date, but she returned to her home in Flint. I didn't know when she would return, but I was certain she wouldn't wear white clothing again should we go out.

Sean went back to work early Monday morning, I wouldn't see him until the end of the day. By then, he was worn out from toting fifty pound cinder blocks up a two-story scaffolding, and mixing muddy mortar throughout his ten hour work day. He wasn't eager to do anything after work, just sleep. The rest of my friends appeared to be in the same boat because they had jobs, too. Complete boredom set in while I waited for them to finish work so we could do something, cruise the lakes, have a beer party, anything that would help me look forward to the end of the day. But that never happened. I decided I'd beg for forgiveness at Snow Kist Tree Farms in hopes of getting my job back.

Marcel 'Buck' Charboneau, a slender, willowy forty-six year old foreman said he'd give me another chance because my heritage was French Canadian, the same as his. "Nous des Grenouilles devons coller, n'est-ce pas? ("We Frogs have to stick together, don't we?") He declared.

"C'est vrai. ("That's true.") I had learned more French in Mrs. Apking's class to go along with the fractured joual dialect Old Man taught us brothers.

The sun was absent but left a brightly backlit eastern horizon painted in streaky magenta, and stretching yellow swaths during the summer when I walked along Lynn Street toward downtown at six am. It began to rain. I took my place against the glossy, wet fire hydrant in front of the Dairy Queen to wait for Mrs. Hanover to arrive.

She came as expected with her two sons, Eric, who was fifteen years old and uncomfortably shy, and Tim, a high school dropout who should have graduated that spring. Eric's clay colored hair draped above his eyebrows in thick, oily strands gave it the appearance of not being washed for some time. His face was flushed red with emerging acne pustules he continuously addressed with his unattended fingernails. Tim was of the same indefinable hair color but had been more attentive to his personal hygiene. I noticed the strong fragrance of British Sterling cologne. He had given himself a good drenching when he left his house. He rode shotgun next to his mother. Mrs. Hanover greeted me warmly, Tim indifferently, Eric said nothing, turning his head to the backseat door window when I sat next to him. The Hanover family survived mainly on government assistance, but worked hard to better themselves. Their 1963 Chevy station wagon was in good condition.

Tim, with his head twisted slightly in my direction, said, "Think you can hang in there longer this time?" His tone was arrogant and challenging.

"I think so. Sure beats doin' nothing all day long like I have been," I replied. I wanted to tell him, "shut the fuck up," but I refrained. I needed the ride.

The spritzing rain changed to a sluicing aggregate and cooled the early morning in a damp but comfortable thickness. The windshield wipers flapped in a monotonous reoccurrence putting us in a pensively quiet mood.

Mrs. Hanover was a large woman of considerable weight. Her round and comfortably placid face seemed quite normal if you refrained from looking at her bulbous entirety. Her quick smile revealed tightly placed teeth, which were short and surprisingly pure moby in color. From time to time, she would put herself on a strict diet of legumes and other low carbohydrate grazing food. She held the steering wheel with one hand, while she attended a leafy head of lettuce with the other. I mumbled an observation, "Lettuce for breakfast?"

"This is my candy," she responded. This particular week she had decided to make iceberg lettuce her main snack choice to alleviate her cravings.

By the time we reached Snow Kist Tree Farms the rain had lessened to sprinkles. Mrs. Hanover asked Eric, "Did you bring your medicine?" Eric replied, "Yes." Other tree pruners, like us, were showing up, awaiting the canvas covered stake truck getting gassed up at a nearby filling tank sitting on stilts.

The stake truck would take us to a distant grove of Scotch pine plantings outside Wolverine, some twenty miles away.   When the filling was complete, we climbed into the back of the truck, like we were members of a chain gang being led off for a day of grueling tree pruning. Ten of us took seats on the long pine benches on either side of the cargo area.   Buck Charboneau secured the canvas flaps at the rear of the enclosure then got in the passenger seat. Henry Platt, an older man, who bore the ruddy wearing of a chronic alcoholic, took the driver's seat. We headed out to a pine plantation at the edge of I-75.

When the truck made sharp or wide turns on the road leading to the expressway, we swayed and clung to the benches so we wouldn't slide into one another.   A collection of machetes scraped against each other in the far corner of the wood-planked truck bed. The truck's exhaust filled the compartment with an offensive stench making our heads ache. Once we reached I-75, the freeway was straight as string, so we were able to unclench ourselves from the bench seat.   The Doppler sounds of cars passing us along the route came and went as we sat quietly, like prison inmates, enclosed beneath the wind stressed canvas covering. There was an uncomfortable, submarine like eeriness inside the dark enclosure. We had no way of knowing where we were to measure how long it would take to arrive at our destination.

When Henry Platt slowed the truck, the transmission and rear differential whined in a dry and tortured cry. It wasn't long after we departed I-75 when he stopped, and Buck opened the rear flaps to set us free. Each of us grabbed a razor-sharp machete. We were soldiers about to do battle with Christmas trees. We stepped into the blinding shock of daylight at the edge of the one hundred acre planting. The Scotch Pines waited for us, whispering to each other in the damp, southern breeze.

There wasn't much to it. Before we lined up at the beginning of adjacent tree rows, Buck gave each of us a brown salt tablet and a gallon jug of water, "Take the salt now so you won't get dehydrated." We began swiping our blades in long, scything thrusts to prune the new, obtrusive shoots spiking from the otherwise conically shaped Christmas trees, one at a time. Throughout the summer they would heal into a splendidly coned shape for the holiday harvest in December.

Pruning wasn't supposed to be a race, but some of the more seasoned pruners, led by Buck, made it one. Buck had been a pruner from the time he was in high school. He had one good arm, his left. Born with a birth defect, his right arm was only half as long as his other and it hinged stiffly at the elbow. Scrawny, short, and permanently bent, the arm was useless. But looking at his left side would reveal how the constant swinging of the machete over the summers had formed it into a grand, almost grotesquely muscled shoulder where his arm launched into rippled straps of tricep and bicep leading to his sinewy wrist. The Hanover boys and I, along with some of the others, refrained from the contest by staying abreast with one another in our progress. By late morning, Buck and two race contestants were a full row ahead of us with him in the lead. Buck didn't mind though, as long as we did a good job, and didn't hack the trees irreparably.

Buck shouted, "Lunch." We stopped immediately to head for the stake truck. Everyone had brought one, but I had forgotten mine. I was thirsty, hungry, and tired. The constant spittle of rain and body sweat had all of us soaked to the point where we didn't know where the rain left off and the sweat began. I sat beneath the canopy of a mature oak tree, while the others ate sandwiches, apples, and candy bars. Eric Hanover saw that I was without food. He split his peanut butter sandwich, and offered half to me. I was grateful and surprised. He never said a word but just walked over, extended his arm, and gave me the half sandwich. Our eyes never met. "Thanks." I ate the half sandwich quickly while waiting for Buck to call us back to work.

We thrashed and stumbled our way through the still vibrantly green, tall grasses growing between the perfect rows of trees to where we left off at lunchtime. We found it hard to regain our rhythm with the machetes. Once it came back, the Hanover brothers and I plodded harmoniously along the tree rows.

The constant thrum of machetes racing through the air ended with the sound of blades slicing and clicking against the brighter green of new offshoots on each bow.

I felt like singing. I had heard about work crews singing to lessen their boredom. I began singing, I Dream of Jeannie, not loudly, just to myself. Someone else joined in with me, it was Eric. This was the first time I ever heard his voice. I was stunned. His clear and perfectly pitched singing rose above mine, much better than I sounded. I stopped singing, he continued. I was witnessing perfection, a voice unequaled by any I had ever heard. His pure vibrato quivered beautifully, without strain. Tim and I ceased our blades so we wouldn't foul the beauty of his voice. When he ended the song he had stopped his blade too but not from the singing. The ugly sound of Eric contorting and gagging during a convulsion frightened us. Tim rushed to Eric's side. I followed, timidly. We found Eric heaving and shaking from the effects of his Epileptic seizure. White froth oozed from his mouth, his eyes inverted and turned to a glassy white. Tim frantically searched through Eric's pockets hoping to find the medicine he had forgotten to take at noon. He found it, but he had to wait until the seizure subsided before he could give it to Eric.

Tim Hanover cradled his younger brother in his arms and spoke softly to him while the attack began to subside, much like a mother does to a sick infant. He sopped the drool from Eric's mouth with his shirttail. "There now, just rest, Eric. Everything will be just fine." Eric's face relaxed, his eye lids opened in a sleepy, dreamlike awakening. He placed a thankful hand on Tim's forearm. Tears began to trickle from the corner of his eyes. Tim's eyes were moist, too.

"I had another one, didn't I?" Eric's voice was apologetic and exhausted.

"Yes, Eric, you did." Tim placed a small, yellow pill to Eric's mouth. "Take this."

We got Eric to his feet. His legs were wobbly and unsteady. We led him back toward the stake truck just as Buck Charboneau cried out, "Quittin' time!"

Tim spoke in a humble pleading. "Please don't tell Buck, Eric will lose his job."

"Of course, I won't."

Tim lowered his head. "Thanks for helping us, Chris."

I continued to work at the tree farm into the summer, hoping something better would come along. I remembered to bring a lunch. Eric remembered to take his medicine at noon each day.

When I got home, I told mom about Eric, and his beautiful singing voice. Eric would become a star at funerals, singing "Amazing Grace", and "How Great Thou Art."

CHAPTER FOUR

Old Man brushed my bedroom door open before the sun came up on Saturday morning. The hallway light and a squeaky door hinge woke me. There had been a call during the night. Eddie Fields had fallen asleep at the wheel, and crashed his pickup into a white pine tree on M-68, east of the Ocqueoc Falls. He sent Ed Lennox and Al LeBlanc to get Fields with our Mercury station wagon. The body was waiting for us on the embalming room table.

"I need you this morning, son. Got ta' get up now." Old Man was often kind and polite in the early morning, before the beer drinking set in. I dressed quickly, washed up, and we headed for the funeral home at five am. Two hours later I was walking back home as the sun rose over the damp streets. Steam was rising where the blacktop was drying. I return to my bed but couldn't sleep.

Charlie Fitzpatrick was coming home in the early afternoon. At noon I hiked up the hill on College Street to wait for him at the Peak. That's what the Fitzpatrick's called their home at the end of College Street, where you could see most of

Chandlerville from their lawn. A 'Welcome Home' banner sagged from the loose twine holding it up between two closely growing crab apple trees on the Fitzpatrick's lawn. Red, white, and blue balloons bobbled on strings and sliver spinners hummed on the wind in the yard for the special occasion, and the 4th of July holiday coming in a week. He finished his boot camp, then advanced military training at Fort Gordon, and was now Charles Dane Fitzpatrick, Private First Class, soon to be a proud member of the Wolfhounds. He would be home for a two-week furlough before he was shipped out to Vietnam. Charlie's older brother, Young Nute, was bringing him home from the Pellston Airport. They were an hour away from the homecoming. Family and friends waited in the old house where we could rush to the lawn and surprise him when he arrived. I was trying to stay out of the way of Charlie's older sister, Cheryl, his aunts, and neighborhood moms who were bustling about preparing a fitting luncheon in the over-crowded kitchen.

Charlie's mom, Jean, who the Fitzpatrick kids called "Big Red," because she fit the description, fretted with brow perspiration while dishing out orders making sure everything would be perfect in the steamy kitchen. Jean Fitzpatrick was the high school's cook. She got the position because of her frugal measuring and experience in making large but delicious meals, a perfect requirement for the job.

The Fitzpatrick's weathered, two-story wood-sided house was rickety, old, and was always in need of repairs. The clapboard siding was separating in places, the window jams leaked cold air in the winter making the curtains dance throughout the house as though someone just rushed by. A faulty foundation allowed snow to drift inside making delicate, white dune wanderings along the kitchen's interior walls that faced west. Every fall, Nute, Sean's father, stacked bales of straw along the outer walls to keep the snow and cold from seeping into the house.

Nute Fitzpatrick fathered a passel of eleven children. He was saving his money to build a new home adjacent to the old one. Sean, and some of the older siblings were sharing part of their paychecks to help. Nute worked at the stone quarry outside of Chandlerville, mining limestone. It was a low paying arduous job, but he had managed to save half of what he needed to start the house. Ten thousand dollars separated him from his goal. He was a humble but proud man in his early fifties.

Cat and Con Fitzpatrick, the twins, were upstairs making a special sign for Charlie's homecoming. They breezed nervously into the living room in a whirl, carrying a sheet of white paper broad enough to cover the front bay window.

"This is going to be so much fun. Con and I have been making this for everyone to sign. Here, you can be the first," Cat said.

She pointed out her design details; an American flag, a few distorted fireworks colored in red and blue, and a heading of 'God Bless America' scripted on its border. There were randomly sketched red stars dotting the sheet reminding me of a kid with fresh case of chicken pox. She handed me a black crayon. "Sign it anywhere ya' want." I signed it, and put a peace symbol below on a distant corner.

"Sean said he's putting a party together tomorrow night," Con said, excitedly. She continued to dish out every thought that had collected in her mind over the past few hours. "Out near Mud Lake, or maybe Bear Den Lake. You know where the old barn basement is? It's just off '33, we've been there before. Remember? Yeah, Mom, I'll be right there. There's gonna' be so many people goin'. Jerry, and Harry, you know, the twins from Posen? Well, them, and John and Andy Foeller, and their sisters. Oh, did I tell you Cousin Mike is coming, too? He's home on leave. What a blessing to have Charlie and Mike here at the same time. He's going to train to be a Green Beret, you know. Yeah, Mom, I'll be right there!" Con sped off, leaving Cat and I holding the placard. My head was spinning trying to absorb the information Con had just unloaded.

"Give me a hand with this, okay? Let's get everyone to sign it before Charlie gets here. Then, we'll put it up in the front room window," Cat was holding a roll of tape and the crayon. We went about the room having everyone sign it. Con finished her duty of carrying two trays of cold cuts out to the backyard tables.

Con returned. "I'll help Cat, Chris. You go and help Sean in the backyard. He's putting up chairs."

When Young Nute drove up to the house everyone rushed to the front lawn. Big Red dropped the record player needle on the 45 rpm disk, and the "Star Spangled Banner" began to play. She and Nute stood by the front door waiting for their son to meet them. Charlie stepped from the car. He looked splendid, dressed in his dress green Army uniform, with a freshly sewn on stripe signifying his rank as Private First Class. He stood by the car, and removed his hat. Spreading his arms away from his body he tilted his head. "Home at last," he said. The crowd swarmed around him like he was a rock star. He made his way through friends and family to greet his parents who were waiting nervously by the house entrance. Big Red was flush with tears while Nute held back and waited for his hug and handshake.

I stayed away from the crowd, finding a shade tree to lean on. I noticed the placard Cat and Con taped on the front window was upside down. Charlie looked my way. "Thanks for coming, Chris. I'll catch up with you in a while." I nodded, and set out for my house eight blocks away, leaving him to enjoy his family, knowing I'd be able to spend time with him at the party Sean was planning. I was eager to find out what military life was all about, and how he felt knowing he'd have to go to Vietnam in a few short weeks.

I was five blocks away from home and I could still hear the Fitzpatrick's homecoming din carried by the warm southern breeze at my back. I was envious of the Fitzpatrick family, they were all together, all as one. It saddened me to know I wouldn't see all of my family together again for a long time, perhaps never again.

Before I reached our driveway on Lynn Street, a truck drove slowly by. The driver gave me the 'evil eye.' I hurried into the house. There was no one home. "They're back at it again."

CHAPTER FIVE

Sean called me later that day. I hadn't left the house. Charlie's homecoming party was carrying on in the background. He cupped the phone with his free hand to shield the firecracker pops, and laugh crescendos rising in a distinct blare behind him. "Ay, where did ya' go? You should 'a stayed longer, Mike stopped by. He and brother Chad shot a deer south of town for the beer party tomorrow night. Chad is setting up his cast iron kettle to cook it in. Remember the one he had at Rainy Lake last summer? We had two deer in it, and half of Big Red's sweet corn crop. We'll have to find another garden to hit sometime tonight or tomorrow. I'm leaving that up to you. Any ideas? You're in charge of the veggies for the stew," Sean said. He went on with the details of where and when; Bear Den Lake Road, at dark, where a spiny two-track trail wound through a stand of Jack Pines leading to a grassy field and a burned out barn foundation. "I'll pick you up."

"What time? You gonna' help with the garden chores? Ay, sweet corn isn't up yet."

"Aw shit! Just figure out who's got the best garden in town, and we'll get what we can get. I'll track you down," he said.   His words nearly indistinguishable in front of the cackles and crackles the partygoers were making.

"I might be with Eddie Fields at the funeral home most of the morning.   I better go out tonight."   I paused on the garden dilemma, considering who had a garden that will be ready to raid so early in July.

"Eddie Fields? What you doing with him?"   He caught himself, Eddie Fields? Funeral home? "Oh, what happened?"

"Ran his pickup off M-68 last night, hit a pine tree. I think he was entertaining himself, though." I laughed.

"How's that?"

Eddie Fields was a forty-something, chore-hardened farmer, with slender sapling arms, and hands the size of bread pans. He owned a small herd of milk cattle, and eighty acres of low lying ground east of Chandlerville. Lucille Fields, Eddie's wife, resembled an ugly fire hydrant, and was always barefoot. She had parted from her marriage to Eddie a decade earlier. She told anyone who would listen that Eddie just couldn't get enough sex, even if it was self-administered. How could she conjure Eddie's libido so feverishly? He really was hard up. After she left, and Eddie added a couple sheep to his fold, did her words find a footing. Eddie didn't care if he was milking his cattle or baling hay, when the urge struck, he partook. Town folks just shrugged and cringed at her tellings, wondering and worrying about the purity of his milk he was selling to the dairy in Cheboygan. Apparently, the local dairy took heed of the rumors, and shied from buying his milk.

"Al and Ed said his pants were down around his ankles when they pulled him from the wreck."

Sean laughed. "Must 'a been spankin' his monkey, ay? Couldn't wait to get back to his she-e-e-e-e-p!"

"Y-a-a-a-a!"

When our stomachs began to ache, we stopped laughing. Sean added, "I bet his favorite song is, E-w-e-e-e M-a-a-d-e-e M-e-e-e L-o-o-v-e E-w-e-e-e."

I replied, "E-w-e-e-e di-i-id-n-n-n-t h-a-a-a-v-e-e t-o-o- do-o-o-o i-i-i-t."

"Stop that! It's not right to make fun of the deceased." Mom interrupted as she passed through the kitchen with Claire in tow. I was still bent over laughing.

"See you tomorrow. Late morning?" I said. I thought about the garden again. "Any idea who has a garden that might be ready to be raided?"

Silence.

Simultaneously, we whispered a frightful name, "Peckwater?"

"Shit, not Baldy Peckwater," I said.

"Yeah, what are we thinking? But...." Sean's voice rose in interrogatory.

Baldy Peckwater was the orneriest cuss who ever put on a pair of bib overalls to groom the ground in Chandlerville. What was also true, he had the greenest of thumbs, and the most succulent garden west of Calcite City. If any garden in Chandlerville were to be pluck worthy it would be Peckwater's. He lived on Glazier Road, on the eastern outskirts of town. There was a significant problem, however. He kept a twelve-gauge shotgun loaded with rock salt on his porch, ready to be used on any crow, critter, or person considering harm to his precious garden. Then, there was his dog, Buckets. Buckets was even more wicked than Baldy.

Peckwater got Buckets from Lester Kraft who found a female coyote pup in a swamp, and raised it. Well, his neighbor's German shepherd hooked up with the coyote, and Buckets was born. He gave the half-breed pup to Baldy. Buckets had the disposition of what you'd expect from a wild animal; he was unapproachable, sometimes even to Baldy Peckwater, and he took care of the garden with the same savage vigilance as Baldy. Buckets never barked, he just chomped on his victims.

"Peckwater's garden is the only one I know that will have potatoes, carrots, onions, and maybe some corn," I shivered, "what's Mike doing tonight?" I needed reinforcement.

"Let me ask," Sean cupped the phone tighter, "Ay, Mike..." I could hear a mumbled conversation behind his hand, "Ok, he'll go, too."

"He knows the perils?" I asked.

"Ah, well..." Sean hesitated, deciding Mike didn't have to know every detail right then.

"Tell him to pick me up at home before dark. And, tell him to bring a couple gunnysacks." I knew I'd be in good hands with Mike.

Mike Fitzpatrick was toughened on the streets of Pontiac, brawling with the Latinos and Blacks hanging out on Wide Track Avenue. He learned how to hustle money with a pool cue at the Club 300. He was of medium height but burly framed. A furrowed scar stretched above his right eyebrow, left by a defeated opponent's knife. His knuckles were permanently etched with the remnants of every blow he dished out. He was of distinctive Irish descent; hair the color of beach sands, an untanned barometric facial paleness when at ease but rising to crimson when he was agitated. He had the uncanny insight of knowing when a fight was about to happen so he acted accordingly and got his licks in first.

Mike was two years older than Sean. He went to college for a year but had dropped out knowing full well he'd be drafted. When he heard the song, "The Ballad of the Green Berets," he became impassioned to become one. After his furlough he was headed to Fort Benning to see if he could make the elite grade. Vietnam was waiting for him, too. He and his cousin Charlie were two of the finest apples ever to be plucked by the draft.

CHAPTER SIX

Just as the sweet light of early evening dressed the neighborhood in glowing colors I heard the rumbling glass packs on Mike's blood-red 1963 Pontiac Bonneville rolling down Lynn Street a block from my house. A dash mounted eight-track tape player boomed, "For What It's Worth." I met him in the driveway. He was eating a brownie when he pulled up. Smiling widely, he left the car idling when he stepped from the hotrod to give me his customary bear hug, followed by the distinctive Fitzpatrick high-pitched laugh. "Ay, little brother, what's happenin'? He nodded to the Bonneville, "Far out, ay? Let me show you what's under the hood."

Mike had worked for his Aunt Verna, who owned a Pontiac dealership on Wide Track Avenue, in Pontiac. Occasionally, he would find an opportunity to cherry pick a groovy car he could soup up. The Bonneville was his latest pick before he went to boot camp. When he raised the long chrome-trimmed hood three brightly polished chrome air breathers sitting upon the tri-power carbs hissed with greed. The engine loped a menacing rattle from the high-lift solid camshaft he installed. "Comes from a totaled 65 GTO Aunt Verna salvaged. Three hundred and eighty-nine cubic inches, four-speed Muncie rock crusher tranny, 411 gears, ooh wee! She's faster 'an any stock Mustang or Charger on the street!"

"Far frickin' out, Mike!" My excitement overtook me. "Man, I'd love to drive it, dude. Maybe later?"

"Hell yeah, man. Let's go for a spin uptown. See what's happenin' before we go gardening." He bellowed another laugh. "You can drive. You know how to drive a stick, right?"

"Shit man, yeah." I was used to driving the Ford stake truck we used for burial set ups. It had a long steel rod shifter that angled toward the driver with a shift pattern that required a two-foot shift distance.

"Get in." Mike said.

I took the wheel, and backed out onto Lynn Street. I placed the Bonneville at the center of the black top pointing toward downtown, and eyed Mike who was popping the tab on a Hamm's beer. "Can I?" I asked, wanting to burn rubber, like I was a kid begging for a free sample of candy at the Dime Store.

Mike tilted his beer for a long swig, smiled a "yes." "Go for it!" he said.

I watched the tachometer rise to five thousand rpms when I toed the gas pedal. The neighborhood kids cringed on their lawns anticipating some kind of explosion. The beefed up

Bonne screamed and took off in a cloud of burnt rubber when I dumped the clutch. The posi-trac rear end fishtailed wildly to each side of the street until I let up on the gas. Wow!

"Fun, isn't it?" Mike tipped his Hamm's my way. "You want one?"

"God, yes!" I said. Mike stripped the tab and handed me a beer across the front seat. I was in hotrod and beer heaven.

I cruised through town a couple times showing off, like I owned the car. Ronnie Gilford lopped toward us near the Dairy Queen in his silver Plymouth Fury, an ex-cop car he bought at a State Police car auction. It had a 383 cubic inch high-performance Mopar motor in it, with over a hundred thousand hard driven miles on it. It was fast but he knew not to challenge the Bonne. I tried to appear tough, squinting my eyes, dangling a Winston from the corner of my mouth. I must have looked like a seventeen-year-old dorky poser.

Darkness was coming soon. I drove the Bonne up Glazier Road to show Mike the layout of Peckwater's garden while there was light enough to figure out a plan. I slowed when we reached the garden where it was laid out in a long rectangle beside the road, growing in lush green, protected by six-foot high, rusting page wire fence. Peckwater's house was within a stone's throw from the garden. The old man was poised on a weatherworn rocking chair, with Buckets pacing the broad reach of the porch. A shotgun was propped against a stone column support. There was a calculating coldness in the man's prickly face, and a restless and nervous wildness demonstrated by the cur while they eyed us suspiciously as we drove by. As though they were waiting for us.

"What the hell? Who the hell was that?" Mike asked.

Sean never told Mike what we were getting into. "Ah, that's old Baldy Peckwater, and he's as mean as his name sounds."

"Yeah, well what about that 'thing' on four legs with him?" Mike gulped the rest of his beer. "Did I see a shotgun by the pillar?"

"Okay, here's the deal." I began revealing the details of what we were facing; the mean old man, the shotgun with rock salt rounds, and the abomination of the ill-bred coyote that was better suited to be in a junkyard. Mike didn't say anything, he just listened, like he was making a plan. He was.

"Keep drivin', let me think this out a bit."

I continued rumbling down Glazier with the solid purring of the Bonne dispersing across the open fields. I turned right at the next crossroad, sipping on a fresh beer.

A bright July moon rose, throwing short, blue shadows over the cornfields and barnyards out in farm country. Not the best night cover to make our raid, but there was a splendid, warm breeze milking its way from the south, which would dash the mosquitos back to the swamps. At least, we would have a beautiful night to be mauled and shot with rock salt.

Mike finally spoke.   "Make a loop through town, and let's head back up Glazier. Did you see that pull off path before we got to the garden?"

"Near that old leaning barn?" I asked.

"Yeah, pull the car in there. But before you get to it, turn the car off, we'll coast in so they won't hear us. I think I know how we'll get this done." He didn't elaborate.

We made our return to Glazier Road. Before I got to the leaning barn I shut the engine down, and turned the headlights off. The moon provided enough light for me to see the path. The knee-high grass whispered in soft scrapings under the car. The car's springs squeaked when we passed over the undulated path. I let the car roll to a stop in the tall grass, not using the brakes that would illuminate the taillights. I took a long breath, and giggled.

"Shush," Mike said. He was trying to suppress his giggling. "Here's the plan."

Mike lowered the glove compartment door. A dim light came on revealing a flashlight, and a plate of brownies covered in cellophane. I was puzzled and worried. I could see the need of a flashlight, but brownies?

"What the hell are they going to do? Buckets would eat them, and then what?" I asked.

Now, I was worried. What kind of plan was this? I began to think of which appendage I would offer up to Buckets for him to start on.

Mike sensed my anxiety. "Don't worry. I got this down, brother. It'll be a piece 'a cake," He laughed quietly. "Brownie cake."

"Oooh-kaay," My face showed doubt with my raised eyebrows illuminated in the dim glove compartment light.

Mike fetched a couple gunnysacks from the back seat. "Let's go."

We crawled through the rolled down windows to keep the interior lights from turning on due to an open car door. We sneaked low on bent knees through the tall ditch grass to the fenced garden a hundred yards ahead of us. A car approached from the south, we lowered ourselves within the cloak of grass until it passed. Peckwater's porch light burned orange across his fenced in front lawn. He was still in his rocking chair, talking to Buckets. "What's the matter? You hear somethin'?" Buckets perked his ears, smelled the breeze with his searching nose. "I don't see nah-thing, you old cuss." Peckwater sounded irritated with the dog's nervousness. , "Shit cabbage. Le's go inside." The screen door spring ached open, and the door slapped shut after they enter the house.

"Perfect!" Mike said. "Let's find the gate and get what we came for."

We found the opening, a tube framed gate with a pressure latch nestled in a notched receiver. We crawled into the garden. It was everything I expected, bushy topped carrots with a glimpse of orange bulging from the ground, heavy leaved baseball sized russets potatoes buried inches below the loamy dirt. There were bright green stems of sweet onions in perfect rows waiting to be unearthed. Through the glancing of the flashlight the rows of corn appeared, standing tall, proud and sprouted with clumps of fodder shooting from the plump ears. We began filling the gunnysacks with fresh produce in the quiet night. Our venison slumgullion would have all the finest ingredients one could ask for, far exceeding Benny McCain's campfire creation I had the pleasure of eating three years earlier.

"This is a piece a cake," I said, in my littlest of voices. "My bag's half-full already."

"We ain't there yet, keep diggin'," Mike hesitated. "What's that? Hear that?"

"No, hear what?" I stopped my gathering to listen. The tattle-tail stretching of the screen door's spring screeched into the damp night air. Then it slammed shut, followed by the sounds of paws leaping, bounding across the lawn's short grass. The paws were headed our way, straight to the garden. The hairs on my neck rose in a spiny awakening when the paws reached the garden fence, and the small opening Baldy Peckwater had snipped through the page wire, just large enough for Buckets to pass through. I scooted across the soft dirt to get beside Mike. We began gulping air like we were being smothered.

"Don't move." Mike was frozen in anticipation for what was going to happen next. He aimed his flashlight at the sound of fur brushing against wire. There was Buckets, paws anchored in the delicate garden soil, teeth presented brightly behind the curled flesh of his frothing mouth. He didn't bark, but he hissed and snarled balefully in white, foaming slurry, inching closer to us, like he was trying to decide which intruder he was going to attack first. Mike slowly reached for the plate of brownies by his knees. He presented one to the dog with a hesitating reach of his arm. Buckets paused, twitched his nose, and inched closer to the brownie. He snatched the brownie with the swiftness of a snake's strike, and devoured it. Regaining his ill demeanor, he resumed his snarling. Mike offered another brownie. Buckets took it, less aggressively than the first one. "There we go, Buckets. Good doggie, want another?" Buckets lowered his haunches and rested his belly on the black dirt, almost obediently. Mike gave him more brownies. Buckets gobbled them quickly, and relaxed briefly, as though he found us as no threat.

"What now?" I wasn't sure what to expect next.

"Just wait a minute. You'll see." He whispered praise to Buckets, who was now sitting next to us, like an obedient house pet. The grimacing snarls had disappeared, replaced by a content glow of peacefulness. What could have come over him? "There now, my angry friend. Ain't they delicious?"

We remained huddled like children playing hide and seek. Mike handing pieces of brownies to Buckets, me stiff with fear, looking like a humped up statue in a garden.

Mike, now confident, reached to Buckets and petted his matty fur. Buckets rolled playfully at Mike's knees, anticipating the next brownie. "Okay, the brownies are workin'so let's get what we need and split."

I began digging fervently, scooping potatoes into my sack. Mike was pulling fleshy carrots from their roots, Buckets was pawing and retrieving onions like he was fetching a thrown ball. I shook my head in disbelief.

When our gunnysacks were full, we made our way to the garden gate, and slipped through, confident, relaxed, and ready to roll. Buckets followed at our heels.

We heard a "What 'ta hell?" echo over the lawn when Baldy Peckwater stomped across his cement porch. "Who's out there?" He saw us and reached for his shotgun.

"Mother of God," I screamed, "he's got his gun!"

"Run, dammit, run!" Mike yelled.

'Boom', then another 'boom' broke the evening's silence. We could hear the rock salt whizzing past us, splattering against our backs, and into the tall grass in the ditch. We sprinted toward the car, slowed by the heavy bags over our shoulders, laughing loudly at our success. Buckets lead the way. He must have known he was in for a serving of harsh treatment for failing his post, should he return to Peckwater.

Mike rushed to the driver's seat and cranked the Bonne to start. I tossed the gunnysacks on the back seat. We began to back onto the blacktop when I saw Buckets, sitting forlorn, abandoned, confused at our impending departure. "We can't just leave him, Mike. He's one of us now."

Mike sighed. "Okay, let him in."

Buckets leaped into the backseat, embracing his freedom. He let out a whimper. He wanted another brownie.

Mike lit up the Bonne, racing through all four gears, leaving rubber behind on every shift. Buckets curled up comfortably between the sacks of garden goods. Finally, we were free to laugh as loudly as we wanted, and we did. I opened two beers. "How the hell could brownies change that dog like it did. I just don't understand."

Mike smiled, a sly, deceitful smile. He knew something I didn't know. "They're magical brownies, dude. There's a dime bag of Mary Jane mixed in them."

I shook my head. "I see. Got any left?"

"Nope."

We leaned back in our seats, and nipped at our beers. The moon began to hover near a drifting cloud, and soon crawled behind it. Buckets began to snore. "What are we gonna do with him?" I nodded to my left.

"We'll see if Uncle Nute wants him. Foxes have been getting after his chickens. Maybe Buckets can keep them away."

We rolled into the night with the glass packs gurgling back at us, bouncing off the buildings in downtown Chandlerville, on our way up to the Peak. A Chambers Brothers song played on the eight-track, and we sang along to it, "Time has come today! Young hearts go their way. Time has come today."

"You don't suppose a fox knows anything about Mary Jane, do you?" Mike laughed with a mouthful of beer, spraying it on the dashboard.

Mike went into the house, and returned with Nute who brushed past the screen door, rubbing the sleep from his eyes for his inspection of Buckets below the glare of his side porch light.

Buckets' matted coat was brindle colored, like that of a summer white tailed deer. A patchwork of deep scars traced across his muzzle from battles with raccoons trying to get to Baldy's corn, and wandering stray mutts he didn't want in his neighborhood. The tips of his ears were missing, and his tail was bent at an odd angle, the result of being run over by car on Glazier Road. He was missing a couple lower teeth, and he smelled like stagnant swamp water. He'd never been petted with a loving hand, so he was reticent to anyone's approach.

"Jeezas! How the hell did you pry him away from Peckwater?"

Buckets sat quietly beside Mike and me, while Nute cautiously eyed the dog from different angles. We told Nute we found him wandering in the ditch on Glazier Road. We fibbed a bit about Peckwater shooting at him from his porch, and how we reasoned it was our duty to rescue him from harm. When we suggested Buckets could keep the foxes away from his hen house, he agreed to take the dog.

I slid over the Bonne's passenger seat so Mike could take me home. The midnight air was thick with humidity, draping the windshield and other horizontal surfaces in fine droplets below a cloud filled sky. Nute was bent on one knee, gently coaxing Buckets to come closer. I rolled my window down, "He really likes brownies."

A dull kitchen light sprinkled through the living room curtains when Mike dropped me off. Old Man must have been having his customary can of peaches and cottage cheese late night dinner. I sneaked to the Magnolia tree to climb to my bedroom window, unnoticed by anyone. An early morning trip to the funeral home was only a few hours away where Eddie Fields awaited his final preparations.

CHAPTER SEVEN

Eddie Fields' brother, Conrad, had picked out a modest casket for Eddie. Not too fancy with ornate handles or gilded interior, just the ordinary cheap variety. We dressed and tucked him inside then wheeled him to the front of the chapel on the bronze tinted bier for folks to visit him that evening. I waited in the chapel for Sean and Mike to show up in the Bonneville. They came. We drove off to Bear Den Lake Road to see if Chad needed any help preparing for the evening party.

"Anyone else there, ya' think?" I asked.

"Probably just Chad. He's getting the kettle setup. I gave him the garden goods this morning so I'm sure he's got something cooking by now," Sean said.

Chad was the second oldest Fitzpatrick brother, behind Young Nute Jr. Bright, pragmatic, eccentric, and annoyingly opinionated, he was one of the first guys I knew to protest the war in 'Nam. He went to Northern Michigan University, in the U.P., on an academic scholarship. He studied chemistry then got a job with Dow Chemical in

Midland when they were making a new chemical called Agent Orange, something the Army was using to defoliate jungles in Vietnam. He said it was nasty stuff, dangerous to work around and could kill people too. So he quit his job that spring in protest making him draft bait. He was a profound party organizer and fire pit cook.

When we drove to the old barn basement, Chad had his new 1967 Chevy pickup backed inside the basement using the tailgate for a table. He was leaning over the cast iron kettle adding vegetables to his brew. He always dressed in bib overalls even on hot summer days. Steam rolled out of the black pot clouding his glasses. He turned toward us. "Voila!" He presented the pot like we were dignitaries attending a state dinner. "Smell it, yet? Mike, you got any brownies left?" Mike told him no.

"Good stuff," Sean said. "Now, Chad. Don't get carried away with it."

"What do you mean, carried away? I've seen you make lots of trips to my pot every time I make one."

"I see those critter pelts on the tailgate. I wanna' make sure I do the same thing tonight," Sean said.

"Oh, those. Thought they'd be good addition. Come on, don't tell me you lost your taste for squirrel?" Chad turned the concoction with a canoe paddle.

"No, I like squirrel, but what about that 'coon sitting there? Yer' not gonna' add that, are ya'?" Sean said.

Chad laughed, stirred the pot, and replied, "Fresh road kill I found on 33. I was thinking about it."

"Come on, venison and squirrel should be enough. The hell with that 'coon. Slimy, greasy bastard."

"No one will notice anything different."

"I will," Sean said. He took the coon before Chad could drop it in his concoction, and tossed it on the fire below the pot. The fire hissed and flashed on the coon's fat. "There. That settles that!"

"Bastards! Now get outta' my kitchen and get some more firewood from that dead apple tree over there."

An overly used Dodge station wagon roared down Bear Den Lake Road coming right at us. It stopped short of where we were standing. It was mid-afternoon, hot and dry, making clouds of powdery sand dust plume in the air behind them. Chad shook his paddle, "You sonzabitches are gonna' ruin my stew with dust!"

The car doors opened. Terry Brown rolled out sprawling on the sand amidst a cacophony of hoots and cursing and empty beer cans clanging together. Butch McGrath and Calvin Van Camp followed as drunk as Brown. The driver, Dick Main, was too intoxicated to find the door handle. He was slumped over the steering wheel. Butch McGrath opened the door and Main fell onto the soft sand. "Get yer' ass up soldier," McGrath shouted, "yer' in the Army now, Main Dick."

McGrath called him Main Dick because he liked how it sounded, and it fit the guy well.

"Ay, I heard there's a party out here?" Van Camp asked, propping himself against the car.

Mike shook his head. "Yeah, but yer' a little early, boys, the party's tonight."

"Never too early...for...a pa...rty!" Brown attempted to rise to his feet. "We ain't got much time, ya' know?"

"How's that?" I asked. It was July, and they didn't have jobs. They were severely intoxicated so maybe there wasn't enough time for them to get sober to get drunk again.

"We all joined the Army on the 'Buddy Plan'. We was gonna' get drafted anyway, so we enlisted together so we can be in the same outfit. Whad a ya' think a' that, you sonzabitches? We're gonna' be Vietnam bound for sure!" Brown said. He searched through the beer cans near his feet. "Where's my beer?"

Dick Main reconstructed himself, wobbled unsteadily forward while he surveyed the bunch of us through his glassy eyes. He wasn't sure of his surroundings. His dull-eyed glare found me looking back at him. "Huh, you lookin' at?" His body was searching for something to prop against. "What tha' fuck you lookin' at, I said?" There was a meanness growing from his unfocused gaze.

"Nothin'. I'm not lookin' at nothin'." I was uncertain what he was thinking. I didn't trust him in his drunken state. I had learned from previous experience, you can't trust a drunk, especially one who didn't give a shit because he was shipping out to Vietnam soon.   He staggered toward me.   I stiffened, readying myself for a physical confrontation.

I had known Dick Main since I began hanging around Hartman's Standard Gas station a couple years earlier. He was a high school dropout, and his father used to beat him silly when he was younger.   But when he was mature enough to stand up to him, his father split town, leaving his mother and him to fend for themselves. The only time I ever saw him was when he was drunk. He wasn't friendly and never paid much attention to me until now.   He was my height, slender but scrappy in build.   His hair was the color of over-used dishwater, oily, and unattractive. When he got drunk he thought he was a hard ass. He took a slow, looping swing at me. I stepped aside, and he fell to the ground. Mike interceded by helping him up. I could have pummeled Main Dick, if I had wanted, but there would be no achievement in beating up a drunken soldier heading for 'Nam.

"Settle down, son.   He's not doin' anything. Besides, we're all going' to 'Nam."   Mike led him back to the station wagon.   "Have a seat. Take a load off."

"I don't like him.   He thinks he's somethin' with that long ass blond hair. Fuckin' hippy."   He slid onto the back seat, searching for the case of beer until he found it. "I bet he's not goin'."

"What's his problem? What an asshole," I said in a small voice to Sean.

"He's just drunk, but yer right, he's an asshole," Sean said. "Mike, let's head back to town. Chad, you need anything from us?"

Chad spoke out, "Not right now, just take those guys out a here when ya' go."

The Buddy Plan boys assembled at the station wagon, Butch McGrath took the wheel. They peeled away leaving a cloud of dust for Chad to bitch about while he stirred the pot. Mike was skeptical about leading the way so we followed them.

We would return at dusk when the party started.

CHAPTER EIGHT

I was finally going to spend some time with Charlie. The Bonne's horn beeped outside my bedroom window just before dusk with Charlie behind the red steering wheel. Sean was riding shotgun so I got in the back seat with Mike. I felt invincible, I had three of the toughest guys I ever knew sitting beside me like over protective big brothers. I wouldn't have to worry about anyone giving me any shit at the party because of my long hair or because I was talking to someone's girlfriend. Chandlerville hadn't embraced the new culture like the rest of the country had, there were still a slew of rednecks around town wanting to get in your face to say, "You need a haircut." Jealousy was never going to change. That's when I usually got in trouble with one or the other. I refused to take any shit from anyone.

The four of us rumbled into the party along the narrow trail amidst left over dust hanging in a dry mist from the cars that came before us. The closer we got to the old barn the better we could hear "Wild Thing" raging on car radios. I practiced my backseat drumming on the top of the bench seat. Mike and Sean and Charlie began singing along,

"Wild Thing, you make my heart sing...Wild Thing...Groovy."

"Shit, man, look at all the cars," I said when we got to the gathering. I stopped counting at twenty.

At twilight the leafy summit of trees swayed on a slight breeze before the fading sun's remains. The fire Chad had built beneath the tripod-held kettle illuminated the basement sidewalls like a glowing alter. Another fire, much larger, crackled and reached out into the night air away from the barn. There were people encircled staring at the flames near the bonfire, couples plopped on car hoods, and others just cruised from one conversation to another. Clusters of people were waiting in line by a beer keg that was nestled in a washtub filled with ice. Others, like us, brought their own beer. A half-dozen car radios were dialed in to WKNR out of Detroit, in a synchronized din. The glowing ends of cigarettes swayed to and fro, held by unseen hands in the darker areas away from the firelight.

Charlie parked the Bonne in a field, far away from any fire embers, and impromptu puking. When we made our way to the party the crowd began cheering. Mostly aimed at Charlie and Mike because they were leaving for Vietnam soon, but I felt a warm sense of significance because I was with them.

Thomas 'Nug' Nugent and his sidekick, Danny Sullivan, emerged from the fallows near the bonfire, running at full speed, each holding a half-downed bottle of Boone's Farm apple wine. The both of them were bandy-framed, barefoot, and shirtless. They ran in circles around the bonfire singing, "I'm E'nery the eighth I am, E'nery the eighth I am, I am," over and over to the point of annoyance. They were in the early stages of their destinies of a downward spiral to become town drunks. But they were happy, harmless drunks tolerated by most, for the most part. Nug and Danny went for their draft physicals that spring but both failed because they had "the shakes," caused by their abstention from alcohol for a few days prior, making them 4 F; unfit for military duty because of chronic alcoholism. They aimed their direction to the basement where the stew pot sat guarded by Chad. This was going to be trouble.

"That's far enough, you two," Chad warned. He stood stiffly between them and his stew.

"Ya' wanna' swig?" Nug offered to Chad as he slowed to a simple stagger.

"No thanks, Nug. You and Danny be careful. I don't want you falling into the fire." Chad was protective, concerned and considered himself their guardian. "You boys should have some stew, and slow down a bit."

"Don't wanna' screw up a good buzz, Chad. Later," Danny said. The boys raced off to the bonfire, pinching their noses and singing, "Winchester Cathedral, yer' bringin' me da..own."

Spark Fallon and Johnny Veihl were sitting on a grassy rise near the bonfire, just out of reach of the light and heat of the flames. I joined them. Charlie came to us with Dean Wilderdpin from Flint, who spent his summers on Black Lake running his parent's seasonal party store on Bonz Beach. He had been drafted and was now in the

Marines. They saw us and came over with fresh beers for all of us.

"You okay?" Charlie asked me. I was in that brief contentment that a few beers provide. "Heard you guys were drafted, too," he said to Fallon and Veihl.

Spark flicked his cigarette into the darkness, "Yeah, I was going to South Macomb College, but the Dean didn't put me on the 'list.' Next thing I know I gotta' report. I'll be takin' basic at Fort Leonard Wood. What a kick in the ass."

"I just got engaged to Jeannie when my draft notice came. Getting married will have to wait now," Veihl said.

"It's not that bad. Goes by pretty fast, man," Charlie said.

Johnny Veihl was a splendid nineteen-year-old athlete. He was a champion high school track star a year earlier, winning in hurdles and cross-country events. Spark Fallon, also nineteen, was another older guy I looked up too. He was a downstate kid who moved to Chandlerville a few years earlier. He learned how to box in Golden Gloves when he lived in Warren. He had taught me a few boxing moves like Booz Danker had done years earlier. Both Veihl and Fallon were fleet and quick despite their long, rangy length of arms and birdlike legs. When Fallon tried out for the high school track team the coach drooled over his ability to run for miles at full speed, never seeming to tire. He and Johnny Veihl, who was his equal, were destined to win any race they entered. But when the coach saw Spark smoking downtown he was dropped from the team. Together, Fallon and Veihl would have been an unbeatable track pair. In response, Spark stood on the sidelines at the next track meet at Maxon Field. When the starting pistol fired he took off in street clothes and boots while puffing on a cigarette. He beat every runner but Veihl, who he tied, by twenty yards in the 880-meter race. When Fallon went by the coach on his last lap he gave him the one-fingered salute.

"I'm gonna miss you guys," I said feeling beer sad.

"Hope you don't have to go, little brother. But, ay, I'm home now, and I want to get as much fun in as I can. Spend as much time with my friends as I can," Charlie said. There was a hint of seriousness in his voice.

"You scared at all, Charlie, about goin' to 'Nam, I mean?" I never knew Charlie to be afraid of anything or anyone. But the confidence that usually bursted through his smile and demeanor was missing.

He inspected the bonfire for a moment, gleaning the people roaming around all of them laughing, having a fleeting good time. "Sure I am. I wasn't before I went to boot camp, but when my drill sergeant called us to formation the last time he walked back and forth in front of us and said, 'Most of you will be coming home in a box.' That's when it really hit me. I'm heading for 'Nam to fight a war thousands of miles away." He sipped at the beer can, and lit a cigarette. "I'm a good soldier, guys. The Army said I was. I'll fight my ass off when I have to." He hung his head. "I'll have to kill people. So will you guys," he said to the others who were going to report for basic training soon.

"Charlie, yer' the best fighter I ever knew. You'll come through it, I know you will, man."

"Thanks, little brother. But if I don't, it won't be because I hid from a fight, I'll go at it like I'm supposed to." Charlie rose with his now empty beer can, "Let's go have some fun."

The five of us walked slowly back to the party. A car appeared in the field above the basement walls, its engine racing full blast, throwing sod and sand in the air, fishtailing wildly toward the deep basement. Chad was dishing out stew in bowls when he heard the car closing in on him. The old station wagon flew over the sidewalls, suspended briefly in air, and crashed on the concrete a few yards away from Chad. The engine continued racing, its headlights piercing past a cloud of dust that obscured its occupants. Everyone gasped, silenced by the violent landing, waiting and wondering if the car doors would open. Calvin Van Camp pried the driver's door open in a cry of metal-on-metal sound. Chad, paddle in hand, said, "You crazy bastards!"

"Airborne has arrived!" Van Camp hollered while holding a beer can in salute.

The party carried on until dawn.

CHAPTER NINE

While Mike and Charlie were home we had a party most every night. Mike's Bonne saw a slew of summer girls come and go, some departing with broken hearts while others marked us as conquests of their own. When Mike and Charlie's leave ended, the summer seamed to drift away rampantly. The remainder of summer was not the same with so many of my friends leaving for boot camp and Vietnam, uncertain of their futures. I wanted to go with them. Maybe we could keep the special summer alive longer if I did.

Bad news showed up in a headline and obituary of *The Cheboygan Tribune*. Le Roy Harland Charboneau, age 20, was killed in action in a place called Pleiku, Vietnam. The hearts of Cheboygan grieved at its first Vietnam casualty. The Calcite City and Chandlerville newspapers had yet to report a local soldier's death, but eventually it would. Whose name would appear first on the front page?

It was now late August, and school was starting the first week of September. The letter I got from Mike was sent from Vietnam. He said he had reported to Fort Benning, and then to Fort Bragg for Special Forces, Green Beret training. He was proud that he made the elite Green Beret unit. He was writing the letter while out on night patrol, hunkered down in the jungle beneath his rain gear. He called it 'search and destroy missions.' The rain had smeared his penciled writing. He said the Army shortened his training to twelve weeks because the 101st was getting their asses handed to them, and they needed troops immediately. He stepped off the C-41 troop transport plane in Saigon to join Charlie Company, 327th First Brigade, 101st Airborne. A day later he was choppered up country to Tuy Hoe, a hot spot Air Force base on the coast of the South China Sea. It was there where the war began for him. His first night on patrol a guy from his platoon was blown into oblivion when he removed some brush on a trail setting off a booby trap mine.

He wrote:

Chris,
This is a lot more dangerous than raiding gardens at night. I hope you don't have to come here, little brother. I'm starting to count down the days before I rotate back home. Some of my buddies here said it was too soon to do that because it was bad luck.

That was the last letter I got from Mike for a long time. Sean, however, was getting letters regularly from Charlie. One letter came with a *Stars and Stripes* newspaper clipping showing Charlie emerging from a tunnel he discovered in the jungle. The Viet Cong used hidden tunnels to wage war against the American GIs. He was with the Wolfhounds up country in a place called Cu Chi. I jotted down Charlie's address so I could write to him. I received a letter from him a couple of weeks later. It read:

August 31, 1967
Dear Chris,
I can't tell you how great I felt getting your letter. About the only joy I get is receiving letters from home. It's a mess over here. Every day we hump through the bush trying to find the enemy, but it seems we only hear them. Short blips of their AK 47 rounds streaking past us. Sometimes one of our guys will fall to his knees with a bullet through his chest after a sniper picked him off. A moment later we'll hear the sound of his rifle. By the time we reach were the sound came from there's no one there. I hate this place.

Save your money, Chris. When I get home I'm buying a car from Aunt Verna and we're heading to California. Write back when you can, buddy, and tell everyone I'm thinking of them.

Your friend, Charlie...

I read, and re-read his letter over the next few days. I found myself praying he'd come home safely so we could go to California together.

California, what would that be like? It was easy to imagine seeing Charlie and me on the beaches, hunkered down near a palm tree, chicks in bikinis everywhere, or cruising down Ventura Highway in his new car. Maybe I could convince him to get a convertible. After all, it was summer three hundred and sixty-five days a year out there, and it never rained. Henry Fraser, a former classmate of mine, moved to California with his mother and her new husband a few years earlier. He came home for his cousin's funeral back in

February. He didn't look or act like the Henry Fraser I knew. His hair was longer than mine, his tanned skin glowed in a color similar to a caramel apple. He was California cool, chrome shades perched on the bridge of his nose making him appear mysterious and secretive. It was Henry who introduced me to my first joint. We smoked it behind the funeral home during visitation. He told me he couldn't wait to get back because folks out there never got old. I believed him.

I put Charlie's letter on my nightstand. Claire came into my room showing the sadness of a child who lost something. She always had something clutched in her small hands, usually Vincent. "You don't look happy, pumpkin? What's wrong?"

She grasped her hands behind her back, her pouting lower lip displayed her frustration. "I can't find Tuhta."

I lifted her to my knee, "Let's see if we can find him. Did you go outside with him?" Tears tracked from her blue eyes and collected on her chin.

"Yes. I put him in my swing, but he left. Now I can't find him." She began sobbing. "Bad man took my Tuhta."

I dabbed the droplets from her cheeks and told her I'd find him. We left my bedroom to search for Tuhta in the backyard.

When I stepped out of the house the early evening air was silent with rain misting the grass and leaves of the maple and elm trees lining the back lawn. They stood lifeless and unremarkable, like a paint-by-numbers painting. Claire clung to my leg, hesitant and frightened to go any further.

"What's wrong, Claire?"

She brushed her scattered bangs to one side, her face revealing fear that I had never seen her show before. She spoke quietly, not to me, but to the hushed evening.

"Tahta's gone now."

She turned her paled face toward me and her voice got louder.

"Please, don't go out there! Bad man hurt Tuhta."

"You stay here...I'll look for Tuhta. I'll find him."

Claire cowered inside the darkness behind of the slightly open metal-clad door, afraid to expose her full body to the outside. I went to the swing set, but I could see across the spread of the wet lawn that Tuhta wasn't where she left him. I walked slowing, searching the bushes near our property line then over to the grill pit Denis and I built last summer out of limestone at the far end of the lawn. When I got closer to the pit I could see what used to be Tuhta lying on the grate. His arms and legs had been dismembered, shredded like corn stalk silage. His head was ripped apart leaving it unrecognizable. In the center of its chest a rusted spike was impaled through a piece of paper. I removed the spike and read the note. It was written in German, "Zeit ist heute gekommen. Zahlen Sie für Ihre Sünden." ("Time has come today to pay for your sins.")

I stuffed the paper through my pocket opening.

I knew this day was going to come. I just wasn't prepared for the realization that my family was once again involved. I didn't know what it said, but I had a good idea what it meant. I would have to visit Fritz Krupp immediately.

I went back to Claire, slowly, deliberately, trying to come up with an explanation of what happened to her companion. She couldn't see Tuhta from where she waited inside the back room, but she knew I had found him. She knew he had been destroyed. She began crying pitifully.

I took her hand and led her back inside the house. I stopped before we entered the kitchen. I could hear the dings and clangs of mom washing the pots and pans from dinner.

I knelt in front of Claire to calm her down so mom wouldn't know what had happened. "Little pumpkin, I need your help. Will you help me?"

She rubbed her forearm across her dripping nose while she snorted a delicate sniff to keep more from escaping, her sobs lessening.

"I know. You don't want mom and pa to know Tuhta died, huh?" she said.

"Yes, Claire. That would make them feel bad. Let's keep this to ourselves."

I searched for something for her to look forward to, "Ay, I bet I can find another Tuhta."

I hoped this would brighten her spirit.

"No more Tuhta, Twis. Bad men will hurt new Tuhta."

"I'll find a new Tuhta, and we can hide him so he won't be hurt."

Claire held her eyes looking directly into mine. We didn't talk for a long moment. What was she thinking? Her look changed to a stare that went through me and beyond. Her eyes narrowed when she spoke.

"Will you look for new Tuhta when you ride on steel to the land of dead, green men?"

I was helpless to answer. What did she mean, when you ride on steel to the land of dead, green men?   I told her I didn't know where I would find a new Tuhta, but I would never stop looking for him.

She took my hand, and led me through the kitchen, passed mom who was consumed by the dishes she was washing. She didn't notice us.

"I want to go to bed, Twis. Will you tell story?"

"Yes, Claire. I will read you stories."

I lifted and laid her on her small bed. I tugged the pink bed cover up to her chin, and pressed it close to her sides. Cat in the Hat was on her nightstand.

"The sun did not shine, it was too wet to play, so we sat in the house all that cold, cold wet day. I sat there with Sally. We sat here we two and we said how we wish we had something to do."

When Claire's eyes closed and her tears dried, I swept her bedroom door to the jam leaving it partially open.

I set out for Fritz Krupp's house in the grey darkness of early evening.

No one noticed me walking through the misty alleys and backstreets until I reached M-68 at the edge of town. A car slowed and stopped behind me. I couldn't see who was driving, but I heard a hesitant, familiar voice call out, "Chris." I was afraid to turn and face the voice until the car door opened. Like a moth attracted to a light of a flame I felt helpless, but faced the voice. It was Hana.

CHAPTER TEN

For the longest time we didn't talk. She drove west out of Chandlerville on M-68, heading toward the muted sunset. We passed Fritz's house, there were two vehicles in the driveway, his truck, and a car I didn't recognize. I sat in the passenger seat waiting for her to speak, thinking of a proper beginning to a long anticipated conversation.

It had been three years since I saw her last at the Millersburg cemetery. I didn't know anything about her anymore. She was a ghost from my past that caught up to me.

"I know, I don't know how to begin either, Chris," were her first words.

I released a pent up sigh, "Geezzas, me too." I turned her way when I couldn't contain my curiosity any longer. The wave of her blonde hair concealed part of her face as I remembered. She flinched her head to one side to remove it from her sight, just as she did years earlier when we were in love. I felt a familiar warmness come over me. I was glad she kept her eyes on the road because I was caught up with her beauty, and stared at her for that short moment.

"You look the same, Hana," I said, but she really didn't. She was a grown woman now, and the innocence she once had was gone, replaced by a certain hardness that shows on a woman's face after she has endured the harsh realness of life's blows. We changed her, the child and me.

She tugged a cigarette from a box of Marlboros setting on the dashboard, never lighting it. She held it nervously between her fingers.

"I have to tell you that I hated you for a long time. But I realized it was my family that made me hate you. What happened to us a long time ago can't be changed, we were just kids who got caught up in an adult's game, and I've paid the consequences.   I don't want the bitterness anymore. I'd rather spend my time being happy for my son's sake."

She fussed over the cigarette, still not lighting it, concern furrowing her forehead.

"I had to see you," she admitted. "You're in trouble. They're coming after you." She parked the car at the edge of the road.

I didn't have to ask who was coming after me. I replied, "I know. Someone made a visit to my house today and left a frightening message. I've seen them coming around more often, too. Here, read this." I retrieved the note from my pocket.

She held it in her cigarette hand, read it, and crumpled it in her palm. She told me what it read.

"I begged them not to do this, but someone else is in charge now, my first cousin, Wolfgang Krieger. He's called Wolf, and it fits him well. He's embraced the old ways of using violence to get justice, no matter what it takes. No matter who it involves. He's obsessed with you, and..." She put the Marlboro in the empty ashtray.

"I love our son, and I'm okay with the way it is, Chris. This is not my doing, but you have to leave here. Now! They want you to pay for what they call, Sünden gegen die Familie, sins against the family. They'll never leave you alone until they get their justice," she took my hand, "and you know what that is."

I knew. They never left Massie Maserone alone, or Angus Fromme. They had murdered Fromme because he fought against killing my brother Denis and me three years earlier. There were dozens of moss-covered headstones in Presque Isle County dating back to the 1800s bearing the names of those they wiped out. Some victims were never found, their names were whispered occasionally at dinner tables and bar top conversations. Coming here from the old country, they were the Bundschuh, the tied boot of wicked vengeance following the motto, "For as long as the sun and moon shine in the sky."

"What about my family? Will they leave my family alone?"

Hana braced her arms stiffly against the steering wheel she was gripping. She admitted, "I don't know. I begged them not to do anything to them, but you must go if you want to stay alive." She retrieved her Marlboro, struck a match and brought the flame to cigarette's end but didn't light it. "What am I doing? I won't smoke with him in the car."

"With who in the car?"

She turned to the backseat, "Kristof."

There came a soft awakening from below a thin blanket that was covering a young boy at the mention of his name. The child rose to sit in the backseat, sleepy, unaware of his surroundings. This was my first time seeing him. His blond hair was sleep-disarrayed. The blueness of his eyes were pooled deeply like the waters of Lake Huron on a calm day. There was a delicate fairness in his skin, like his mother's, and a slight indentation in his chin, like my own. He surely was our son.

He spoke, "Wo sind wir Mama? Wer ist er?" ("Where are we, Mama? Who is he?")

"Dies ist ein alter Freund. Englisch sprechen, Kristof."

I couldn't take my eyes away from the boy. I breathed, "He's beautiful, Hana. Beautiful."

"He's very smart, too," she said, "like you. He's already reading."

I reached across the backseat, more hesitant and afraid than he, "Can I..."

"Of course you can."

In a child's natural response he raised his arms toward my outstretched reach to be lifted. I brought him to the front seat where he stood between us. I could smell his breath and skin. He had the familiar fragrance that only a small child has. I asked him, "Do you like stories?"

His face brightened. He studied my face, and traced his small hands over my nose and cheeks in discovery. He touched the crease on my chin, he felt his chin, "Butt crack, too."

Hana and I erupted in laughter at his candid appraisal. "I tease him about his chin all the time," she said. "Sorry for the butt crack thing."

I touched my chin and said, "That's okay. Sometimes I get teased about it, too. It is what it is, I guess." I placed my fingers on his temple and dragged them delicately over the contours of his face and said, "Manouge," like my father had done to me as a child. The gesture was a French endearment of love expressed to a child.

Hana and I played and laughed and teased the young boy for a brief time while we were parked on the edge of M-68 outside of Chandlerville, almost like we were a family. She was excited about a job interview she was having in Alpena in a couple days.

Kristof asked me to tell him a story. I constructed a children's story about a boy who loved his polka-dotted puppy. He asked if I knew a "skrary story." I told him a scary story about monsters walking in the woods that climaxed with me screeching, "Rahhhh!" When he nestled close to me seeking protection I felt a bond forming between us. He was briefly afraid, but sought the comfort of my protective hug. That's when I knew I could be a father who would do anything to protect his son. I could sense his acceptance of me, even though I was a stranger to him. He knew I was someone who he could trust.

When it was time for our visit to end, our conversation stalled while we absorbed what we had just experienced, neither of us trying to put words to it. There was joy and sadness blending ominously together. Like a rubber band that had been over-stretched, or a jumbled ball of twine seeking to be rewound properly, we could never make our lives the way it once was. We were too late for a ship that had already sailed.

Hana drove down Fritz's bumpy driveway while Kristof giggled sitting on my lap, enjoying the carnival-like ride. She stopped short of the house, away from the back porch light.

"You know, he's in danger, too."

I believed her. Fritz was involved in the battle against the Bundschuh three years earlier, along with Murdy St. Germaine who came to my rescue out on Black Mountain. Murdy killed Hana's estranged father, Gunther Haupt, saving my life.

"I need his advice more than ever, Hana. I don't know what to do. He's the only one I know I can trust right now. He and Benny..." I stopped short of saying the name, Benny McCain. Folks around Chandlerville said he was dead, a ghost lurking in the burned out Lobdell factory ruins no one ever saw, except me.

"Please don't stay around Chandlerville too long, Chris. They will come for you sooner than later. Leave tonight, if at all possible."

When I stepped from the car she gave me a small wallet photo of her and Kristof standing in a field of black-eyed Susans.

I began to wonder how I was going to put my departure together. Where the hell would I go? I stood the boy in front of me and hugged him.

"You be a good boy, mon petite chou "My little cabbage."). Listen to your mom, okay?"

He nodded.   Hana leaned toward me and closed her eyes. We kissed and embraced with Kristof between us.

Fritz answered my knocking quickly, as though he had been waiting for my arrival.

CHAPTER ELEVEN

Fritz stood in the dimness of his porch where the outside porch light failed to reach. He opened the door for me to enter. He still wore the moose foot he had made to replace his missing foot three years earlier. It had held up better than he had. I hadn't seen him in a long time. His face still plumed with a fully silvered beard, now reaching to his chest. His hair was the same shading of his long beard, and uncut like a horse's mane. He had reached the point in his life when there would be no more physical transgression of age degrading his face. He reached for my hand. When I extended mine he pulled me close for a hug and patted my back. I sensed his concern.

"I've been waiting for you, young Christophe. We have much to talk about. Come in."

"Hello, old friend. It's been awhile, ay? I should have come to see you more often, Fritz," I said. My hesitant smile apologizing for past visits I never made.

"I understand, son.   I was your age once. Youth and youthful decisions often dismiss or delay good intentions for another day."

I felt guilty, like a dismissive driver ignoring a needle pointing to empty on his gas gauge, only to run out further down the road.   His beloved wife, Evie, had died two years earlier, and I never attended the funeral.   I was camping at Shoepac with friends and didn't know what had happened.   I never went to Fritz afterward to give my condolence.   This was my dismissal of good intentions, the paved road to hell it often makes. "I'm sorry about Evie, Fritz.   I should 'a been here after Evie..."

"Don't punish yourself.   I know you thought of us, and that's what counts." He put his hand on my shoulder, "Have a seat, I'll be right back.   How about a cup of coffee?"

"Sure."

"What color?"

"Black."

He stopped at the interior door,   "There's someone here I think you'd like to see."

The door widened, Murdy St. Germaine appeared like an aberration who had been holed up in obscurity for three years. Where? I only heard rumors.   The last time I saw him we were on the craggy bluffs of Black Mountain. He saved me from Gunther Haupt, who was going to kill me. I tried to fight Haupt but I was losing.   Murdy came to my rescue and sliced Haupt's throat, but not before Haupt buried his knife into Murdy's chest.   I held him while he lay dying on the crest of the mountain. I believed he would die, but later I found out his father-in-law, Chief Ten Bears, took Murdy and his family to his Drummond Island reservation where the tribe of Odawa-Annishinabe Indians could shield them so he could recover. I never got a chance to thank him. He was back in Presque Isle County now, on the lam. He, too, trusted Fritz. If the Bundschuh knew he was back in the county they would kill him.

He was smiling when he approached me. "Aanii (hello), my friend," he said. When he spoke, his chin rose, his coal shaded eyes looked down at me, like he was peering from within a dark cloud. "Remember me?"

"Murdy," was all I could say. "Murdy, you're okay! I can never tell you enough times..."

He interrupted, "Say nothing, Chris. I'm glad I was able to help you and your friends."

We met in the middle of the room and gave each other a strong embrace. The smell of tobacco and campfire smoke clung to his clothes which comforted me.

Fritz returned with coffee. We sat at the pine table. Fritz and Murdy doused their coffees with a splash of brandy. I held the warm coffee to my mouth, waiting for Fritz to speak.

The damp night air squeezed through the porch screen chilling the room. The intermittent zooming of nighthawks attacking airborne bugs interrupted the evening's silence.

"Once again we sit at this table facing the same opponent. We know them now. We know they will not rest until they have taken care of old business. I'm surprised it has taken them this long to emerge. Tell me what has happened to you." Fritz looked directly at Murdy.

"I came back because I can't live on the rez anymore. There's no work. This is the only place I can find work, working for you. Mary's father didn't want us to leave, but I had to. I've only been here for a week, and nothing has happened, yet. Fritz and you are the only ones who know I'm here," Murdy finished.

"They, at some point, will know you're back." Fritz said. "Now, what about you, Chris? I can tell something occurred. You have the smell of fear on you."

I placed the coffee cup on the table, and reached into my pocket. "This was left at my house today. There was a spike driven through my little sister's shredded stuffed toy with this note attached."

Fritz read the note, and palmed the stray hairs away from his face. The deep trenches of skin near his eyes collapsed tightly. "We need to know who Is now the fuhrer."

"I know his name, Wolfgang Krieger, he's called Wolf. Hana told me about him tonight. She's the one who dropped me off here." I told them more. "Hana said he is after me and probably made the visit to my house, leaving that." I pointed to the note still in Fritz's hand.

Fritz sipped his coffee and revealed, "Wolf Krieger, ay? I know about this man. He's a descendant of one of the original Bundschuh members who took Alois Molitor's life back in the 1800s. I believe he's a commercial fisherman harbored out of Seagull Bay, outside of Calcite City. He sells most of his catch to stores in Alpena. Rumor has it he killed his deckhand for disobeying his order while they were miles out on Lake Huron. They never found the deckhand's body. After that he couldn't get anyone to work for him, so he and his dimwitted son manage the boat. The boy is obedient but doesn't have the sense to come out of the rain. Did Hana tell you what the note said?"

"Yes, something about having to pay for sins against the family."

Fritz leaned in his chair, and poured a splash of brandy in my coffee. "You'll have to leave Chandlerville, Chris. You know that, don't you? You should leave, too, Murdy."

"I'm not afraid of them. I'll be ready if they come." Murdy's usually relaxed hands collapsed into fists.

The brandy bypassed the coffee exuding its fumes and clearing my nostrils, it burned pleasantly as it went down my throat, warming my stomach. "Hana said I should leave tonight. She told me you were in trouble, too, Fritz." I rested my face against my palms, my mind spinning with uncertainty and confusion and fear. "Dear God, where the hell will I go?"

"We'll figure that out, Chris. Try not to worry. You need to have a clear head. I know you are afraid, but there are solutions to every problem. Let's think this out," Fritz said.

He rose from the table and went inside his house. He didn't return for a long while. Murdy and I sat studying the top of the old pine table as though it held answers.

When Fritz returned I was pacing the floor, mulling over his reasoning of a solution to every problem. I could think only of a problem for every solution. I raked my thoughts of how to get out of town, which was the first difficult dilemma. Sure, I could step onto M-68 or M-33 and start thumbing, but that would only make me obvious and anyone could see me. The only way I knew was jumping the D&M Railroad. If only I could find Benny McCain, he knew how to do it. He could school me again like he did three years earlier.

McCain never called folks traveling the railroads, 'hobos', he called them travelers. The travelers left unobtrusive signs and symbols for other travelers, carved on fence posts, sidewalks, walls of building, or trails telling 'go this way,' or 'cop unfriendly here,' and 'danger.' Cryptic designs only other travelers would understand. I knew some of the signs, but not enough to be well versed.

"Come and sit, Chris. Let me tell you my thoughts."

I told Fritz and Murdy I felt the only way to leave without being seen was to hop the D&M. Murdy liked the idea, but Fritz cautioned me, "There are loads of perils doing this. Did you ever 'catch out' before?"

I didn't know what that meant and said no.

"That's what hopping a train is called. I did it for a year before I met Evie and settled down back here. There are a few things you have to know before you catch out, if you want to be safe."

Fritz made more coffee and brought out bologna sandwiches with mustard for us to share. He spoke for a long time, sharing his smarts on the ways of the rail. Like which end of the car to get on and how to get off. He also told us which cars were safer to ride and which ones would be dangerous. He drew crude sketches I could take with me. He told me of what to be aware of when entering a 'hobo jungle,' a camp where travelers met near the tracks, or outside of rail yards. "Be especially wary of other travelers, trust no one," he said poking my shoulder with a stiff finger. Rail yards had cops he called bulls who could be indifferent to hitchers or mean as hell. He told several stories about how bad they could be after he witnessed a bull drag a man he found under a car hauler as the train was departing. He beat the traveler to death with a Billy club.

When Fritz was finished he stood beside the table, "You'll need this. Keep it in your shoe, and this close by." He handed me two twenty-dollar bills and a yellow handled jackknife. Murdy took out a ten, but I refused, forcing his fingers shut with mine. I knew it would cause him hardship if I took it.

While we talked I realized an assassin could wipe us out in one swift dispatch should they show up. I knew I had to leave right then. I wanted to go home first and gather some items to take with me.   Fritz told me it wasn't a good idea. "You'll only bring danger to your family," he said.

CHAPTER TWELVE

In a moment of weakness I went home to get a few things and say goodbye to Claire. I couldn't face Mom, she'd know the jig was up. I would write her a quick note telling her I had to leave, but without much explanation. I was as discrete and shy to the open areas of town as an alley cat prowling at night. Storm clouds were cruising in from the west darkening the late summer evening earlier than usual. It was the bleakest night of my life, even the neighborhood dogs warned of my passing raising their suspicious imaginations every block I sneaked through. A telltale trail of barking and howling followed me from Fritz's house to mine, but I made it to the magnolia tree entrance without incident.

Nine o'clock, Mom was in bed with her nightstand light on. I knew she was reading her Bible. She didn't hear me climb into my room from the tree, but Claire did, she stood in the doorway and watched as I quietly pillaged through drawers and the closet tossing only a few items on my bed to wrap in a bindle for my travels. One change of clothes and a small Monkey Wards flashlight was all I took. A lightly worn pair of Red Wing boots, my size, was sitting near my doorway. Mom put them there for me after a family wanted nothing to do with them after Bobby Marks died in a boating accident. I changed into them. The leather was stiff but dry. I had nothing else of value to take with me. When I finally looked at Claire I knew she had figured out I was leaving, her eyes showed fear and suspicion, gathering moisture like a glass of cold water beading up in the sun. I knew she wanted to go with me. I sat on my bed with Claire on my knee, both of us cried quietly.

"I'm scared," she cried.

I gave her a long and smothering hug. "I am, too."

"Bad men down there, Twis, real bad men everywhere. Don't go."

I explained as best I could, reducing the 'why' part in a child's naive telling. She understood. I trembled at her admonition because she had been right every time she revealed one.

I scribbled a hasty note to Mom, and left it on my nightstand, she would find it in the morning. My note was as elusive as my words to Claire. By the time she found it, I hoped to be miles away from my home.

When I stepped through the window opening Claire clung to my leg. She was crying more implacably and forcefully. I shushed her and gave her another hug. I told her I would come back and she shouldn't worry about me. Before I lowered the window she reached and showed me a piece of Tuhta she had salvaged, "Don't forget my new Tuhta."

I set out for the Lobdell Ruins in the dark, briefly spraying the flashlight beam only when I reached the seldom used trail at the edge of the immense concrete remains looming against the faded evening, like tombstones in a lost cemetery. In the deepest part of the Ruins I would look for traveler signs, perhaps a traveler who could help me. I hoped I would see Benny McCain.

A small campfire was burning in muted flames, ricocheting off the hard cement walls of what used to be the heart of the steering wheel factory. I could hear the faint sound of a harp playing sad quivering tones to an unfamiliar song. When I reached the border of the fire's light I waited until the player saw me, hoping he would invite me over. He quieted his playing when he noticed me. "Coming or going?" he asked.

"Going," I replied. I approached slowly and cautiously. Propped in the fire's coals was a can of beans gurgling hot, seeping over the edges into the fire, its lid bent back. The traveler was wearing a dull green Army issue shirt with the sleeves removed and well-worn blue jeans in need of washing or disposal. He was sitting on a tattered Army jacket. A nametag on his shirt read, "Stokes." The tips of his combat boots were worn past the outer layer of leather. An opened bindle was lying next to him bearing very few items; an Army issue canteen, flashlight, crumpled road maps, some canned goods, and a knife. His dark, stringy hair was parted in the middle and draped haphazardly about his unshaven face. His dog tags dangled around his neck with a P-38 can opener between the tags. He looked to be in his middle twenties. His voice carried the familiar U.P accent

I had been around most of my life. It was similar to my own.

"Yer' welcome to join me at the fire, ay." He pointed to a broken piece of concrete where I could sit. "You been on the road long, man? Oh, my name is Randall Stokes. Call me Rand, ay, that's what my friends called me." I told him my name, then we shook hands. He looked to the fire for a memory, while crossing his legs. His arms and hands were locked above his knees. "That's what my friends over there called me, that is what's left of 'em." He slapped his harp against his open hand to dislodge any spit collected on the reeds and stuffed it in his shirt pocket. A glossy pink scar scattered like spilled wax from his right bicep down to his forearm. Above the scar was a healed black and red lettered tattoo reading, "I Made It" struck through a green, yellow, and red banner.

"I'm just starting out," I replied. "What happened to your arm?"

He ran his palm and fingers over the old wound, "Shrapnel I took at a place called Dak To in the Kontum Province." He changed the subject. "Know where 'yer headed yet? Lots a space out there, man."

"Not yet." It hit me. I really didn't know where I was going.

"Best to head south. At least you'll be warm when winter hits around these parts. I'm catchin' outta' here soon for the end of the line in Mackinaw City. That's as far as the D&M goes. It's departing Chandlerville around eleven tonight. I got off to get some sleep and eat somethin'. I only came through with half of my plan. I haven't slept yet.

I'm from the Soo. I got out last spring," he said pointing to his shirt. "101st Airborne, Vietnam. I rotated in January, and spent my last days at Bragg. I kicked around the south a bit just for the hell of it. Now, I'm gonna' visit my family in the UP, then head out again." He tugged the boiling can of beans away from the coals with a stick to let it cool. "Ya' hungry? Say, you wouldn't have a watch, would ya?"

I was starving, and didn't have a watch, "Nah, I'm fine," I lied. "I don't have a watch, I must have lost it, sorry."

He asked more questions while he ate his beans, "So, you plan to catch out, but you don't know where yer' goin'? That's cool. There's a lot a guys out there doing the same thing. Nowhere to go but they're goin' just the same." His spoon scraped the remaining bean juice from the bottom of the can. He licked his fingers. "You must be runnin' from somethin', maybe to somethin', ay? Which is it, Chris?" He realized he was getting personal, and corrected himself, "Aw, man, I don't mean to meddle. You don't have to say. It's just that you look a little young to be hittin' the rails and roads, dude."

The night was getting cool so I hunched closer to the fire. I didn't tell him the real reason why I was leaving. There were ongoing articles printed in *The Chandlerville News* every week that told where area soldiers were stationed. I decided right then I was going to visit Spark Fallon at Fort Sam Houston in Texas before he shipped out. He suspiciously understood and commended me for being considerate and loyal.

"Think they'll let me on the base?"

Rand reached for his right boot and dislodged a small cotton pouch from his sock. He untied the bag strings to retrieve a rolled joint. He lit it, and dragged deeply, forcing a stressed voice, "Hard to say. Better to let him know yer' there so he can come and see you." He exhaled fully, and pointed it my way.

I had only hit a joint once before when Henry Frazer shared one with me. I didn't get much out of it, probably because I didn't know to hold it in my lungs long enough to have an effect. I took a deep pull and held it like Rand did. I spoke with a pinched voice, "Hope he can. He doesn't know I'm coming." I exhaled, and held the joint while considering the fire.

"It's all groovy, dude. It'll work out. Peace."

Rand Stokes watched me watching the fire, still holding his joint, taking several hits, not sharing it.

"Bogart." He laughed at my naïveté.

"What's that?"

"Dude, yer' Bogarting." He explained that it meant I was hogging the joint and not passing it back.

"Bogart? I love it! I'm a frickin' Bogarter. Cool. Sorry." The joint was taking hold. Our laughing echoed off the thick concrete wall in our hazy mirth. The fire lulled to short yellow flames as it died. "You got any more beans, man? I'm starving."

"Munchies," he laughed. "Always happens." He fetched another can of beans from his bindle.

Rand Stokes and I talked for a while after the joint and fire embers ceased. He told me I should catch out with him to Cheboygan. I would have to catch out on the NYC Line where it would go south to Bay City. I'd have to find my way from there. "You'll be able to find a train that'll get ya' further south. As far as you wanna' go."

We collected our meager belongings and set out for the tracks beneath the loneliness of a midnight sky. When we reached the siding near M-211 the main locomotive was pulsing low hanging purges of diesel smoke at the head of twenty or so cars. A headlight atop the hardhat of a night worker grazed the tracks and train in quick glimmerings while he inspected the train's assembly. We hid inside a damp crop of cattails waiting for the train to begin thrumming away. In a lowered voice Rand said, "Take hold of the front of that open car like I do. I'll help you aboard."

The steel wheels rolled like giant round feet digging in on the tracks. The pounding of the diesel's pistons powered the train forward. Our shoes were like shovels spading into the pea stone as we trotted in time over the poplar ties until Rand gripped the ladder to swing on board an open framed car hauler. I followed close behind until he reached and tugged me aboard.

The wind tossed our hair behind our faces when we stood and watched the blackness of the west coming straight at us. The hauler rocked and swayed like a canoe on the uneven tracks so we spread our stances to get balanced. Rand stooped to relax against the outer bracing of the car. The night was cool, nearly cold, but we were warmed by our efforts. I turned to watch the town lights of Chandlerville diminish until all I could see was the tall spire beacon of the courthouse burning out like a falling star. My heart felt its absence, my life in Chandlerville was over. Would its memory fade like the light on the spire which had now disappeared?

We set out on the warm steel tracks like all other travelers do, going to any place but here.

CHAPTER THIRTEEN

There was no talking. The click-clack of the wheels and track had us thinking of places beyond the pine forests and low lands hurling behind us unnoticeable in all directions. We didn't speak until the train slowed near the Waveling Plains outside of Cheboygan. The damp, night air brought the spicy smell of Snyder's swamp to us. Its peppery smell dissipated to the briny wafts of cattle huddling in barnyards waiting to get milked in the near hours ahead. Rand seemed at home on the rail car, lying on his side pillowing his bindle, seemingly asleep, but aware of the train slowing. "We'll have to get off at the south edge of town where there's a depot. I'll head north when it picks up again. I'll show you where to catch the NYC, it'll take you to Bay City. From there you can hop on another southbound."

We departed the hauler with a gentle jump onto the forgiving pea stone bedding between the tracks as the train crawled ahead. Stout pressured blasts of air relief valves spit the moisture from hoses attached to each car pissing loudly below the cars startled the hell out of me.

Rand led me along a trail heading away from the tracks to an opening cleared in a growth of stunted alders. There were three men hovering over a bright campfire. One of them, a rail-worn man looking to be in his fifties, stirred the small pieces of a burning pallet with a long stick. They rose suspiciously when we approached. The other two were younger, perhaps in their thirties, stood separate from the older fellow. One of them was balding with a high forehead, the other wore a dirty cap disguising the integrity of his hair. They must have been traveling as a pair, while the other was alone. The man in the cap kept his eyes on me, watching me steadily, making me uncomfortable. Rand noticed.

"Evenin' brothers. Mind if we join you 'til we catch-out again, Captain?" Rand said, with a disarming tone aimed at the older man, believing he was head of the camp.

"Come on in. Nice night to travel, don't 'cha suppose?" the older man said not looking away from the fire. His initial assessment of us saw no threat.

"Thanks," Rand said. We quietly joined them, but I could sense Rand was unsettled. There was something about the two younger travelers he didn't like. We took knees close to the fire, away from any proximity of the pair.

The older man spoke, "Name's Babin, Jules Babin. I goes by Uncle Boogie, 'atz what most calls me. I'm an' ol' boomer from Luzeeana," he said. He flicked the errant shards of tinder back to the greater fire with his stick.

"This here is Chris, I'm Rand." Rand nodded to the men.

"Howdy." Uncle Boogie returned a nod. The other two nervously paced the rim of the fire, and didn't reply, mumbling to each other secretly. The capped man became more noticeable with his inspection of me.

"You two brothers?" Uncle Boogie asked. His pale grey eyes looked tired but gentle, set inside the deep, corrugated wrinkles surrounding his eye sockets.

Hurrying to correct him I tried to speak. Before I could, Rand quickly replied, "yes" for reasons I wasn't sure of.

"Fuck you are!" The man in the cap blurted, challenging Rand's answer. "Don't look 'atoll like you."

Rand took his gaze from the fire to the doubting man who was standing defiantly across the pit. "That so? Yeah, he's my little brother. He wants to learn the way of the rails so I told him I'd take him on a trip to Bay City." Rand narrowed his focus directly toward the man. "I'm gonna' make sure he's safe, ya know? Lots of bad people out here, haven't you heard?"

"Sounds like you know how things are out here, don't 'cha? Yeah, good yer' watchin' over such a tasty little Angelina like him." He licked his lips, looking straight at me while he palmed his crotch. He reached in his pocket where he retrieved a black handled knife he flipped open with a quick wrist snap. He began scraping at the black filling beneath his fingernails, smiling openly, displaying rotten teeth resembling burnt tree stumps.

"Now Clarence, you might be scaring the young lamb," the bald man said, nudging himself between Clarence and the fire.

"Aw, Bruno, I was just gettin' ta' know 'em is all," he said, flipping his wrist again to set the blade back into its pocket.

Rand stood and stretched, like he was going to begin exercising. He walked to Clarence, facing him close enough to smell the stench of his tortured clothing. "Good thing that's all it was, Clarence. For a moment I thought I was gonna' have 'ta go back to war. You know, killin' people and all."

"Fah..," Clarence replied defensively. Bruno put his hand on Clarence's shoulder, and escorted him away from the fire where the alders grew. They disappeared down a trail that led to the purring clamor of a train's diesel engine.

There was silence that smoldered like the fire over the camp. Uncle Boogie spoke, "Good riddance ta' them two fuzz tails. That itchy one's a trombo lookin' ta fight, or sumpin' else. They's what makes travelin' wicked." He directed his words my way, "Good thing 'yer brother is here, son. They had evil 'tensions."

"Not gonna' happen on my watch," Rand said, breaking into a confident smile, giving me a reassuring nudge with his shoulder.

I made a frightened smile, beads of sweat had nervously formed on my forehead. "Sonzabitches."

I knew what was going to go down if it weren't for Rand. "Thanks."

Rand kicked at a piece of charring wood back to the fire. "Shit, man, I can't let you catch-out on yer' own, little brother." He sat next to me, and declared, "I can always head back up to the Soo some other time. Not much there for me anyway. Where did you say you wanted to go, Fort Sam Houston in Texas? Your buddy gonna' be a medic, or somethin'? That's where they get their training."

"Yeah, that's what the newspaper said."

Uncle Boogie began telling his story, his hands palsied while he spoke. I had a hard time understanding his deep-south Cajun drawl and cryptic traveler terms. It was hobo language told by a Cajun.

"Times is tough down 'nar. All over. I'm on the hummer, but not down and out," he said, meaning he had been hoboing well. "Mais, I'm still able to gandy dance and mush fake a bitz when I getz a chance to earn a fin or a sawbuck when I needs dough. I know hows to find a mark for grub, too. Life's good since I split the pogey down on Hadley Road afta' I loss it back in 'fitty-two. Bank took it all. Yeah, bess' times a my life was when I had a young Creole wife, name a' Rainy. She was sumpin'. Legs as long as da' highway 'ta heaven, skin like cream on a fresh bucket a chocolay milk. We'd take that ol' pirogue back inna' bayou fah' crawfish 'til her spell takes me over like the smell a' new gumbo and we moss up on a dry ta' makes the love. Now, I'z don't mean ta' sagebrush heah' likes those fella's from the west, but I'm meanin' ta' say she was all a man needed fah' all times."

Uncle Boogie pulled a cotton pouch from his shirt pocket, and poured some tobacco on a Zigzag paper. "Excuse me fellas whilst I twist a dream." He fashioned a cigarette and touched the end with the burning stick. He took a long pull, exhaling a long plume of smoke through his nostrils. "I'z sayin' about Rainy. We was goujon fishin' an' she got her han' inna' wahdah. The Devil putta' gree gree on her and me right then an' theyah'. Jus' en' a cotton mouf bites her han'." Uncle Boogie stirred the fire, and wrung his trembling hands, "She gone nah'. Fah all times, 'cept when I try to fais do-do or when I can't. I gotza' picture heah, see?" He held a dog-eared photo of Rainy over the fire for us to see. She was all he had described.

I wanted to cry, but we sat quietly watching the fire crackle into ashes. I thought about Hana, Kristof, and everything I was leaving behind. I wanted to tell the travelers my story, but it would have to wait for another time.

Rand took his harp out, "You mind?" he asked Uncle Boogie.

"Nah, you go ahead, son. Make the night beyahn."

Rand blew softly across his harp, making sounds like a lonesome train sadly crying away in the night.

When dawn began gathering around us we picked up and followed the path to the southbound NYC where it was ready to head out. Uncle Boogie said it was a 'redball', and we'd have to run like hell to catch it.

CHAPTER FOURTEEN

Run we did, as fast as we could to catch the swift moving NYC when it barreled outbound from the siding at daybreak. Rand helped me lurch over the metal edge where an eight by four foot platform gave us just enough space to plant ourselves at the front end of a bright white grainer. We hauled Uncle Boogie's' light frame up and over when he caught up. He was exhausted, so was I. We fidgeted about the platform to get comfortable for the three hour ride to Bay City. None of us had gotten any sleep over the long night. I braced against a steel pillar with my feet dangling over the lip of the platform, watching the ties blurring below me as we gained speed. Rand and Uncle Boogie bunched over their bindles and were soon asleep. Uncle Boogie was holding Rainy's photo close to his chest with a high-knuckled hand.

It took some time for me to sleep. I watched the sun rising over a promontory jutting into a lake whose name I didn't know. The strong southern wind joined force with the whir the train produced scattering my hair about my face. The lake showed glistening whitecaps splashing against the shore, swirling a frothy flotsam near its sandy beaches.

We sped through the vast pine forests of Crawford and Otsego Counties, through the unremarkable towns of Gaylord and Grayling, then Roscommon and West Branch, never stopping. I stirred occasionally to see what was causing the change of mid-morning scents emitting from the wood mills of Gaylord into the whiff of stone dust plumbing out of giant stone crushers in a deep gravel pit near West Branch. I didn't wake fully until the train reached the starchy wafts of endless sugar beet fields in Saginaw Valley; the fertile heartland of Michigan's stellar crop farms where migrant Mexican families congregated every summer to collect the harvest. The aroma of Mexican food blended inharmoniously with the stench of acrid water waking my two companions when we reached the stagnant canals near Saginaw Bay.

"Must be close to the Bay." Rand rubbed the sleep from his face that was showing a definite outline from the lid of a can of corn he had buried inside his bindle. The noonday sun blistered down on the grainer bringing us back to full awareness to our surroundings. We were at the end of line and would have to hop off soon. Uncle Boogie rose and stretched and made the sign of the cross. Rand leaned over the platform to see behind and ahead of the long scything trail of boxcars and open trailers.

"I was here a few days ago when I caught the D & M to head north. There's a camp near the river just over that bridge ahead. We should get off here before we reach the yard." I leaned outside the grainer to see the busy rail yard a half-mile ahead. "The bulls are active up there. We don't want any of their shit. We can settle here until we find a southbound, but we'll have to hoof the tracks at dark to the yard," Rand said. He pointed beyond a black-framed trestle rising over the Saginaw River.

The train slowed over the rail bridge. When our grainer cleared the last framing of the bridge we dropped to the tracks near a trail that led to the camp Rand spoke of. I was stiff and tired but renewed once my feet met the ties and soft mush of stones. Rand and Uncle Boogie maneuvered down the steep bank away from the tracks. I followed close behind giving assistance to Uncle Boogie when he slipped on the scattered stones.

The clay path coursed through a web of low growing willows near the river. Discarded cans and weather-cracked tires and whiskey bottles Uncle Boogie called dead soldiers lay strewn beyond the path's edges. Skunk cabbage and ivy enveloped the junk nearly concealing its existence. A long dead carp of considerable size drifted belly up on the putrid green water near the bank. We walked for a hundred yards or so until we could see a tight congregation of men, women, and children surrounding a fire built near the river's edge. Beyond them was another band of men separated from the first group like different tribes thrown together by happenstance. We could see Clarence and Bruno among the other group of men. Uncle Boogie and I paid little attention to them, but Rand grimaced intentionally their way. We halted near the first group.

Uncle Boogie greeted the group with "Hola" when he saw they were Mexicans.

"Gu tal?" a slumping older man said, who bore the riddling effects of his many years being hunched over crop rows collecting fruits and vegetables. He was wearing a sweat-darkened cap, its logo worn past its readability. His protective but amicable stance told me he was clearly the leader of the migrants. He appeared to be Uncle Boogie's age. His greeting was friendly. The rest of his group grinned and humbly nodded to us. There was a girl in her teens among them that receptively caught my glances. She was wearing loose fitting jeans and a tight, partially buttoned, blue blouse that bulged from her ample braless breasts. She was beautiful and unassuming, if that was possible. We continued to exchange interested glances while three women fussed over the fire preparing lunch on what looked like an old oven rack. A large cast iron skillet crackled when one woman dropped a thin pizza sized yellow paste into the scalding pork fat oil. I had never encountered an aroma, or brown skinned beauty such as this. My stomach and loins ached simultaneously, reminding me how hungry and horny I was at the same time. Hana came quickly to mind shedding half of my urges. I prayed they would offer food to us, maybe an introduction to the girl, too.

"Buenas tardes," Uncle Boogie responded, "Podemos hablar a Inglés para mis amigos?"

"Se," the older Mexican replied, "English for your friends."

The Mexican spoke to his group, and they responded collectively, "se." He turned to say, "We welcome you to our family, my name is Jesus Santiago."

We told them our names, and where we were coming from. Rand kept the disguise of introducing me as his younger brother for reasons of protection.

When Jesus introduced his family, I only recorded the name Maria to memory. I wouldn't have been surprised if he said her name was Rainy. Jesus said he'd been Up North before but only by accident when he slept through his intended stop in Saginaw. He'd been coming to the tri-cities of Bay City, Midland, and Saginaw area for many summers to work in the fields with his family. The summer crops had been harvested, now they were returning home to Palomas, just over the New Mexico border. He said his family could safely ride in a boxcar in the northern states, but would have to purchase tickets when they reached the dicier rail yards in the south. He showed us his master key which was a rail spike welded on a small square plate that would open most any boxcar door should it be locked. Uncle Boogie produced one of similar design that worked for him. Jesus asked Uncle Boogie why he had gone so far north. He said he wanted to see the Mackinac Bridge, something he had wanted to do since it was built in the '50s. Rand said we were joy riding for my benefit.

The children gathered around Rand like shy inquisitive puppies, wanting to inspect the remnants of his army shirt, tattoo, and the blatant scar on his arm. "Go ahead, you can touch it." A small girl dashed up and touched the scar and tattoo then bolted back to the group bellowing a high-pitched yawp. The rest of the children inched forward for closer inspection. Rand played a quick rendition of Camp Town Races on his harp further enthralling the kids.

When Jesus's wife declared lunch was ready he motioned for us to come to the fire. I wiped the drool from the edges of my mouth when Maria handed me a generous plate of crispy tortilla chips covered with sizzling pieces of pork and a lumpy green paste Rand said was guacamole. The plate was drenched in salsa and finely shredded lettuce sprinkled over the top. I wasn't sure if my masticating apparatus was drooling because of the food or Maria's close proximity. My first mouthful made me put the thought of Maria behind my hunger. My mouth began to burn in a pleasantly divine numbing that made my forehead moist. I was in Mexican food paradise.

I voraciously gobbled away at my food. Maria brought another portion noticing I was still hungry. She sat beside me. I contained my eating to a lesser bohemian appearance. She spoke in passible English telling me she was "Seeksteen." I asked her to tell me her age again so I could hear her intriguing accent. She thought I was teasing her, smiling bashfully.

After the splendid lunch we succumbed to the tiring draw a full stomach brings. I was burned out completely, rode hard and put away wet, Rand said. We all found places to flop for siesta. Uncle Boogie propped himself against a Mulberry tree, its fruit plucked away at arm's height. Rand and I found an adequate spot to sleep on a ragged green couch that was still damp from rain the day before, caring little about the rancid smell of the couch and nearby canal.

A whispering breeze chatted through the willows and alders cooling the camp and the clinging afternoon humidity. I made a furtive glance toward the other group where the two scoundrels were playing cards. I felt safe with Rand being an arm's length away. We dozed off, waiting for the sun to go down when we could catch-on a southbound.

Hours later I awoke to Rand tugging at my sleeve, telling me to get ready, it was time to hit the tracks. The camp was dark and empty and lonely. Lazy puffs of smoke trickled from the spent fire. The southern sky glowed like a distant great fire from the many lights in the yard where trains were being assembled for departure. The Mexicans had left earlier, so had the other group. By now they were preparing to catch-out somewhere down the tracks. Uncle Boogie handed me a folded piece of thin cardboard from a raisin box, Maria's address was written in pencil below a message saying to look her up if I was ever in Palomas, an unlikely occurrence. I would never see Maria or the other Mexicans again.

We returned to the tracks. Rand used my Monkey Wards flashlight to find the path from the camp. We walked between the ties toward the amber radiance of the rail yard with our boots slushing in the fine pebbles. The blunt yellow glow of moonlight grazed the steel surfaces highlighting them like long strands of gold ribbon. I thought of the Wizard of Oz; Rand was a reconstituted brave Lion, Uncle Boogie was the Tin Man who possessed the grandest of hearts, and I was the equivalent of Dorothy, who could not go home again.

I danced along the top of a rail and mumbled, "We're off to see the wizard."

I thought about wicked, flying monkeys.

CHAPTER FIFTEEN

The closer we came to the yard the brighter it got, despite a sullen, opaque sky. Our steady free-for-all pace lessened to a cat-like cautious crawl when we saw a man strolling separately from the workers whose purpose was attending to the rail cars. "There's a bull," Rand whispered. He halted and drew us into a sharp shadow of a boxcar. We bent beneath the car's frame and watched him tap his thigh with a stubby nightstick between steps. He paced further away down the long line of cars, tapping and stepping forward in his evening ritual of searching for guys like us. When he became small in the distance, and the work crew advanced beyond our view we sneaked forward along the hooked freight cars that occasionally jerked back and forth without warning.

Rand flashed a quick blip of light on the boxcar's logo to find out if it was a NYC train, it was. He and Uncle Boogie said it would carry us to Detroit. "Good. Once we're in Detroit we'll have to switch out on a west bound to Chicago, probably a Grand Trunk. From there we'll find one that'll take us toward Fort Sam Houston."

The train lurched again. "Dis un' as good as it gets," Uncle Boogie said. He tried sliding the heavy metal door but it was locked. He had has key ready and turned the tumbler where it opened easily. A short but heavy blast from the train's horn hooted out when the train inched forward with a quick jerk. We climbed into the dark opening, helping each other inside just as the train began rolling away.

Like creatures of the night, small groups of shadowy figures emerged from the darkest reaches of the yard, hunched and loping over the tracks like hobbled contestants in a race for the train. Two of the shadows reached our car before we could close the door; it was Clarence and Bruno. Rand jumped to his feet when he recognized them, "This is a private car, find another!" he shouted, pushing them back on the tracks. "Assholes!" he screamed.

"I'll find you pricks down the line! You'll pay for this!" Clarence yelled, his taunts tailing off as the train picked up speed. Rand drove the sliding door closed with a grunting shove, and latched it tightly against its frame.

The enclosure was as dark as a tomb, the only sound within was our breathing and the under carriage leaking in the distinct din of the steel wheels thrumming along the tracks. Uncle Boogie's match flamed against the wick of a candle, and the car brightened to reveal our faces, our eyes peering into the dark to examine the warm interior of the empty boxcar. The wooden interior walls and floor were scuffed and scraped from the wear of past cargo hauls. There was a faint smell of Cosmoline still lingering inside. We sat near the candle Uncle Boogie had provided, its stem welded on a small dish with melted wax drippings. The trip would be a short ride of less than two hours to the greater Detroit hub where other trains would meet and leave from all parts of the country. We were going to enter a vast jungle of concrete, iron, steel, and the hordes of people who created it.

We sat silently inside the boxcar. The mesmerizing song of steel on steel put our minds in separate worlds from each other. Rand sat cross-legged studying the candle's steady flame that moved only when he breathed a memory's sigh, perhaps reliving his Vietnam War days. Uncle Boogie studied the darkness beyond the candlelight. Was he seeing his Rainy? I wondered. I remembered the photo Hana gave me, I held it in front of me with both hands, staring at it until I thought their faces moved, but they hadn't. It was just my mind being fed by the emptiness gathering in my soul. We were all fighting separate wars inside the candle's flame.

"What's that you got?" Rand asked, waking from his candlelight dream. I tried to put the photo back in my shirt pocket, but Rand asked if he could see it. Uncle Boogie looked at it, too. "Who are they?"

"Hana and my son, Kristof," I admitted.

"Are they who you are running from?" Rand asked, returning the photo.

"Not them. I'm running from her family. They want to kill me for getting her pregnant. I'm worried about my family, too. That's why I left, so they would be safe with me gone," I said. A floodgate of tears gushed open as I told them the story of all that had happened.

Uncle Boogie rolled to one hip, and put a hand on my shoulder, "Some 'tings you run from, some 'tings run to you, no matta' how fah' away you 'ah. You got 'ta meet 'dem someday and settle it, or else you dies inside. I'm runnin' in one di 'reckshun, but I knows I won't find my rainbow until my time has pass."

Rand slapped my arm with a quick snap of his hand, "You gotta get tough, little brother. This is no place to be weak, you'll get eaten' alive by guys like those two assholes back there. Before this journey is done you'll learn how to do it. Damn good thing you got someone like us to get ya' started. We've been around enough to show ya' a few things." He finished by drawing me close with a strong shoulder to shoulder hug.

I smeared the tears away with my damp palms, "I have a bad habit of not saying thanks soon enough. Thanks, fellas."

"I broke a pretty important rule, back there when I tossed those guys outta' our car," Rand said. "Out here it's easy to make enemies. I just hope we don't run into them two again."

"It needed doin," Uncle Boogie said. "Sooner or later we was gonna' have trouble wit 'dem fuzz tails. Jus' be ready if we see 'em again."

The train sped toward Detroit without any stops. Uncle Boogie had replaced a new candle in the puddle of the old one, telling more tales of his travels. He said he was in Dallas when President Kennedy was assassinated. He was watching the caravan from a grassy rise when the shots coming from behind him made him run and hide near a parking lot further down the road. There were two men dressed in grey suits who fired rifles over his head. After things settled, he returned to the place where he had witnessed the shooting to place a sign of four lines crossed with another four lines like a tick-tack-toe puzzle. I knew this traveler's sign, it meant a terrible crime had been committed there. He didn't stick around Dallas for long, there was too much sorrow.

"She's slowing," Rand noticed first. "We must be coming through the north end." We slid the door open for a glimpse of my first view of Detroit. It looked like it was still on fire after the riot on 12th and Clairmount streets a month earlier.

"So this is Detroit?" I said, leaning outside of the car to the length of my out-stretched arm to look south. The first thing I noticed was the pungent smell of the city's conglomerated breath. Cars, busses, and tractor trailers hauling heavy loads swarmed on the sun-weakened asphalt, shaping its surface into potholes. A stack of discarded tires burned in blackened flames near a lone house standing in a cleared field that had long been vacant, never to be a home again. A bell was tinging in the distance at a road crossing further ahead. Abandoned buildings of concrete and broken windows lined the outer tracks like old soldiers who lost a battle, their threadbare uniforms spray painted with humiliating vulgarities. Four dark skinned men sprawled slovenly across the broken stoop of a two-story building watched us pass by. It was safe to stare back at them from our rolling haven. Their empty eyes and glowing teeth pulsed like small candle flames inside a dark, ominous cavern.

"We'll get off before we get to the main station downtown," Rand said.

We bundled our bindles and were ready to depart from our decent accommodations. We would get off the train in the deepest trenches of the rancid city where only ragged and dangerous people gathered.

"Stay close to me, Chris. You, too, Uncle Boogie."

CHAPTER SIXTEEN

The train was moving faster than we wanted when Rand decided we had to get off at a less bright section of tracks within the city. Rand and I jumped first and jogged beside the train to help Uncle Boogie get off. His old knees failed slightly, he stumbled when he landed. He winced when one knee nicked a wooden tie making him limp away toward the vacant buildings beyond the outer rail boundary. I knew he was in great pain but he didn't show it. We held him up when he fell behind, scooting him along like we were stealing him. We could hear sliding boxcar doors yawning open behind us, and the crunching sounds of shoes splatting the stone bedding against the steel rails as they ran for cover.

We retreated behind a fragile decommissioned boxcar that was set beyond the tracks. It appeared to be a perfect gathering place, but Uncle Boogie said it was a trap, and we shouldn't stay there. Yard Bulls would surely pounce upon any traveler that fell for the ruse. We followed a trail that went beyond the boxcar to a fallow field where eye-level grasses and weeds cloaked our presence. The silhouette of a clumpy Chinese elm tree blocked the streetlights of a distant street where houses were stacked beside each other like books on a shelf. There was a well-used hobo camp below the sprawling tree's branches where the ground was scorched with black patches from past campfires. It was unoccupied, and looked adequately safe for our temporary holdover until we got some sleep before searching for a Chicago bound Grand Trunk train.

There was no silence to be found anywhere in the throbbing, illuminated city. Absent were the sounds of a northern Michigan night I was only familiar with. The zooming wings of diving nighthawks and screeching owl yawps were replaced with echoing sirens wailing out, announcing a crime or a grave illness. The far off warning and threats from car horns replaced the evening laughter of children playing kick-the-can, or anti-I-over. Loud and vulgar voices carried over the rooftops of a nearby neighborhood, unlike the gentle hailing from mothers calling their children in from their late dusk play as it was done in Chandlerville. Missing was the soothing amiable breezes that brought cooling comfort into Chandlerville homes during the night. Here, there was only the pulse of sweltering breath carried past boiling heat of the concrete and steel we felt but could not see.

"So, what do you think of the big city?" Rand asked.

"It's not what I expected," I said.

We built a small fire from brush and broken pieces of wood others had left below the canopy of the Chinese elm. We wouldn't need much, only enough to heat several cans of food, and bring more light into our camp. There was no need to get warm as it must have been one hundred degrees with the humid night air.

A block away stood a small neighborhood market, its windows and door clad in rigid steel mesh. A faded sign above the entrance read, "Stosh's Polish Market." Below it was a broken, amber neon sign reading, 'old Beer and Wine,' the letter "C" was indistinguishable. Uncle Boogie noticed it too. I had the money Fritz gave me, and it was burning a hole in my boot, as they say. "You thinking what I'm thinking?" I asked Uncle Boogie.

"Sha' could use a cold drink right nah. Mais," Uncle Boogie said. He wiped his brow with his sleeve. "Hah 'bout 'chew, Rand?"

Rand made a quick, cautious glance over his shoulder toward the market. Suspiciously, he warned, "I don't know, Chris. This is no place to get separated."

I pleaded with Rand, reminding him that we had no water and he must have been thirsty, too. I certainly was, not having water since our lunch with the Mexicans the day before. We were also excitedly hungry. Uncle Boogie knew the dangers but was a seasoned traveler. Rand wasn't worried about him, but he was concerned Uncle Boogie couldn't defend me. "Okay, we'll all go."

I removed my money boot to get a twenty. The bills were damp and soggy from sweat. I waved the twenty over the fire to wick the moisture out of it. Uncle Boogie stood and finally winced in pain from the swelled knot that formed on his knee. "I better stay heah', I don't think I can walk that fah," he said, scissoring his stiffened knee trying to loosen it.

"Tend to the fire, Uncle Boogie. Anything I can get you?"

"Somethin' cole an plenny wet. Maybe a bite 'a somethin'," he said.

Rand and I stepped into the high wavy hair and foxtail grasses where there was no trail, and made our way toward Stosh's Polish Market.

"Ah, shit!" Rand moaned, seeing the closed sign on the front door. "What time is it anyway?"

We had lost track of time. We were mid-way through the night, but neither of us could prove it not having a watch. Rand cupped his hands and peered through the crosshatched screen covering the door. A clock hung on a wavy plaster on lapboard wall far in the back of the well-lighted store. "Two o'clock, damn!" A radio was playing muted songs from within the narrow aisle store. There were loaves of bread, boxes of cereal, bags of potato chips, rows of canned goods, and stacks of other staples everywhere. An aroma of smoked meat and garlic leaked past the loose door frame coming from rows of dried sausages, smoked hams, and Kabonosy Hunter's sausage hanging from racks above the counter, all ready to eat. We drooled at the sight and smell.

"So much for something to drink and eat," Rand despaired.

I suggested, "How about we knock on the door?"

"Smart, little brother. Guess it couldn't hurt."
Rand gave a progression of sharp whacks against
the mesh with the rim of his fist. A head bobbed
into the doorway of a back room and then
disappeared. Rand thumped the mesh again. The
head turned into a man who scuttered cautiously
toward us from behind the long counter, dipping
his head to one side like a puzzled dog. He met us
at the locked door, holding a sawed-off side-by-
side shotgun cradled in both hands. He was broad
and heavy-built with brutishly rounded shoulders
leading to his thick arms. The tops of his hands
and between his knuckles were as fury as a dog's
paw where he was squeezing the shotgun like he
was waiting for water to trickle out of the barrels.

"Chew guys want? Go away, wur' closed." he
said tilting his bushy grey and brown covered head
back and forth, trying to look through small
keyhole sized voids in the mesh. He looked at
Rand's army shirt with interest.

"Sorry to bother you, friend, but this old
soldier and my little brother haven't eaten in a
while. We got money," Rand said. He kept his
hands cupped against his face and the door. I
waved the twenty where he could see it.

The door jiggled when he turned several
deadbolts to open it and removed a long horizontal
bar that was securing the door. He spoke in an
accent I had heard most of my life, having known
many Polish families from Posen, Calcite City, and
Chandlerville. Their words were clogged, harsh,
and displaced front to back sometimes when they
spoke English. "Ah, what 'da hell." He spread the
door open for us to enter. "Only 'cause yousa' a
vet, like me. Where was you from home?" He

meant to say, where are you from, where's your home. I became an interpreter for Rand's sake.

"We're from up north," I said. He was pleased hearing where we were from.

"Oh, ya, up nort. Love 'dem folks up dare'. I'm Stosh, Stosh Kuznicki, what's youse guys name? Youse know I got family up 'dare?"

"I'm Chris, this is Rand. Yes, I believe I've heard of them. Posen?" I asked.

His doubting face brightened. "Ya, dat's 'da place, Posen. You boys come in here, we'll talk, 'en I'll get 'sum food for youse."

We stepped into the market, and he led us to a backroom kitchen where he made his products. The full force of Stosh's hand-fashioned recipes of various sausages and aged meats overwhelmed our empty stomachs. It was marvelous. The smell brought me back to a Polish funeral I had helped my father on. The family wanted the wake held in their home. They had prepared a grand feast of Polish food, just like I smelled inside the old market. I felt a tinge of melancholy building inside me, but soon put it away when he began cooking long strings of Kielbasa and Kiszka blood sausage in a large frying pan. He went to his coolers in the back end of the store and brought back milk, fresh bread, and a large bag of Better Made potato chips. "Dare'." He divvied pieces of caramelized sausage on our plates. "Dis' week I jus' made it."

Rand sliced the bread to make sandwiches. I spread a thick slurry of grainy mustard on top of the meat and covered it with thin slices of sweet onion. I asked Stosh if we could bring a sandwich to our friend, Uncle Boogie, who was across the street at our camp. He said, "Fur' sure." He went to his counter and got a large grocery sack. When we finished eating, Stosh wrapped a couple sandwiches in cellophane, and stuffed them in the bag, along with the potato chips, bread, and dried meats he took from the hangers above the counter. He set two one gallon jugs of water on the table for us to take.

We finished our sandwiches and relaxed in wood-framed chairs at the table, content as lions after a feast. Stosh brought a bottle of vodka to the table, setting three glasses out for a toast. He poured generous glugs into Rand and his glasses, and a lesser splash into mine. "Na zdrowie!" We tinked our glasses together and drank the vodka in one gulp. It went down my throat in a pleasant burn, its fumes tracing back to my nostrils.

Rand and Stosh spoke about their military service. Stosh had been in the Korean War, a Marine in the 7th Infantry, but spoke of it as though he was reminiscing a schoolyard fight that was broken up before there was a clear winner, but he was proud to have served his country. Rand's experience was different. He returned home to hate crowds waiting to curse and pelt returning Vietnam veterans with rotten eggs, shouting "baby killers", and "murderers." But Stosh understood, and said, "They ought not to be doing that." There was a mutual respect between the two ex-soldiers who fought in separate wars, regardless of where the wars were or the popularity.

We thanked Stosh for his gratuity when he wouldn't accept any money from us. He led us to the door, carrying his shotgun, where we could re-enter the ominous night waiting beyond the market's facade. I hefted the bag of groceries against my stomach. Rand toted the water jugs.

When we crossed the threshold of his doorway a spotless blue Buick rolled to a stop when its two occupants saw us. The passenger's window buzzed down, and a black face leaned through the opening, "Wha' cha' gotz in a bag, mutha' fucka'?" I froze in place, caught completely off guard by an obvious threat.

Rand stepped ahead of me, "Just some food for the road, brother. Nothing of any value."

"Who you callin' brotha', peckawood? I ain't yo' brotha'. Now, lemma' see tha' bag, fuckas'!" he demanded.

Stosh came forward with his shotgun held waist high, pointing it at the car, "Youse boys better get on down 'da road."

The black face disappeared behind the dark glass when he buzzed the window closed. They drove slowly away down Mulberry Street, the blue Buick's shiny chrome sparkling below the humming streetlights.

When we crossed Mulberry Street we gave a quick look back to the market. Stosh was still standing in the doorway with his shotgun ready should we have any more problems returning to our camp. I waved goodbye, Rand threw a quick hand to his forehead in salute, Stosh did the same, nodded and stepped behind the door where he latched it shut.

We walked toward the faint glow of our campfire, peeling aside the tall foxtail weeds with our free arms. Uncle Boogie was at the fire talking to another figure who was bent to one knee. We had company, friend or foe, we weren't sure.

CHAPTER SEVENTEEN

The new guy shied away from the fire when we approached, keeping his back slightly turned our direction, like a mistreated and doubting stray dog being coaxed to 'come' by an amiable stranger. He wouldn't let Rand and me see his black eye and facial cuts and bruises he got at his last stop when he was jumped and beaten by some unfriendly wiz tails who robbed him of his money leaving him with only his fatigue clothing in his duffle bag. The only other thing he possessed was his driver's license and orders to report to Fort Gordon in a few days. The uniform clung on him like an ill-fitting glove. He was thin and gaunt like an unremarkable hazy mid-day shadow. I got the immediate notion he knew who we were, and he was caught between deciding to escape or confess, considering his rock and the hard place he was sandwiched between. Uncle Boogie called him back to the small fire. "We got company, fellas. This here young soldier says he knows you..."

"Dick Main?" I said, before Uncle Boogie could fully introduce him. I wanted to say, Main Dick. I found myself in a similar sandwich he appeared to be in. I didn't know if he had searched me out to follow through with his threats he made at the party back in early June, or wanted to apologize for being an asshole. Neither was the case when he settled in at our camp and began telling us why he was there. I kept a cautious eye on him, just the same.

"I just finished boot camp," he said. His shyness coagulating between anger and disappointment. "Them lyin' sonzabitches said we were gonna' stay together when we enlisted in the Buddy Plan. But when boot was over, we all had different orders. Lyin' bastards!" he repeated. He was agitated because he, Calvin Van Camp, Butch McGrath, and Terry Brown had been split up. He regarded me with an apologetic remorse when he timidly looked my way. He must have remembered the party.

"I see." Rand glanced at his sleeve that was void of a chevron stripe. "Can only go up hill from there, son. When you gotta' be in AIT? What fort?"

"Well, my orders are to report to Fort Gordon in a couple days," he said, but not confidently, the word "well" rose in a noncommittal hesitation while he fidgeted with the bag of chips Uncle Boogie had passed his way.

Rand cautiously studied Dick Main, finding fault with his lack of confidence, his indifferent attitude. Missing was the bravado of a fresh-out-of boot camp soldier that was common among those he knew in the past, like he was when he completed boot camp. Rand was suspicious of him traveling the rails, too. "So, you're on to Gordon, ay? That's where I got my AIT, too." Rand paused to pose an obvious question that was more of a statement, "You know where you'll be goin' from there, don't cha'?"

"Yeah, I know. That's sorta why I'm here. I ain't goin'. I ain't puttin' my life on the line for nobody!" he said in a matter-of-fact admission. "I'm heading' to Canada. Fuck that war. I got a cousin up in Chapleau who's got a sawmill. I can go to work for him. Fuck that war," he repeated, louder.

Dick Main was a deserter, regardless of its consequences. I didn't believe he thought it through thoroughly because he was without a credible answer when Rand asked him, "You know what they do to deserters, don't 'cha? Have you considered you'd be locked up in a brig for bein' AWOL, if they catch you? Do you want to live the rest of your life on the run, never able to go back home again?"

"Don't matter to me. I'll get by."

Dick Main and me were on a similar path of sorts. Neither of us could go back home again but for different reasons. I suppose I was a deserter, too, like him. The only difference I could see between us was my departure was for what I believed were honorable reasons while his was that of a pussel-gutted coward. I wanted to punch him. I think Rand did, too.

We mulled over the fire for the rest of the night in a sober, uncomfortable silence. The presence of Dick Main had managed to drain dry the comfortable camaraderie we had before his arrival. Even Uncle Boogie felt the tension of disappointment the deserter had brought with him. I knew he was contemplating his departure from the group when he said, "Wonder what the weatha's like in the Smokey's rat' nah'?" We weren't going in that direction, but he was a traveler who disdained being in an uncomfortable surrounding like he was currently drenched in.

It was then, at the rising of the sun over the rooftops, where the Chinese elm brightened like a prolific shrine in our urban desert was I struck with an epiphany that made me shiver. What if I became Dick Main, and he became me? We were about the same in size and frame so the uniform should fit me. Could I put on his uniform and follow his orders to report to Fort Gordon? Could I become a soldier without training?

The more I thought of it, the more I was convinced I could do it. I had Rand there with me, maybe he could give me a crash course on how to be a soldier? Hell, we had time, I was a quick study and I was a damn good shot with a gun too. Surely it wouldn't be that difficult if I learned how to take orders from someone other than myself?

As much as I hated the idea of becoming and being known as Dick Main, a guy I considered to be a cowardly prick, I made my announcement for the group to consider. I was immediately met with a contentious list of why it couldn't and shouldn't happen by Rand.

"Just think about it for a while, Rand. Just give it some thought. There's a way, I'm sure," I responded.

Rand shook his head in dumbfounded amazement, but he said he would think it over. Dick Main was indifferent to the idea, but once again said, "Hell, I don't give a shit. Go for it.

Here, try it on." He handed me his jacket. When I put it on another feeling came over me. Suddenly, I felt like I was a soldier, proud to be wearing my country's uniform. I must have given reason to Rand to think even harder about my proposal. He said it fit me well. But then he laughed, "That hair has to go, little brother. You certainly couldn't go to Fort Gordon looking like that. You'd never get passed the front gate."

I paraded around the camp mimicking a soldier marching, standing at attention as best I could. Rand rolled on his side laughing heartily at my counterfeit soldiering. "No, no, no, not like that." He jumped to his feet to show me the proper way to salute and march. I knew I was enlisting his training subversively and subliminally by doing everything wrong. Before he knew it, he was teaching me what I had asked him to do. He asked me, "Are you sure you wanna' do this?"

"Rand, where the hell am I going to go after I meet up with Spark Fallon? What am I going to do, keep wandering around the country on a train to nowhere? I don't wanna' do that."

Uncle Boogie watched from his perch on a cinderblock, "Mais, I never heard such a ting'." He looked over to Dick Main, "You should be thankin' yah' lucky stahs, son. This heah' boy gonna' make ya' life a ho' lot easiah'."

Dick Main remained indifferent, unconcerned about my outcome, or his. Rand asked him for his military ID and orders and driver's license. He asked for my driver's license. He studied them, "Not that much of a similarity between you two, but enough to get you by. That's okay, Chris, when you get to your base tell them you lost your

ID and they'll issue you another one."   Rand palmed the sweat from his brow and shook his head, "Man, I can't believe we're doing this. Shit, man, this is a long shot at best."

Dick Main and I exchanged clothes. His boots and uniform fit like they belonged to me, but his hat floated and bunched awkwardly over my over-grown hair. When the transformation was complete, Dick Main and I looked at each other suspiciously. The only resemblance I could see of Dick Main to myself was my clothes. Rand confronted the deserter, "Feel better, now that you're free to be somebody else?" he asked.

"This will do," he said in the same disenchanted indifference he had showed all along.

"That's good." Rand grabbed the new Chris Cosette by the shirt with both hands, like he was going to toss him to the ground. "Now, you get your fuckin' chicken shit ass outta' our camp right now! I don't want you around us no more."

The deserter picked up what belongings I had, now that they were his, which didn't amount to much. He started out toward the yard, but turned to us, "I ain't got a dime, can I hit ya' up for some change?" I pulled a twenty out of my pocket and walked over to give it to him. He didn't say "thanks," he just stuffed it in his shirt pocket.

"One more thing, dude." Rand rushed over to him. I could hear him warn the deserter. "You better not betray him or I'll hunt you down and destroy you. You got it?"

"Won't happen," he said. "You can trust me."

CHAPTER EIGHTEEN

The camp returned to being pleasant and comfortable once the deserter left. Even Uncle Boogie seemed relieved. I began putting the complete uniform on, tucking the soiled shirt into my pants and straightening the wrinkles, Rand tugged my tie into place. I spit polished the boots enough to clean the dust and smudges and debris away from the toes. They weren't perfect but it added to my overall spiffiness.

"Okay, get ready to march," Rand said.

I gave him a puzzled look, "What?"

Rand pointed to Stosh's Polish Market, "We're gonna' pay a visit to Stosh. I'm sure he's got scissors and a razor, yer' gonna' get yer' ears lowered, soldier."

"Oh, shit. I forgot about this," I said, fishing my fingers through my near-shoulder length hair.

Uncle Boogie laughed, "Mine if I come along to see this?"

"Hell, no, Uncle.   Yer' leg up to it?" Uncle Boogie took a few tender steps and nodded. "Let's go."

We set out for Mulberry Street under a noon sky that was trying to melt everything in the city. I was leading the way when Rand called out, "Halt! Get yer' ass back here, Private Main!   Drop and give me twenty."

Private Main? That's me. I didn't like the sound of Main, but private sounded distinguished. I was now a soldier by the name of, Private Richard Main, United States Army. I was a bit confused when he said, "Give me twenty." Did he want the last $20 bill I had? I figured it out when he pointed to the ground.

"Count 'em off, grunt."   Again, my name changed momentarily, I was Grunt Main.

"One, two, three," and so on went by easily until I got to fifteen. Now I knew why he called me "grunt."   I pressed and push and strained and grunted, "Eighteen, nine...teen, tw.......enty!"   I sprawled on the ground, steaming with sweat, melting like an ice cream cone in a Finnish sauna.

"Whatcha' doin' soldier, takin' a nap? You ain't a bolo, are ya?" he growled like he was barking backwards in time when he received his training. A bolo was a fuck up. I wasn't going to be one, he made sure of it. "Get on yer' feet and hit it double time." He swirled his finger like he was stirring a cocktail, which meant I was to jog in a circle around Uncle Boogie and him on our way to the market.

I trotted in circles under the baking sun while they strolled in wandering strides, like they had all the time in the world to get to the market. By the time we crossed Mulberry Street the ends of my hair were dripping with sweat and my face was as bright as a fresh carrot. Rand called out, "At ease." I stood on the stoop, breathing heavily, anxious to go inside the cool market for a rest. Rand held the door for us to enter.

Stosh was behind the counter waiting on an old lady who was fraught with indecision between purchasing fresh Kielbasa, or the ring of bologna she was juggling in her hands.

"Afternoon, Stosh, how goes it?" Rand asked. Stosh met us with a broad smile. There was an aroma of clove, celery, and allspice tapping into the fragrant, cured meats hanging on hooks above his counter.

"Youse boys lookin' for lunch? Come on back," he said motioning for us to come around the counter to his private kitchen. He saw me, "Wait a minute, what we got here?" I tried not to look embarrassed. I went back to attention, but I couldn't keep the fraudulent impersonation intact when I looked at him. Stosh let out a shy giggle.

"May I present, Private Richard Main. He's a little rough around the edges, but I'm hoping you can fix him," Rand said seriously. Stosh must have figured we had paid a visit to a Salvation Army store to get ready for Halloween.

Stosh gave me the up and down examination one gives to validate authenticity. "Is this the 'new army'? Boy, things have changed since my days."

He tilted his head, trying to figure out the missing ingredient which was a buzz cut head.

"He needs a GI cut, Stosh, you got the tools back here?" Rand asked.

"Sure do, have a seat private." He went to a backroom office and returned with scissors and shaving kit. "Now, youse guys gonna' tell me what's goin' on?"

Stosh clipped away at my hair with the skill and patience of a butcher, while Rand explained to him what was happening. Stosh nodded here and there throughout his labors, not taking his eyes from the job at hand. I felt my ears cooling pleasantly, and my hearing improve while they were being lowered, as Rand had described. "There!" Stosh said as if he had just mended a broken wing on a disabled bird. He brought a hand mirror from the bathroom for me to see the bona fide Private Main.

"Jeezus! Is that me?" I examined the mirror at different angles, hoping to find my old self somewhere between the smooth contours of my temples to the split in my chin. My cheeks seemed higher, my eyes were bright and unrestrained set modestly below my brow. The hockey stick scar on the bridge of my nose was more defined and prominent. My tanned face ended abruptly, well below my hairline where the sun hadn't been able to reach, like someone had spray-painted a pale white ring at the edges of a mask. My sideburns were gone, having been shaved clean to match my bald skull. The skin near my ears looked like two creamy and delicate bluegill fillets with their hides gone. I stood in the kitchen and brushed the wisps of hair away from my shirt, feeling like I had lost weight.

"How do you feel now, Private? You look like a soldier, son," Rand said appearing proud as a father seeing his son in uniform for the first time.

"When does he have to report?" Stosh asked.

"In two days, at Fort Gordon." Rand looked closely at my orders. He read them more carefully. "Damn! 11B," he noticed wearily.

"What's wrong with 11B?" I expected it to be bad news.

"11B is infantry, little brother. Means, most likely, you'll be goin' where I just got back from. Vietnam. That's where most infantry are headed these days. Stosh, we've got to get this kid up to speed and fast."

The spirit in the room lost its frivolity, as though a broom brushed away dust from a vacant floor, replacing it with a sheet of ice. I wouldn't know for a long time what Rand's concerns really were.

"Takes all kinds," Stosh said. "You won't be alone, for sure." He changed the subject. "How 'bout some lunch, boys? Ever had czarnina?"

"I have," I said having had duck blood soup at the Polish wake. "It's delicious."

Stosh ladled generous scoops of the swampy soup into four bowls. We dipped torpedo bread rolls into the rich, amaranthine colored broth where the allspice and cloves burst their flavors on our pallets.   Uncle Boogie and Rand had never tasted the bold concoction of duck blood and breast meat, raisins, heavy cream, apple slices and celery until now, their faces rocking delightfully with each dip and sloshy bite.

Stosh began to reminisce about the great battle he was in at a place called the Chosin Reservoir. He said it was bloody, brutal, and cold as a well-diggers ass in the Klondike. He told me, "If yer' gonna' go to war, youse might as well fight it in a warm place." He said he still disliked the communist Koreans for devastating his division in Korea. "Slant-eyed bastards!"

"A warm place? Oh, yeah, it'll be plenty warm over there, but don't get fooled.   When the monsoon season comes it's a goddamn nightmare. You'll wish you never saw a drop 'a water again." Rand caught himself when he saw I looked a little forlorn as he tried to find something positive to say about Vietnam.   "It's not like yer' alone in it, there'll be thousands of drenched rat grunts just like you over there, but the weed is mighty groovy."

The straight and square Stosh stretched his smile. "Youse boys were lucky 'cause all we had was piss poor hootch to drink in a frozen foxhole. It worked 'probly as good as that weed stuff youse smoked to forget about the war when youse got a chance." Stosh took our empty bowls to the long white sink and said, "Let's get started on him."

My training resumed. Stosh got a notepad and pencil for me to take notes. I wrote down every command and their meanings, as best they could recall.   The one piece of advice both of them repeated throughout my impromptu schooling was,

"Learn your dog tag numbers because you are a number now, know your General Orders, and never volunteer for anything!"

Rand said I was shaping up nicely, but I needed to know how to handle a rifle. Stosh brought his shotgun out and handed it to me. I got a bit sassy telling them I had plenty of guns in my hands before.

"It's not a gun-it's a rifle!" he shouted. "Left shoulder...Arms!" I braced Stosh's 'rifle' to my right shoulder. Rand adjusted it properly. "Order...Arms!" I placed the rifle butt on the ground beside me. He continued shouting commands, correcting me occasionally when I was wrong, like he was a handler in a dog show, and I was a stand in contestant.

This went on for most of the afternoon. I marched in place with the shotgun displayed as he commanded. Finally, he ordered, "At ease." I took a step toward the table. "Keep that right foot down, soldier!" He screamed. I was supposed to wait for the command of, "At rest," a big difference to a drill sergeant. I ended the afternoon's training by doing another twenty pushups.

I was tired. I looked ragged in my soiled uniform that showed dark blotches of wetness around my collar and torso. Stosh said he would wash it so I would look presentable when I got to Fort Gordon. I wore a stained meat cutter's apron while I waited for the uniform to be ready. Rand let me walk "at rest" back to the camp. He said I had had enough training for the day.

Uncle Boogie lit a small fire with dried branches and charred ends of larger kindling, just large enough to provide conversation light. I rested on a slice of moss-covered carpet that had been bedding for many previous travelers, the folded duffle bag served as my pillow.

The night halo glowed above the city's lights, always dingy yellow, no matter what time of night it was. Still, the sirens and wails of far off emergencies clamored above the constant muted rumble that belched from the gut of the great metropolis of Detroit. Trains came and went like impervious couriers whose mission was to deliver and pickup products and people, no matter the condition or their worth or desperation. I pondered our worth in the scheme of life. Were we mere bolos, the flotsam of despair and failure, washed up on a jagged shore of a concrete, steel and asphalt sea?

My near asleep mind rehearsed commands, marching, saluting, sweating, and swearing until I passed into a dreamless void. That is, until I heard Rand shout harshly, "What are you fucks doin' in our camp?"

When I rose to my feet I could see Uncle Boogie gasping with blood pulsing in wide gushes from the knife's trench in his neck. He rolled on his side, heaped up and convulsing near the fire, like a dying animal. Bruno continued his assault, thrusting his blade into anything that yielded on Uncle Boogie's body. He was already dead from Bruno's knife slicing his throat, but his body reflexes hadn't given up yet.

Clarence had one arm around Rand's neck from behind, pushing his knife deep into Rand's back and shoulders repetitively. Rand cried out, "Run Chris, get outta' here now!" Rand managed to pull his knife and drove it deep into Clarence's forearm. Clarence screamed, but continued stabbing him from behind. I could hear the blade entering Rand's flesh where it crunched against his ribs.

I ran to the fire and grabbed a burning piece of kindling and stabbed it against Clarence's face. He cried out in a deep shrill of pain and pulled his closed arm away from Rand's neck. Rand broke free from Clarence and faced him. "Get out 'a here, I said! Go to Stosh's!"

I raced as fast as I could for Stosh's Market. Tears peeled away from my eyes back to my temples. I didn't want to leave Rand, but I knew Stosh could help.

I franticly pounded the mesh screen covering the market door until my palms bled. Stosh rushed to let me in, carrying his shotgun. "They're killing them!" I cried, "Uncle Boogie's already dead!"

We charged to the camp, like soldiers desperate to save comrades.

The attack was over. Uncle Boogie was dead. Rand was holding him across his lap, comforting him as though he was guiding him with soft breathy whispers, wishing him peace on his next journey at life's end. I heard Rand say, "Rainy." Blood bubbled at the corners of Rand's lips where it spilled downward to his shirt when he coughed. Clarence and Bruno had done their bidding, and were limping away toward the rail yard. Bruno was doing most of the work, hauling Clarence who was doing the limping. Rand's knife was lying near the fire, its handle drenched in wet blood.

"Holy God in Heaven!" Stosh cried. He rested his shotgun on the ground. "How can I help, Rand?" Rand only returned an exhausted gaze.

Stosh leaped to his feet. "I'm goin' to call an ambulance, you stay with Rand until I get back."

I sat beside Rand, pulling him close to me. I could feel the warm, saturated blood soaking his shirt when I put my arm around him. He continued to cradle Uncle Boogie, still spread across on his lap. All I could do was cry, there was nothing I could do or say to help him. He tilted his head toward my chest, and looked up at me. The brightness that once burned through his eyes was fading like an evening sun settling to night.

"Be strong, you can make it, little brother. You have it in you. Be strong." He closed his eyes for the last time in this world.

I wept for Rand and Uncle Boogie, like I had never wept before. The demon in me found life and I wasn't afraid of him. I let him take over me. I welcomed him like a lost brother.

I could hear Clarence and Bruno, still thrashing through the tall weeds and foxtail grass on their way to rail yard where they sought the cloaking darkness of an empty boxcar. I wasn't going to let them escape. Stosh's shotgun was within arm's reach. I broke the gun's breach, there were two double-aught buckshot rounds sleeved in the barrels. I snapped it closed and slid the safeties forward past the red warning. I set off through the high foxtail grass cover, following the wispy sounds of their bodies slicing through the tangle. Their silhouettes got larger as I advanced closer, crouched and bent at my knees, I was ready to strike when I could hear them breathing. Bruno struggled to help Clarence forward.

"Ay!" I shouted when I was within range of the short, sawed-off shotgun's pattern. They turned, looking surprised and stunned when I brought the shotgun to my shoulder, aiming it at their faces.

"Aw, now, you wouldn't hurt a fly, Angelina. Why don't you hook up with us, we'll show ya' a real good trip. What 'a ya' say?" Clarence said. He braced himself on Bruno. His shirt was drenched in blood from his neck down to the belt. Bruno was without injury, but breathing heavily under the load of hauling Clarence.

I studied them as though they were dangerous wild game, my prey. All I could say was, "Fuck you!" Bruno began to haul Clarence forward, toward me.

I killed them both. The twin blasts I fired were sucked into and hidden within the uncaring city's ears, unnoticed by anyone, not Clarence or Bruno, only me.

I returned to the camp and waited for Stosh and the ambulance, but not before I put the shotgun inside the unlocked market without Stosh noticing.

I regretted not bringing Rand's knife because I would have taken their scalps. That's what Murdy St. Germaine would have done.

I became a soldier that night.

CHAPTER NINETEEN

After the ambulance left I sat at Stosh's kitchen table as upright and rigid as the chair, staring at the eggs and toast he had made for me for some ethnic mourning reason unknown to me. I wasn't hungry, how could I be? I had just lost Rand and Uncle Boogie in a most barbaric way. My ears still rung in a constant squeal lingering from the aftermath of the twin blasts. The only solace I found was the actions I took in revenge. I had no regret for what I had done, but it bothered me that it didn't bother me. There was no siren screaming either, only it's spinning lights streaking silently across the field and buildings and decrepit houses on Mulberry Street when they took my friends to the morgue. There was no need to hurry anymore.

The Detroit Police where questioning Stosh near his store counter. I could hear him tell the officers he heard loud voices and cries coming from the field, followed soon by a man covered in blood, pounding on his door, pleading for someone to call an ambulance. He didn't let the man inside his market, but he called for help. "Wish I could help you more," Stosh explained. He kept me entirely out of the story so they would never know I was there. Stosh was unaware what I had done to Clarence and Bruno. There was no mention of two more dead bodies in the field. They were yet to be discovered.

Stosh closed the market door that rattled loosely until he turned the twin deadbolts tightening it to its jam. I heard his cushioned footsteps approaching across the sunken oak flooring. He had put his shotgun behind the counter, but retrieved it and brought it with him to the kitchen and laid it across the tabletop. He joined me at the table.

"Not hungry I see." He noticed I hadn't broken my sunny-side-up eggs. "You should eat. It will take your mind off them, and you have a long road ahead of you."

"No, but thanks, Stosh. Maybe in a while."

"I'll call the train station shortly to see when you can catch a train to Savannah, Georgia. I'll give you a lift, too," he said.

He reached for the shotgun lying between us, and unhinged the breach. Two empty shells ejected landing in his lap. He said nothing. He knew there were live rounds in the chambers when he left the gun at the camp. In a look of despair, he sighed, "You took care of business, didn't you?"

I slid the chair closer to the table, "Do you have any salt and pepper?" He got them from counter cabinet, and I gave the eggs a generous dose and began eating them. "It needed doing, Stosh."

He nodded in agreement.

"It needed doing."

Stosh beheld me differently now. On our Sunday morning ride to Michigan Central Station, on 15th Street near the area known as Corktown, we spoke sparingly, his and my answers to insignificant questions amounted to yeses and nos. Tiger Stadium loomed above the stunted skyline where the Tigers were playing the White Sox. Stosh knew I was at the doorstep of another world, another life, separate and alienated to the present. His newer model Ford Galaxy smelled of smoked Polish meats, rode smoothly across the intertwined roads and expressways leading to the train station. The particulars of the trip faded behind us, unrecorded to my memory, interceded by my daydreaming. It was useless knowledge to remember the turns and road names and exit ramps for I doubted I would ever have to retrace its path.

"My mom was born here," I said in afterthought of driving through Corktown. "I always wondered what it looked like." Every neighborhood I had seen in Detroit thus far looked remarkably the same, and Corktown's huddled houses and vacant lots was no different, except for the connection I felt for mom's history of growing up there. I searched the houses imagining and wondering if one of them was once hers. I remembered her telling my brothers and me about my grandfather, an uneducated Irish immigrant, and how he died in his bed after he tried to cure himself from a terrible flu that had stricken him. They were too poor to get proper medical treatment. Desperate to get well, he tried an old time remedy of drinking kerosene. He drank too much and it destroyed his kidneys. He agonized in his bed for a week before dying in her arms. Mom said there was a wet, yellow ring surrounding his body where he laid. Gruesome and ironic was his fate, because Grandpa Cosette, my father's father, was a medical doctor of great intelligence and cures for most illnesses. A strange and tragic fate awaited him, too. He died of shock lying beside my father who was giving him a direct blood transfusion. I knew my father carried that image with him for the rest of his life. It was no wonder why he drank. What is my fate to be? I questioned, alone in my thoughts.

"Dare' she is," Stosh remarked. We turned onto 15th Street and rolled slowly ahead weaving his car between others that were letting off and picking up passengers. He curbed his Ford in front of the ornate station's once ablicant now greying facade next to a 'No Parking' sign. The greater portion of the station rose behind it with more floors than I could see from my rolled down window. The building was grandiose and harsh in design, with replicating floors stacked on each other until it reached eighteen levels. He opened a folded sheet of paper containing the notes he had penciled down, and read the information to me. "Your train will leave in about an hour. This is the departure number."

I took the paper and studied it. I saw forty-three dollars written in the center. "Shit! I don't have enough money."

"Here." He handed me a fifty dollar bill he had ready, concealed in his curled hand. "This 'ul take care of it." He nodded and forced the bill in my hand.

"I will come back, Stosh. I will come back and repay you for all you've done." I was humbled by his grace. "I have another favor to ask you."

"Anything, Chris, just say it."

"Will you call the police and tell them who they are? Rand has family up in the Soo, and Uncle Boogie comes from Louisiana. He once lived on Hadley Road, near Baton Rouge, he told me. I don't want their bodies lying in some lonely grave in Zechariah's Potter's field."

"I'll make sure of it, my friend."

Stosh remained parked illegally at the curb, watching me walk away to the train station. A security vehicle pulled beside him advising him to move along. I turned back to see him one more time before I went inside the station. I cupped my hand and placed it near my right eye, the finest salute I had ever made and given. He did the same in return. I would, forever hold a special place within me for Polish people, for here was the finest example of his kind.

This is what a train should feel like; comfortable and legal, I thought reassuring myself when I found my place inside the rail car. I put my duffle in the overhead compartment. The car wasn't a sleeper, just rows of frugal cloth-covered bench seats on each side of a narrow aisle. A frail, birdie woman, dressed in a long, dark, tweed overcoat intended for winter use was sitting across the aisle from me. She was holding a collection of magazines stacked on her lap. She mumbled to herself, never taking notice of me. She had a brown grocery bag spread open between her feet, standing upright like a rectangular wastebasket.

She began speaking a low, quivering voice, while she tore each page into precise squares not much bigger than a postage stamp and dropped them into the bag. "You'll have to wait, now. The doctor is coming soon to give you medicine." She never took her eyes from the magazines, or the tedium of her hands rendering each page into squares. I found it hard not to watch her intermittently, while the flat fields of Ohio and northern Kentucky cruised by my window. I missed seeing the Mississippi River too. Her chores went on for the entire trip to Union Station, in Savannah, where I would board a military bus for the trip to Fort Gordon.

CHAPTER TWENTY

The military busses were not far from where I got off the train. All I needed to do was follow the other soldiers who were getting off the train, and heading for Fort Gordon. My nerves prickled my skin in uncomfortable goose bumps. I didn't know what the hell I was doing or how to do it should I be asked. I felt the best plan for me was to follow the others until I found my way to the busses.

"AIT?" A smiling fellow soldier, not as tall as me, with thick, grainy, sand colored hair said. He was dressed in an identical uniform. He hurried to catch up to me. Hell, we all looked the same, but I think he was as uncertain as me and needed someone's company. There was a stream of us all converging to a row of busses further down the terminal.

"Yes, sir." I turned to look his way. Sir? Shit. I didn't need to say that. He was a ground pounder like me. He smiled. "Sorry, I'm just trying to get used to saying 'Sir.'"

"Yas, I know what yah mean, bettah' say suh', jus' in case. We be goin' to the same place, fah' shuah'."

I thought God had delivered my guardian Angel, right then and there. His warm Louisiana accent flowed gently, pleasantly like a song summonsed every time he spoke; just like Uncle Boogie's graceful words. "Henrah Boudreaux, heah'." I liked Henry Boudreaux immediately. I knew he would become my trusted friend throughout AIT, I just knew it.

This was the first time I was to say my new name, "Dick Main." I felt like I was swearing. I pointed to my shirt, just to make sure he believed me, and assure myself who I now was. "Nice to meet you, Henry."

"Pleasure's mine," he said. We shook hands and continued to the busses.

"Where in Louisiana you from, Henry?"

"Gosh, all. How'd you know 'dat I was from down 'nare?" he asked.

"I had a good friend from Baton Rouge, and you sound like him."

"Well, ain't that a sweet somethin'? Double howdy to ya. I'm from Gonzales, jus' outside a' Baton Rouge, Ascension Parrish. I'm a proud Coonass Cajun, mais." His smile spread, showing his perfectly spaced teeth and cerulean eyes as green as any spring wheat field I've ever seen. He shook my hand again with the intensity of an orchard hand rattling apples off of a tree branch. "Shaw' enough, ain't 'dat a sweet somethin'?"

Feeling somewhat challenged by my accurate guess he took a whack at my origins. "You a northenah, fah' shuah. Not shuah what state, though."

"Michigan, up by the Mackinac Bridge." I held my right hand upright, and pointed to the tip of my index finger showing him where Chandlerville was, something every Michigander does by habit.

"Cain't get anymore Yankah' 'den 'dat, I suppose." He laughed. From that time on he called me "Yank" and I liked and accepted it because it was without the dual meaning that the name "Dick" could conjure.

We reached the slew of idling military busses that had Fort Gordon pasted in wide letters above their doorways. We choose the newest looking bus and stepped in. A silent older black fellow wearing army fatigues nodded over his shoulder toward the back of the bus. I imagined how many soldiers he had seen coming and going over the course of his career. His silence was for a good reason I suppose. Many of us would eventually go off to a faraway place where some wouldn't return the way we left— alive. Better to not know any of us, I reckoned.

We took our seats midway in the bus, thirty-eight other soldiers followed until the bus was full with exactly forty men. The bus's brakes hissed and we were off.

Soldier chatter carried above the low-backed seats from a bevy of different conversations and dialects going on at the same time inside the bus. Henry and I had our own conversation and we learned more about one another. It dawned on me that he got off the same train as me. What was he doing up north when Fort Gordon was closer to Louisiana than where he was coming from?

"How is it you got off my train coming from up north to Fort Gordon? How come you didn't leave from Gonzales?"

Henry stirred uncomfortably in his seat. He took some time before he answered. "Well, ya see, there was a wee bit of a problem back home. I been visitin' relatives in Looahville. That's where I got on last night."

"I see. I don't want to intrude or anything like that," I said. I didn't want to press him on an obvious sensitive matter.

"Ah, hell. I guess it don't mattah' if I tell you. I got out 'a Gonzales 'cause the poleese was aftah' me for some guy gettin' his nose broke. Maybe a crack rib or two. Ah, maybe a couple black eyes throwed in. But I tol' them I didn't know what they was talking about," he said aloof in his narrative recount. I noticed fresh scabs on his knuckles.

"Too bad for that sorry son-of-a-bitch, ay? Probably deserved it, my guess."

"Oh, boy, did he evah'. He should not have done 'dat to my sistah', Claire. Mais! I served him a good plate a' comeuppance." Henry made two white-knuckled fists.

"Your sister's name is, Claire?"

"Yessah', Claire."

I was taken aback once again by Henry Boudreaux. What are the chances I meet another endearing Cajun, and he has a sister named Claire? "You don't say. That's my sister's name, too."

Henry got all warm-looking and fidgeted happily in his seat feeling as pleased as me knowing our similarities like I was a Godsend to him, a new brother, and meeting up with each other so far away from our homes by way of our past predicaments. Our bond of friendship grew as we exchanged stories of our previous lives during the short ride to Fort Gordon. He showed me a photo of his girlfriend, Adele, whom he called Dele, but it sounded like he was saying Dale in his heavy Cajun accent. He was an avid crawfish and catfish fisherman in the muddy, citrine colored bayous near his home. I told him about fishing brook, rainbow and brown trout on the Black and Rainy rivers where you could see the bottom of the streams on a sunny day.

While the other troops quieted and slept during the short trip we kept talking and laughing. Sometimes we lamented, having been displaced from our homes which both of us missed with inevitable lassitude. I never told him about my whole mess up north, just the good things. I hoped Henry and I could stay together through AIT, and I told him so. He said he hoped for the same. We planned to go to Gonzales after AIT so he could show me what it was like in the bayou, and all the Cajun food his maw-maw was going to make for us.

The bus turned sharply and swayed entering the gates of Fort Gordon at three-o'clock in the morning. The compound was enormous. There were long rows of identical barracks about twenty yards apart flanking either side of an immense grassy field when the bus stopped. Behind them were two-story buildings used for the military police trainees and Signal Corp officer candidates. A single lamppost lighted the entrance at each barracks. A square-jawed drill-sergeant, the cadre, dressed in fatigue greens and a stiff, green campaign hat was waiting outside the bus. When we stepped off each of us showed him our orders and he checked our names off his long list.

The humid Georgia night air clung on everything in a blanket of steam. Crickets spoke to us briefly but hushed when we assembled after the cadre standing in front of us loudly prompted, "Form a line, troops!" Another cadre separated us by squads of eight men, five rows deep. We stood at attention until all five eight-man squads were assembled. Then it was a run to the barracks.

Henry and I were in C Company, Charlie Company as it was called. I was assigned the bottom bunk three bunks down inside the well-lit, narrow barracks. A stack of neatly folded bedding was on each bunk, and we had thirty minutes to assemble our beds. Henry was above me. Each of us had a footlocker at the end of our bunks, the right locker was for the floor bunk, and the left locker was for the top bunk. Following Henry's actions, I removed my fatigues from my bag and stuffed my fatigues in the locker next to my duffle bag. I would be wearing them soon.

I was heavy with exhaustion. Several nights of scant sleeping and the deed of revenge justice began to weigh on my thoughts, like an anvil had been dropped on my head. I dipped inside my covers hoping I could displace the encumbrance with a quick hour of sleep before first call whistles sounded.

The lights went out and the entire barracks quieted on queue.

CHAPTER TWENTY-ONE

Fort Gordon was a training preliminary center for airborne soldiers and those of us who were considered regular infantry, the 11b ground pounders. In the early sixties, the fort had become the home for the Signal Corp and primary school for military police. Those soldiers who chose a Military Occupation Specialty, MOS, to go further in the airborne jump school program would take their advanced training at Fort Benning and Special Forces Green Beret training at Fort Bragg after they left Fort Benning. I had no interest in airborne and advancing to Fort Benning or Bragg, in spite of Barry Sadler's song, The Ballad Of The Green Berets, that inspired guys like Mike Fitzpatrick to enter Special Forces jump school and the Green Beret program. I felt I couldn't be that caliber of soldier. They were truly America's finest soldiers.

The lights came on with the first-call whistle screaming through the barracks at five AM. A crisp, rude blare erupted from every barracks on the compound screeching distinctly across the entire grounds. A black, medium built cadre emerged from his room neatly dressed, poised like a statue at the far end of the barracks, holding a metal garbage can lid in one hand and his night stick in the other.   A whistle hung on a green lanyard around his neck. His skin was so dark all I could see was the yellow-white surrounding his ebony pupils.   He sashayed down the center path between the two black lines at the end of our bunks, banging his stick against the lid.

"Wakey, wakey, you dreamers of a past life. My name is Drill Sergeant Jones. You will call me Drill Sergeant," he shouted. "Do NOT call me sir, I work for a living. Everybody up and at 'em. Today is the first day of the rest of your life in the United States Army. You WILL become well-trained, well-oiled life takers and heartbreakers. For the next eight weeks you will learn advanced individual training.   Get your shit, shower, and shave done, grab your duffel bags, and assemble outside."

"What is my name?" He screamed louder.

We responded, "Drill Sergeant Jones!" in one joint, loud voice. The entire barracks came to life in a rush to get dressed.

Our routine was shit, shower, and shave every morning at five o'clock.   We raced to our footlockers to put on our fatigues and fetched our duffels, as though the barracks was on fire.   Then it was a hasty platoon assembly in front of our barracks to begin our first day of AIT. Sergeant Jones led us on a run to a barracks further inside the camp for our military equipment we would have with us throughout AIT.

The equipment barracks was crowded but orderly. We shuffled inline in front of long rows of supply tables and were given a canteen, ammo pouch, steel helmet, compass, field jack and rain poncho, and a fragmentation vest. Item after item was handed out, ingredients of which I had no idea what they were or how to use them. We packed the equipment in our duffel bags as neatly as we could. I got excited when they handed me my brand-new M-16 rifle. Most of the other companies where given M-14s to train with, but we were one of the few that received M-16s. It was light and compact and wicked looking, as black as Sergeant Jones's eyes. I couldn't wait to fire it.

When our duffels were filled with everything the Army said we would need as a soldier, our drill sergeant brought us outside. "Ten-hut!" he ordered. We formed our squads. "About face!" I was ready for the order and never missed a movement. "Forward, double-time."

We ran as a platoon of forty men back to the barracks, our rifles and duffels slung over our shoulders, all stepping in time with each other. The equipment was heavy and awkward, but I managed to keep it from sliding away from me. Henry ran beside me, smiling as broadly and proudly as I was. We gave each other a quick look of confidence and respect. I began to feel like I was going to make it, to be a part of the group, and not stick out like a petunia in an onion patch as the song went.

The drill sergeant called out to Henry during our run. He couldn't pronounce his last name correctly, which should sound like "Boo-drow."

"Bowdrux, tighten up your formation."

As time went on during our training Henry and me became known as Hank and Yank.

We packed our footlockers with our new gear. Some of it stayed in our duffel bag. There were hooks at the end of our bunks where we hung our bag and rifle. We would learn how to use our equipment and rifle in the days ahead, but for now it was back out on the concrete road for the next phase of our first day of training.

The training field lay in front of us, lighted by tall streetlights, like a football field, but there would be no games played there. Out to the field we marched, eight rows deep, five soldiers wide. The other barracks met on the field at the same time showcasing four platoons that made our one hundred and sixty-man company. We began our first hour of training with calisthenics consisting of leg stretches, arm swirls, deep-knee bends and jumping jacks, and pushups. It was difficult for me because I was without the benefit of having had basic training. I lagged behind a bit, showing my lack of conditioning the others had, but I tried as hard as I could and made it through the first hour before the sergeant called out, "At rest." Then it was a five-minute rest and formation again for a half-mile run to the mess hall for breakfast.

The sun began to rise over the tall southern pines beyond the barracks drying the heavy dew on the grass, spilling long streaking shadows around us.

"You okay, Yank?" Henry asked. He was standing next to me as I was breathing heavily in a fast moving chow line.

"Yeah, I'm fine. I just feel a little tired today. I haven't gotten much rest in last few days." I was sweating like a stuck pig tangled in a fence. "I'll be fine."

I wondered if I could make it much further in my training and not be discovered as an interloper. I knew we would have to run much further than a half of a mile soon, and that scared the hell out of me. I recalled my gym teacher back in high school, Mr. Nixon, telling us, "The body can take much more than the mind can. Take control of your mind and your body will follow." I fought to remember his words for the coming weeks.

We shuffled our way down the chow line where there were soldiers dressed in white tee shirts and wearing white caps, who ladled out scrambled eggs, sausages, biscuits, pancakes, grits, and toast on our trays behind rows of deep, stainless steel containers. We took seats at a busy table to eat, one of dozens inside the chow hall. I was reminded of lunch hour back in high school. There wasn't much difference, only we were all dressed the same at Fort Gordon.

The hall was loud with conversations going on at each table. Private Ezequiel Walls, a tall, well-muscled, wide-shouldered fellow from our platoon, was sitting directly across from me. He rose from his seat defiantly holding his tray above his head. He announced in a loud voice, "These eggs are burnt and dry and the sausage tastes like shit!" The entire mess hall quieted in astonishment.

Henry looked at me and whispered, "Mais, he gonna' regret dat."

The head cook charged from behind the mess counter in a furious pace and tore his hat off and threw it on the floor. "What did you say, boy?" the cook said.

Every cadre in the hall stood erect at once. Oh, boy, the shit is going to hit the fan, for sure, I thought.

"I said, the eggs are burnt dry and the sausage tastes like shit!" Private Walls smiled adding, "Just the way I like 'em, sir."

The entire mess hall ignited in favorable laughter, even the cook and the cadre were disarmed and laughed along with the rest of us. The cadre returned to their breakfast plates, all of us finished our meals. Private Walls was right about the eggs and sausage, they were awful, but I ate them in great haste because I was hungry.

Over the course of the next eight weeks we would struggle to like every meal, even the horrid ground beef and white paste intended to be gravy that settled between layers of yellow slime and putrid grease. I guess the concoction was the Army's way of keeping our bowels regular. But we ate it because we were famished at the end of a long day of running and PT workouts.

We were called back to formation for another run back to the field. It was time for the cadre to choose squad leaders. When we reached the field, Sergeant Jones held us at attention and walked slowly around our parameter. When he returned to face us he called out, "Private Walls, up front and center!"

Private Walls shrugged, exhaled, and stepped forward expecting a dose of discipline from his actions in the mess hall. Facing straight ahead, not looking at the sergeant, he shouted, "Yes, Drill Sergeant!"

"Drop and give me twenty!"

Walls dove to the grass and pounded out twenty pushups faster than I'd ever seen before. He rose to his feet, back to attention.

"Private Walls, you will be this squad's leader. Do you read me, private?"

"Yes, Drill Sergeant." Walls' face leaked a smile.

"You will be responsible for the performance of your squad. If one or more of your men performs above and beyond the standard, your platoon will be rewarded. If one or more of your men underperforms, and you do not fix it, you will be held responsible. Do you understand, Private Walls?"

"I understand, Drill Sergeant! Thank you." Walls fell back into rank with the rest of us. Walls would get a fifteen-dollar per month pay raise and the rank of corporal.

Ezequiel Walls hailed from New York City. His olive skin and dark brown eyes came from his Puerto Rican mother, the rest of him, starting with his dish-water blonde hair was heavily diluted with traces of his European ancestry. His father was an inner-city high school English teacher. I expected to hear a New York accent but his English never missed a distinctly sounding 'R'. Behind the facade of his impressive physique lay a gentler person showing a pleasant smile and easy going friendliness. We called him Zeke, for short, and he didn't mind.   Some of us sensed there was something else less definable than his outward amiable appearance but wouldn't discover his flaw until later.

A few years earlier the Army had "recommended" that stand-out individuals should be selected to become trained squad leaders in a three week program called, Leadership Preparation Program: LPP.   There was a shortage of cadre because of the Vietnam War, and they needed help at AIT school.   It was entirely up to the base cadre if they wanted to implement the program, but Sergeant Jones was old school and would personally guide Walls on his new adventure. Walls had to take on extra duty to learn from Jones how to be a squad leader.

The rest of the morning we worked out on the obstacle course, climbing a high wall using a thick rope dangling from its top, traversing over balance beam logs, and crawling under barbed wire while machine guns fired rounds over our heads in a mock battle.   The exercise was frightening with yellow tracer rounds flashing every fourth round above us as we hugged and crawled under the razor sharp wire.   I knew the overhead rounds weren't too close to us when a greedy crow was caught feeding on someone's puke under the wires. The bird got about ten feet in the air before it turned into a fog of black feathers that fell on us like fall leaves. By noon it was another run to the mess hall.

Fun came in the early afternoon at the firing range. It was a mile run from the training field. I was able to keep up with Henry's encouragement and prodding. "C'mon, Yank. Pretend there's a fahn' piece a poontang at 'da end 'a 'da road."

Drill Sergeant Jones led us with a descriptive cadence that ended on an upswing note, "Holy moly, who do I see?" We repeated his verse as we ran in time. He followed with the answer to the first line, "Viet Cong are chasing me." Our boots smacked the concrete road in time sounding like a drummer whacking a muted snare drum. "We got rifles, they got guns." Again, we repeated his words, "Rifles for killing, guns are for fun." Each day Drill Sergeant Jones had a new cadence for us to march to.

Every day we ran wherever we were going, whether it was to the chow hall, the training barracks, or the rifle range, I always ended up lagging slightly behind the others in my squad. No matter how much encouragement and assistance Henry Boudreaux and Zeke Walls gave me, I was not getting up to snuff with the others. Slowly, I was becoming conditioned, despite my less-than-perfect heart, but I still was not as strong as the others. I was not a well-oiled, well-conditioned, strong soldier that the sergeant promised I would be, and I knew it. It was an impossibility I could not overcome. I couldn't fix my rheumatic heart, no matter how hard we tried. I was like Humpy Dumpty and all the King's horses and all the King's men could not put me back together again. I got the feeling that others were taking notice of me and not in a favorable way either.

I had performed above average at the firing range with my M-16, but that wasn't enough to make me an exception. The M-60 machine gun, which we called The Pig, was truly exhilarating to fire, it was a real insatiable eating pig because it devoured everything in front of its self when we let it loose. It was heavy but its effectiveness far exceeded its encumbrance. The M-79 grenade launcher was an all-together different beast.   It could be used at close quarters beyond thirty feet or long range, effective up to six hundred feet.   We called it a 'Thumper' or 'Blooper' because of the distinct 'bloop' sound it made when fired.   Private Dempsey, from Pennsylvania, got so good with the Thumper he could drop a round in an empty trash can one hundred yards away.

We spent a lot of time in classrooms.   I learned how to navigate maps and use a compass proficiently, we were taught how to use the PRC-25 radio set.   Some of the cadre who were in Vietnam, called it a "prick."   I became as knowledgeable and proficient as any of my fellow soldiers at every school aspect in AIT.   Henry ran at my side trying to help me along on our runs, he was a true friend and cared about my wellbeing.   But my biggest enemy was myself and I could not run further than a mile without breaking down.   I prayed for my salvation to come in the form of finding my specialty, which until now was hiding within me.

It was now mid-October, our sixth week of AIT.   The white oak, beech, and box elder trees began hinting of an early fall. That's when the pressure began to mount on Zeke Walls to get me up to speed.   If he didn't, he would be demoted from squad leader.   He had been promoted to Corporal when he became a squad leader, and he had it in his mind he wasn't going to relinquish his position because of me.   I had to exceed at something.   I just had to find and show them what I was good at.

CHAPTER TWENTY-TWO

A Sunday morning rain pelted and pounded the tin roof of our barracks as loudly as Drill Sergeant's nightstick whacking against his garbage can lid. I was relaxed on my bunk reading The *Fort Gordon Rambler*, the on-base newspaper. The articles were about base life, really boring shit written by "commu guys," Signal Corp trainees trying to hone their journalism skills. Some of them would be going to Vietnam to write for *The Stars and Stripes* newspaper. Most of the churchgoers hadn't returned from Sunday morning service yet. Others in my platoon who stayed behind had radios playing their definable music preferences. The black guys were listening and dancing to Motown songs, snapping their fingers and parading and dancing about in practiced routines, like the Temptations and the Four Tops did on Ed Sullivan's stage. Their dancing was polished and impressive to watch. A group of southern boys were dialed in to twangy, Nashville heart-wrenchers, played by Hank Williams and Patsy Cline. I hummed along to My Girl and tried to block out the depressing country western lyrics played by the fellows I called Grits, in protest to their muddy and soiled drawls, and meal choice tendencies. God-awful stuff. Henry was above me cleaning his M-16.

"What you reading' there, Yank?" Henry asked. He racked the action back and forth on the M-16 he had just reassemble.

"Oh, just some meaningless drivel in the Rambler. Says here that base life can be exciting and good for your spirit."

"Mus' be wrote by some fella' who ain't on this base, fah' shuah." Henry laughed and placed his rifle back on its hook.

The black guys turned the volume up above the Grits' radio loudness and began maneuvering to Bernadette. The Grits then wheeled the volume up on Merle Haggard playing The Fugitive. The black dudes dialed louder and danced in line while the Grits toe-tapped with their hands propped on their waists, shuffling across the barracks floor like make believe fugitives. One of the Grits belted out, "Hee haw!"

"I should write an article about how a soldier can learn ethnic dances here on the base, a real study in American Anthropology. Now, that would be interesting, don't 'cha think? Isn't there somebody here who likes the Beatles?"

"You a hippy, Yank? I bet you can't write no article about nothin'," Henry said.

"Fah' shuah', ya' head sucka'. I'll write that article, but you gotta' submit it for me, okay?" I teased mimicking his Cajun accent. Henry said he loved to partake in crawfish head sucking, the only way to enjoy them.

"Well, it's about time you learn how ta' talk, Yank. You write it and I'll be shuah' to take it the Ramblah." He tossed his oil-soaked rag down on my face.

"Yer' in for it now, Bow-drux." I jumped from my bunk and reefed Henry onto the floor. Damn, he was strong, but so was I. We wrestled like kids on a playground, each of us gaining the upper hand during the fun match. I was able to pin him when I feigned being hurt. I cried out in an awful yawp, like I was seriously injured. He released his grip. I put him in an inescapable headlock. "See? You should never fall for that old wounded bird routine. Don't let it get you killed, son."

"Damn Yank. 'Dat won't happen again."

We laid on the floor laughing as though a hilarious joke had been played on someone else. I had to relieve myself so I headed down the barracks to the latrine.

While I walked away the Grits turned their radio full-blast.

"Hey, Yankee?" A voice came from behind while I stood at the urinal. I turned toward the voice and saw three Grits braced and bristled for a fight.

"What do you boys want?" I said.

A red-faced fellow with blotchy patches of excited skin and rabbit sized ears stood defiant, and cock-sure as he gripped a towel in his fists. His friends called him Blab. He stepped toward me. I zipped and faced him. They were up to some kind of shit I needed to get ready for. I took a deep breath and tensed my muscles.

"You a bolo, son. You holdin' us back, don't cha' know? We ain't gonna' stan' for that. Purdy soon we gonna' have to pay for yer' sorry ass laggin' behind. You need a lesson, you bolo mutha' fuckah'!" Blab said.

The three of them rushed me head on. I threw a straight right-hand punch that flattened Blab on the floor. The other two overpowered me and pinned me to the damp tile floor. Blab recovered, rubbing his jaw. He sat on my chest and began punching me in the face. It didn't matter which way I turned my head, I couldn't dodge his fists. I felt blood rushing from my nose and eyebrows. The other two held the towel over my mouth, while the red-faced Blab smashed me with his fists. I was able to free one of my arms and grabbed for whatever I could get my hand on. It happened to be one guy's crotch. I squeezed with all of my strength. The son-of-a-bitch screamed in agony and folded up like a broken kite. Through my tearing eyes I saw a flash of a fist collide on Blab's temple with a ferocious thud. Henry had thrown the knockout punch that laid him unconscious on the floor. Henry began punching the third guy in a furious barrage of roundhouse blows until the guy begged him to stop.

Zeke showed up at the end of the fight. He rushed to pull me off the floor to a sitting position to survey my bloodied face.
"Dammit! I told those yahoos I'd handle this my way," Zeke apologized.

Blab, who was coming to, moaning and looking terribly sick, hoisted himself to his feet and staggered back on his heels. Zeke gave him a swift kick in the ass and told him to take his buddies back to their bunks. They had to drag the ball-crushed assailant, who hadn't revived yet, out of the latrine.

"You a part of 'dis, Zeke?" Henry challenged. His adrenaline fueled temper showed in his excited eyes. He was ready for more fighting and wasn't afraid of the bigger squad leader. "If you a part a 'dis bullshit, you and me gonna' have it out right now!"

I knew right then and there Henry was my best friend and wouldn't let harm come my way again. I would stand by him no matter who, what, or where trouble came from.

"Settle down, Hank. No, I wasn't a part of this. Those assholes told me they were going to get the Yank to keep up on our runs, but I told them I would handle it. I just wish I could have gotten to you before they did. For that I am truly sorry, Yank."

My eyes were swollen nearly shut in the aftermath of the brawl. I don't know if the fists to my eyes were causing my tears or the emotional relief I felt when I confessed where I came from and what I had done to get there. Henry and Zeke listened without cross examination. I was busted now. The truth came out. I was an interloper who had wagged his way into the Army by deceit and lies. I begged Zeke not to turn me over to the cadre or the base commander.

The three of us sat on the damp latrine floor. None of us spoke. Zeke gently dabbed at the blood that was still running from my nose. "Hold your head back. That should ease the bleeding. Damn, Yank. I am so frickin' sorry," he said.

"I will accept your apology if you don't narc on me," I said while managing a painful laugh.

Zeke held the bloody towel firmly against my nose. "Okay, I promise I won't say a word about this. I'll help you get through these last weeks as best I can. You better try as hard as you can, Yank, my ass is on the line for you," Zeke said.

"You can count on me too, Yank. If any of 'dem bastards try anything again, I'll take care of it." Henry made two white-knuckled fists.

"I know you will, ya brawlin' Coonass. I don't know what I'd do without you, Henry. Thanks, man."

They helped me to my feet and brought me to a sink basin where I washed up. I looked in the mirror. "Damn! There ain't no poontang out there could love a face like this."

Zeke walked away and returned to his bunk. I caught up to him before he left the latrine. "Ay, thanks for stretching your neck out for me, Zeke. Between the Cajun and me, I'll get through these last weeks thumbs-up, Okay?" I told him.

Zeke turned and gave me a strong hug, kissed my swollen cheek, and walked back to his bunk.

Henry and me gave each other uncomfortable gawps, "Dang, Yank. What 'da hell was 'dat?" Henry said, surprised as me. "Dat Zeke really likes you, too much fah' comfut, ya' axe me."

Zeke's flaw had now been exposed. Later that night I would do as I promised, I wrote a short story about how I learned how to march at Fort Gordon. I came up with some cockamamie stuff how my life at Fort Gordon had improved my marching by watching the soul brothers' dance. Henry submitted my story to, *The Fort Gordon Rambler*.

CHAPTER TWENTY-THREE

The swelling on my face retreated but a blue streak still laced below my left eye after a week or so. Henry and I privately joked about "the moment." We didn't regard Zeke Walls less respectfully because of his flaw. If Drill Sergeant Jones caught wind of it and told the base Commander, Walls would have been dishonorably discharged. We couldn't let that happen to Zeke. Hell, he was a good squad leader, and we worried about the extra baggage he was taking on between carrying me and his flaw around like a boat anchor. So we watched his back so the others in our platoon wouldn't get suspicious.

We were let off base one Friday night to go up town after Private Dempsey won a bet with Drill Sergeant Jones at the firing range. He said Dempsey couldn't hit his helmet with an M-79 round. Henry took Jones' helmet and ran up a hillside a couple hundred yards away and dropped it. Dempsey 'blooped' his first shot right on the helmet blowing it to hell. Jones kept good on his word and let us leave the base. The eight of us took cabs up to a Western Sizzlin on Sunset Boulevard for steak dinners. A big breasted, red-haired waitress, Delores we learned, took our food orders. Henry and I took it upon ourselves to hook Zeke up with her for a good and solid, all-American, heterosexual encounter.

After her shift, she and Zeke met at her old Chevy Impala parked at the end of the lot for a romp in the back seat. The rest of the platoon and me witnessed his accomplishment by peeking through the breath-fogged restaurant windows for verification. In a strange way Henry and me were delighted Zeke could bat from either side of the plate.

Zeke would become a good soldier, and it would have been a loss for the Army if he had been discovered and discharged. If there was any cleaning up to be done in the ranks it should have been directed at the thugs in Camp Crocket, a secret hell-hole airborne training camp about six miles deep within the pines and swamps at Fort Gordon. The 82nd Airborne Division was taking training there, mostly inner-city criminals and perverts thrown in with some naive white guys who feared for their lives. We heard about the rapes and assaults at Crocket through the rumor mill. We heard that some of the more vulnerable troops would smuggle live M-14 rounds from the range should they encounter any nighttime assault in their barracks. The only time we came close to the new camp, which had just been built that summer, was on an over-night training maneuver where our company was used as bait for some "shake and bake" NCO's in the 82nd to set up a surprise attack. They knew we were coming, but we didn't know a damn thing about the planned ambush. I had never witnessed so many screaming black faces at once in one place. We had no chance. Many of us hated the 82nd after that, and it led some in our company to change their MOS to Airborne jump school before they left Fort Gordon. They would go on to Fort Benning and Fort Bragg for Special Forces training. If they were going to 'Nam they wanted to be trained and prepared as much as possible. Henry and I stayed the course for plain old infantry training.

We had one week of AIT remaining. Graduation was coming up soon. I had improved my conditioning and wasn't falling behind as much as I had in the early weeks of training, but I still must have been noticeable on our running exercises. I was on my knees attending my footlocker when Drill Sergeant Jones stopped at my bunk standing firm and proper as he always did. "Private Main, the base commander wants you in his office, pronto," Drill Sergeant Jones said.

My heart skipped and sweat formed immediately on my forehead. Dammit, I had come so close to completing my training, but I knew I was going to meet my doom in the Commander's office. I got angry, but kept cool. "Yes, Drill Sergeant."

Henry approached us from the latrine just as Jones walked back to his room.

"What's goin' on, Yank? Why'd the DI talk ta' you?" he asked. I think Henry knew it wouldn't be good news.

"I've been told to report to the base commander. Fuck!" I bent to tie a loose lace. Henry knelt beside me, his face as drawn out and long in the tooth as mine. "You know what this means, don't ya'? I'll probably be out of here before nightfall." I rose and tucked my shirt neatly inside my pants. "How do I look?"

"Like a well-oil soldier, Yank. You get yer' tail back heah' and let me know what happens as soon as 'ya can, podnah'," Henry said.

"I will. I gotta' split, Henry."

There was a stoic NCO waiting for me in a Jeep outside the barracks. "You Private Main, soldier?"

"Yes, sir, that's me."

"Get in."

The NCO was in a hurry. He drove the Jeep like a maniac through the coursing roads leading to the Commander's office inside a two-story brick building set far away from our barracks. I slumped in my seat, my worrying intensified because of the hasty way in which he brought me there. The Commander must really what to get me off the base post haste. I'm in for a real shit sandwich, delivered by none other than the biggest bad ass on the base, Post Commander Major General Richardson.

The NCO led me to the major general's office. We scooted past a secretary when she looked up from her Corona typewriter and read my name patch. "He's waiting for you, Private Main," she said.

The NCO knocked and peeked behind the post commander's door after he heard a stern "yes" come from the other side. "He's here, Sir."

I went into the office alone.

The post commander was sitting behind his desk paying more attention to a file folder he had in his hands than me. He didn't look up when I stopped at attention near a wooden visitor's chair near his desk. "Private Richard Main reporting, Major General, Sir." He continued studying the file, which was mine. I wished I had the chance to go over it too. I didn't have the slightest notion what was contained on the pages. I was a stranger to myself.

A brand new black Nikon F 35mm camera with an assortment of lenses was on his desk next to a stack of three-and-half by five color prints. Richardson's office walls held a collection of photos from his earlier days when he was Lieutenant Colonel Walter B. Richardson, during the Second World War. There was an aerial photo of the beaches at Normandy, France showing thousands of landing craft approaching the barricaded beachhead. Soldiers, looking as small as ants, dotted the beach invasion by the thousands. He was among them. Another photo showed Richardson standing with General Patton in the forests of Ardennes after the Battle of the Bulge. His Class A dress coat was hanging neatly on a coat tree behind his desk. I had never seen so many different medals displayed on a soldier's uniform before. He was a true war hero.

I remained at attention for what seemed an eternity. He never looked at me until he said, "At ease, Private. Now, have a seat."

I took my seat timidly. My mind was racing to recall if I ever heard of a fake soldier being executed by firing squad. His eyes went back to my file. He was handsome and framed like a hero behind his modest, wooden desk. He didn't have to say much to command respect, his bravery and guts in battle was all in his deeply piercing eyes. "It seems you haven't been forthright about yourself with the army, Private Main," he said.

I sneaked a slow, deep breath. I knew there was no bullshitting this guy. I didn't know where to begin my confession. "I am sorry, Sir. I know I haven't," was all I could say.

"Well, now is the time to come forward about yourself, Private. Your file doesn't match up to you in my mind," he said. My heart sunk deeper. I lowered my head in shame.

"I have tried with all of my heart to become a good soldier, Sir. Please forgive me."

The major general lifted the latest copy of *The Fort Gordon Rambler* from his desk to display the front page toward me. There in bold print was the title of the story I wrote and Henry submitted. Holy mother of all saviors! My sails re-inflated like a giant spinnaker caught in a windstorm.

"Why didn't you tell the army you had this skill?" He demanded. "We are always looking for talent within the ranks. What you wrote here is a prime example of how the Army can be made better here at Fort Gordon. Brilliant, son!"

My ass slid deeper in my chair upon hearing his praise. I was elated with pride where a moment earlier I was at death's door. The Army could do that to young soldiers, I would learn.

"Now, tell me truthfully. Do you have any other skills you are not telling us?" he asked.

I looked at the new Nikon F camera, and its handsome lenses. "I may have another skill you may be interested in, Sir."

"Well, what is it, son?"

"I know my way around that, Sir," I pointed to the camera and lenses.

"You know how to take a good photo do you?"

"Yes, Sir. I was my high school's yearbook photographer. You might say I have a passion for photography too. I used that same camera you have there, Sir. Oh, and I can speak some French." I didn't tell him I knew how to embalm bodies.

"Vous parle-vous, Francais?"

"Oui, puisque j'étais jeune (Yes, since I was young)."

"Tres bien."

The major general leaned in his chair, "Damn, son. Get over here and show me how to use this thang. My pictures look like crap 'cause I don't know what the hell I'm doing wrong," he said with a Texas drawl crawling forward like a kid who emerged from hiding under a porch. He shifted his interest to the camera. "Take a look see at these," He said as he spread his photos over his desktop and reached for his phone to hail his secretary. "Hold my calls, Jill."

I went behind his desk to look at the photos he had taken of flowers, kids, and a kind looking, graying woman, who I assumed was his wife. Most of them were under-exposed, or over-exposed and poorly cropped showing too much background. I was amazed how he had butchered his photos when he was using one of the finest camera assemblies money could buy. Being careful not to insult him, I gave him a few pointers on using the spot meter to get better shots on backlit subjects, how to crop vertically and horizontally. I suggested he use the 135mm lens at a wide-open aperture to mute the background for people shots, and the wide angle lens stopped down for sharper scenery shots. He became puzzled when I tried to explain the two-thirds, one third cropping rule I had learned from Ray Beauregard back in Chandlerville when I was cutting my teeth with a camera. He finally got it when I placed a few upside down prints over a photo of a beach scene with the sun rising to crop extraneous areas out of the frame.

We must have spent an hour going over his photos. I was relaxed in his presence because I knew what I was talking about. That's when it dawned on me—I found what I was good at and it showed. I knew the major general, and the army believed and accepted me now.

Our meeting concluded with him saying, "I've got plans for you, Private Main. You will immediately be transferred to the Signal Corp where you will be trained further in your talents. The NCO waiting in the lobby will take you back to your barracks to get packed and moved to another barracks."

He wrote my new MOS, 84B, and 71Q on a form and had me sign it. I was so flabbergasted I didn't read it carefully. I was delighted when I learned 84B was Still Photographic Specialist and

71Q meant Journalist. I would now be shooting at the enemy with a camera and writing about it after. I was thrilled and frightened at the same time. How was I going to protect myself should I be sent to Vietnam with a camera and pencil?

Secretary Jill made a copy of my new orders for me. When I was about to leave his office he added, "I'll be watching your progress, Yank. Don't let me down." He knew more about me than I did. How the hell did he know I was called Yank? Maybe he came up with that after listening to me talk. After all, he was a Texan.

I thanked him and promised I wouldn't let him down. The NCO rushed me back to my barracks in another mad dash. He said he would return in an hour to get me. I hoped he didn't regard his watch with the same quick intensity in which he drove, I wanted to say goodbye to Henry and the other guys in my platoon.

CHAPTER TWENTY-FOUR

Henry was as nervous as a long tailed cat in a room full of rocking chairs when I returned to the barracks. He met me half way down the corridor before I reached my bunk. His hand was dipped inside a brown paper bag full of hog cracklin's his maw-maw had sent him. "Come on, son, what happened? You in or out? Have a cracklin'," he said.

"No thanks, Hank." I continued to my bunk without saying anything about my meeting with the Major General. I was reenergized with my new MOS and feeling confident knowing I could finally handle what the army said I could do. I didn't like the fact I would have to change barracks and leave the protection of Henry and Zeke, but at least I wasn't going to be ousted completely from Fort Gordon. Word had traveled fast in the barracks, most of the guys who were still hanging around huddled around my bunk, even the Grits. It was a rare event when a soldier was called up to the stand in front of the post commander. It most always meant discipline or discharge. They waited for the skinny.

"I ain't going anywhere, brothers, sort of," I said coyly. Some of the soul brothers made their way through the huddle. Lardanian "Lardy" Jefferson was holding a copy of *The Fort Gordon Rambler* showing the article I had written.

"Can I see that for a minute?" I asked. Lardy handed it to me. I held it over my head. "This saved my ass."

Henry decompressed, relieving his angst with a long-winded breath. "Nah, come on, tell us everything 'at went on, Yank. What he said?" Henry asked.

I told the crowd of grunts about the photos on the wall in Richardson's office. "He's a frickin' war hero, man. You know he was wounded four times in the war?"

"Neva' mind about the big guy, we wanna' know what happened," Henry said. The rest of the guys thought I was up in front of the man because of my less-than-perfect stamina short comings. Only Henry and Zeke knew of my real identity and fears.

I plopped down on my bunk to get comfortable, like I was going to tell a bedtime story to group of children. "Well when I went in his office he had my file opened and was reading it. I thought to myself, he must have my discharge papers ready and was making sure he had my numbers and name written correctly or something. Then he told me I was holding out from the army. Hell, I didn't know what he was talking about until he showed me this," I said as I held the Rambler newspaper and pointed to the piece I wrote on the front page. I did a tongue-in-cheek impression of the Major General, "The Army is always looking for talent within the ranks. Brilliant, son!" The guys laughed. The soul brothers slapped hands in a cryptic routine smiling at me, impressed that I had written about them. "Oh, then he asked me to show him how to use his new Nikon. He called me Yank, can you imagine that? You know, I was the yearbook photographer back in the real world? Anyway, it all worked out, man."

"So he's lettin' you stay in our outfit?" Henry wondered.

"No, sorry to say."

"What? I thought you said everything is hunky dory?"

"The commander changed my MOS to 71Q and 84B. I'm transferring to the Signal Corp today. I got a ship outta' here in an hour."

"What's the new MOS?" Zeke asked.

"Journalist and Still Photographic Specialist. That's my new bag, man. I'm a one-of-a-kind specialist."

"Remarkable! You must be one talented soldier, Dude," Zeke said, sarcastically. "I can just see you now, running through the jungle and screaming, 'I just want to shoot your photo, Gook. Oops, that was my M-16, not my camera!'"

Everyone hollered in laughter. Zeke gave his best rendition of a motorized camera that sounded like the rapid firing of an M-16 rifle. "Smile, you're on Candid M-16. Rat-a-tat-tat!" The entire group rattled off their expressions of wild gunfire with a few grenade sounds mixed in.

There were some sincere well wishes from the crowd afterward. The soul brothers gave me a "it's cool, brotha'" nod. The Grits even seemed relieved, probably knowing they wouldn't be punished because of me. Henry wasn't all that happy.

I began packing when the guys left. Henry sat on my bunk, watching me fill my duffel bag, not saying anything. "You okay, Henry?"

"I'm happy fur' yah, Yank. At least you ain't been drummed outta' heah' with a boot up ya' ass. I guess 'dis the end a the line fuh' us, mon ami," He said.

"I think so. Ay, but we'll hookup on the weekends, maybe go downtown again? What you going to do when we're finished here? We still going down to Gonzales, like you said?"

"Fuh' shuah', Yank. You gonna' love it. Don't you go droolin' too much on my sweet Dale," Henry said just as the NCO entered the barracks to take me to my new quarters.

"Bet I will," I joked.

"Okay, jus' a little," Henry smiled, "keep yer' boots dry, son."

"You, too."

I hoisted the duffel bag over my shoulder and slung my M-16 over the other. While I walked away with the NCO, I could hear Henry crunching a brittle cracklin'. The soul brothers turned their radio on, Buck Owens was singing, "I Got A Tiger By The Tail." They scrambled madly to return the tuner back where it had been. Apparently the Grits pulled a trick on them, Blab was slapping his knee and laughing like Bugs Bunny.

The following week Henry changed his MOS to Airborne. I wouldn't find out about it until after graduation from his AIT, where I would have been if not for the base commander. I was still in school and couldn't attend. He came to my new barracks and delivered the news. He was going back to Gonzales for a two-week furlough. His next stop was Fort Benning jump school then on to Special Forces at Fort Bragg, North Carolina, a place called Smoke Bomb Hill. He would end up in the 173rd Airborne Brigade when he arrived in Vietnam.

I never saw him or Zeke again during my Signal Corp training that lasted longer than their AIT at Fort Gordon. Henry and I never hooked up for Gonzales, either. By the time his furlough was over I was on my way to California to catch a plane to Vietnam. I fretted over the reason why he joined Airborne. Was it was because of me leaving our Company so abruptly?

Signal Corp was a breeze compared to ground pounder training. I got to use my mind more than my body which was just fine with me. About the only problem I encountered was writing and that amounted to spelling. My instructor said my writing was good, but I needed to brush up on spelling. He gave me a pocket-sized dictionary I kept with me like some of soldiers kept a Bible.

Photography classes were interesting and easy. We worked with most every film format out there. We had two-and-a-quarter square, German made Rolleiflexes, the faster F 2.8 models. Ray Beauregard taught me how to use one the previous winter. Ray taught me solid darkroom techniques too. I was well prepared for the photo school when I got there, more than most others in my group. There were a few old bulky four-by-five inch Graflex press cameras hanging around the photo department but they were slow to use with sheet film holders that slid into the back of the camera. It was easy to forget to take the dark slide out of the way when you took a photo. The quality was outstanding so we used them on large groups of people where detail was important. My favorite camera was the Nikon F 35mm. It was light and compact, and the images were sharp as a tack, but it was rare to get a chance to use one. Most of us would have liked several around our necks. My wish was a set up with a 35mm, 80mm lenses, and a second camera fitted with an F2.8, 180mm lens. The army gave us Bessler Topcon Super D 35mm cameras to use during training. I kept a Leica M3 in my pocket. Although it was a rangefinder split image focus style, its images produced the crispest, detailed negatives in the 35mm lineup. It was quick and quiet with a barely noticeable shutter click. We could cover most any shot anytime of the day with these elite cameras. Some of the guys used zoom lenses, the lazy man's choice, but the images weren't as sharp as the fixed lenses. If it got damaged you were lost to cover an assignment.

One of our instructors, a wild-eyed college dropout by the name of Ray Loop, had been a newspaper photographer. He told us, "If you ever go out on assignment and it doesn't come together always take a shot of something, anything. Don't ever come back without at least one shot. It'll prove you were there." I took his advice to heart. There were a few guys in my class that had trouble with exposures like Major General Richardson did. Finally Loop just told them, "F8 and be there," referring to a basic, somewhat safe aperture setting on the camera. He added, "And show up for your assignment."

My extended training in the Signal Corp lasted until the first day of November. I graduated as a Specialist E-3, Private First Class. I was proud as hell to have the chevron and rocker patch on my sleeve and being part of the 160th Signal Brigade. Two days later I was headed to Vietnam to join up with the 221st Signal Company (Pictorial), in Long Binh.

CHAPTER TWENTY-FIVE

Our Company waited in a lobby at Los Angeles International Airport to board a government contracted Pan Am Boeing 707 bound for Vietnam, via Anchorage, Alaska. Frank Sinatra was singing about strangers in the night throughout the terminal's loud speakers. Our flight wasn't scheduled to leave for another hour. There was a strange, unpreventable, complacent silence held within all of us who were shipping out, not unlike students who have studied for the most important exam of their lives. Our test would be waiting for us when we reached our destination. It was the fear of going to war, the unknown waiting for us, and many of us would fail the test.

The Los Angeles sun streamed through the terminal window after a maintenance worker dragged his squeegee over the soapy glass. Those of us soldiers sitting nearby watched the old man skillfully weave the squeegee back and forth keeping the suds below the rubber's edge not leaving an errant trace behind. It is amazing how the most mundane action can captivate on-lookers like being mesmerized by a campfire's flames.

Some of us conversed about our MOS and what to expect when we arrived at Tan Sun Nhut airport in Saigon. There were 'commu' guys I trained with at Signal Corp spread out in the waiting area, but they were radio and telephone specialist. I was the only photo and pencil specialist in the mix. I had read most of the dog-eared magazines lying around the boarding area for the past hour and was getting restless. There should have been a sign reading "Boredom Area." Across the lobby was a long row of pay phones being used by guys in uniforms like mine. I sat and stared at them thinking it was time to call home like they were doing. It had been three months since I departed Chandlerville on the fly. During that time I fought the temptation to call. I was too busy it seemed to follow any obligation to explain to my parents what was going on. Where would I begin? I was certain I didn't want to talk to Old Man, but I missed Mom and Claire. If I called maybe I could get some information about Hana and Kristof too. I hoped. I had kept their photo with me all this time tucked in my back pocket when I wasn't in ground pounder training.

I told myself, Make the call, soldier.

I got four dollars in change from a restaurant near the boarding gate. The cashier, an older woman in her fifties, asked, "Calling home? My son's over there right now. He's stationed in Saigon. I worry all the time about him. He's with 101st Airborne."

I felt the anguish she was masking. Mike Fitzpatrick was in the 101st, but he was further up country near Pleiku. I asked her if he ever called home. She said, "Once a month. Not often enough."

I poured the quarters into my pocket and went to a phone. When I dialed the operator asked for half of my pocket change for four minutes phone time. Mom answered while I was dropping quarters through the slot. I hoped she wouldn't hang up while the eight quarters splashed inside the phone's collection box.

"Hello... Hello... Cosette Funeral Home, hello?"

"Mom, it's me." There was a long silence.

"Chris? Is that you? Oh, my word. Chris?" Her voice was getting frail, and I could tell she was welling with tears.

"Yes, Mom, it's me," I said bashfully in an apologetic confession.

"Dear God, are you okay? Where have you been, why did you leave? You know I've been going through hell wondering if you're okay? Where are you?" she asked. She was in full-blown confusion now, caught between interrogation and delight.

"Slow down, Mom, I'll explain. Are you okay? What about Claire, is she okay too?" I followed with a similar barrage of questions. I was relieved to hear her voice again.

"Oh yes, she's fine, I'm fine, but what about you?

"Did you find the note I left on my nightstand?" I asked.

"Yes, but you didn't say where you were going or why. Are you in some kind of trouble?"

"Not anymore, I hope. I've got a job now and am making some money is all I can tell you. I'm getting by just fine." I couldn't tell her I took someone else's name and that I was in the army. That would only confuse her more, and I didn't have enough quarters to get through that explanation. "I just wanted to let you know all of this so you wouldn't worry. I can say that I'm in a warm and sunny place where it doesn't snow."

"How can I get in touch with you? You are being very selfish, Chris. How can you do this to us? I wore out the beads on two rosaries praying to Saint Christopher and the Blessed Mother for you. I've had Father Brown hold countless masses for you. The whole parish has been praying for you, son. Please come home." There was a long silence while she cried. "There's something else you probably don't know, and it breaks my heart to tell you."

I felt my gut ache immediately. I knew she was going to tell me something very bad. "What is it, Mom?"

"Hana Haupt was killed in a car accident near Alpena the day after you left. It was very tragic. Of course we didn't get the funeral. Gatske did in Calcite City. We found out about it in a strange way. An old woman, with a heavy German accent called to tell us. She didn't give me her name, but she said she felt obligated to tell me that Hana was killed and not to worry about Kristof 'cause he would be taken care of. She began crying when she said she was too old to take care of him so he was being put up for adoption."

My knees weakened, I held the sides of the phone counter so I wouldn't fall. Mom didn't say anything, letting me process the heartbreaking news. She didn't stop there. There was more bad news to follow.

"There is something else I have to tell you. Charlie Fitzpatrick was killed in Vietnam on Halloween day. His funeral was last week. He was shot by a sniper, it was just heartbreaking. We had to have a closed casket, even your father cried, Chris. The whole town is in shock. The Fitzpatrick family has been asking about you. Sean and the twins called most every week to check if I heard from you. I couldn't tell them anything at all. I'm sorry to tell you this. Please come home now."

Mom must have heard me sobbing. She knew not to talk.

Inevitably, the operator spoke, "Please deposit one dollar for the next two minutes."

I placed the phone in its cradle, and walked to the nearest restroom down the long corridor. I closed the stall door and sat on a toilet holding the photo of Hana and Kristof. I wept like a child who just lost his family. I just wanted to go home, damn the consequences.

I tried to be the last one to board the 707. I went directly to the back of the plane as far away as I could get from the other troops. My seat was in the last row in the tail section of the plane. An overhead light said to fasten my seatbelt. I turned to the dull, smoky white wall to shield myself from anyone who wanted to converse on the long flight to Alaska. There was no privacy. Being engulfed with my anguish I paid little attention to the thrill of takeoff or the crunching sound the landing gear made tucking itself inside the craft's belly.

Private Larson, from Minnesota, a chatty Swede with albinic eyebrows and hair to match was sitting across the aisle from me. He wouldn't shut up during the flight even when I turned my body to the small window to watch the Pacific Ocean gather below me and the clouds at thirty-five thousand feet. I swallowed a few times to equalize the pressure in my ears. I should have left the packed feeling intact so my hearing would stay impaired. He never picked up on the overt indication I didn't want to talk as I was overwhelmed at the loss of Hana and Charlie. My eyes were blushed from crying.

"Ya don't have to be an asshole, buster," he said when I didn't respond to his chatter. "Hey, look fellas, this dude's so scared he's crying." There were a few laughs but most of them were dealing with their own anxiety and understood mine.

I continued to ignore Larson, the last thing I wanted to do was hear someone tell me about his problems or concerns, and his meaningless talk I would be expected to care about. It dawned on me that he was more frightened than any of us. I was crushed by the losses of Hana and Charlie. I wondered if I would be able to find my son when I rotated back to the world. I started caring about him more than I had before. How would he fare after losing his mother? Would his new parents care for him properly? Would I ever see him again?

My life now was without a future. The plans to go to California with Charlie Fitzpatrick came to an abrupt end. The possibility of me hooking up with Hana after I got back home were destroyed at the same moment. All coming to a swift demise by means of a two-minute phone call. Folks run out of life too quickly, sometimes you never see it coming, leaving the rest of the living desperately searching for something or someone to grab on to replace it. I didn't have much to choose from at this lowest point in my life.

When the plane's jets quieted, and cruised at a reasonably denuded sonance, I fell asleep.

Alaska was four hours behind me now. My company was headed for Vietnam, flown by the Military Air Transport Service, MATS, the army had an acronym for everything. The brightly polished aluminum C-141A Starlifter had one hundred and fifty troops onboard. We refueled in Okinawa for our final destination of Tan Son Nhut Air Force Base, Saigon. The only thing that stood between war and us were thousands of miles of Pacific Ocean and the South China Sea.

CHAPTER TWENTY-SIX

Saigon was a disorganized smelling mess of four million people, half of them refugees, all frantically going somewhere at the same time. The city had doubled in size when refugees flooded in from the northern provinces speaking four different dialects and seeking relief from the brutal North Vietnam Army and the Viet Cong. Three-wheeled Rickshaw taxis, pedaled by small men, and large military vehicles clogged every street in an endless traffic jam of honking horns and agitated hand gestures. Lambretta and Vespa motor scooters, sometimes carrying families, frantically dodged in and out of traffic like fighter pilots battling everyone and everything. Street vendors lined the sidewalks with their carts holding flaming woks and grills, boiling indefinable meats while rancid, deliquescent seafood dripped and dried on thin wires for display. The wafting aromas of pungent spices and peppers along with human excrement gave the city a special essence I had never experienced before.

An M-35 A-1 deuce-and-a-half cargo truck picked up a dozen of us from the process and replacement center at Tan Son Nhut for a steamy trip down Highway 1 to the Long Binh Base, a virtual military city by itself thirty-three "clicks" east of Saigon. The base entrance was completely fortified with sandbags stacked ten feet high and razor wire rolled in intertwined bundles that resembled tumbleweed brush. It held sixty thousand troops and was the largest US military base outside the United States. I had a job waiting for me with the 221st after a few guys in the pictorial company rotated back to the world. Most of the photo guys came in from the Signal Corp in Fort Monmouth, New Jersey. They came over in four packets of twenty men each.

We were dropped at the 221st Signal Company's headquarters inside the sprawling complex. Lookout towers were placed throughout the post standing ominously above the base perimeter. Three rows of concertina, and barbed wire placed five feet apart, stretched around the rest of the base. Each tower had a manned M-60 machine gunner ready for any attack, which happened frequently, mostly at night. I pondered what my job would be if we came under attack. Would I be pressing a shutter button or squeezing a trigger? I had to be ready for either one.

The heat and humidity was overwhelming. I was drenched in sweat when I entered the air conditioned headquarters of the 221st. The canvas strap on my duffel bag was saturated and dug into my shoulder. I handed my orders to an E-6 named White for processing. He was dressed in jungle camouflage fatigues and was sitting behind a green desk puffing on a Marlboro. He gave me my barracks and platoon assignment.

"How do I find it?" I asked.

"Look on the wall, Main." He pointed to the 221st camp layout diagram tacked on a wall near the exit. My barracks was only a few hundred feet from 221st HQ within the city block sized 221st encampment.

When the 221st Signal Company, Pictorial, had arrived at Tan Son Nhut that spring there were no barracks' ready for them. For the following three months they constructed ADAMS huts, hooches that came in kits like toys that bore ambiguous disclaimers, "Some assembly required." The poor bastards had to build forms, pour concrete pads, and construct twenty-one ADAMS huts. In the meantime they slept in tents that were like mini infernos until they had the aluminum buildings erected.

When I found my bunk, an E-4 was sprawled on the lower bunk reading *The Stars and Stripes*. He appeared to weigh all of about one hundred and fifty pounds, if he was soaked, carried on his light six-foot athletic frame. His sandy shaded hair had begun retreating higher on his tanned forehead. He bore an early term mustache perhaps hoping to give himself an older appearance. The rest of his face showed a few scars from the chicken pox welts he scratched at some point when he was a kid. His bright blue eyes were deeply set within their sockets like two flashlights beaming friendly and peacefully. When he smiled his face lit up in a disarming child-like grin that made me feel comfortable.

A small transistor radio was kicking out a Cream jam, "In A White Room," full-blast, far down the narrow barracks. There were louvered blinds behind our bunks but they helped little to cool the hooch. There wasn't one soul brother in the platoon to play Motown songs I had become so used to back at Fort Gordon.

"You just in, hey? How was life back in the real world?" Mike Breshears said flipping through pages. When he spoke, his voice sounded out words in a relaxed and subtle delivery.

"Just groovy, brother. How's it going, man? I'm Main. Guys got to calling me Yank back at AIT. What's yours?"

"Mike Breshears, from Oregon. Welcome to heaven," he said.

We both nodded.

"Heaven? This isn't at all how I pictured it," I said throwing my duffel on the upper bunk.

"I got pictures to prove it, you're smack-dab in the middle of it now. Isn't it far out?" He laughed, I laughed.

He pointed to a wall locker near our bunks. His had a Peace symbol on it. "Store your shit in there. You'll find it's a step above the footlockers back in basic and AIT. Really the same thing but only different, if you know what I mean. Everything here is frickin' wonderful, man. You'll see, " Mike said with a hint of sarcasm.

I emptied the duffel on my bunk and stored its contents in the grey locker next to his. "So, if this is heaven what time are the girls showing up for the dance tonight? Where's the dance hall, Mike?"

"Oh, hell. It's just down Highway 1 at Mamma San's Inferno where Victor Charlie's band is playing. They flew in from the north just for our enjoyment. Can you imagine that?" Mike laughed going along with my ice-breaking humor. He was as sarcastic as I was. Funny, too.

"I bet they play those Chinese guitars that look like AK-47s," I said.

"No sound like it, Yank. But they only know one song, 'The Green, Green, Grass Of Home'."

"I know that one. Isn't it by Tommy Gun Jones, that English dude?" I replied.

"Yep, that's the one. When the band's on break, me and some of the other fellas play, 'Light My Fire,' on our harmonicas and M-16s. The crowd loves it."

"Wish I knew how to play one. Can you teach me?"

"M-16 or harmonica?

"Harmonica. The army said I was already a life taker on the sixteen, even gave me a Marksman patch."

"Sure, but not for a while. I lost mine on the last assignment in a tunnel up in Cu Chi. Some gook is playing it now, I suppose," he said.

I thought he was kidding. "You really know how to play one?" I remembered Rand Stokes playing his harp the first time I met him. The memory softened my humor briefly.

"I learned how to play back in high school," Mike said.

"Well I'm a damned good dashboard drummer, and I know three guitar cords too." I rapped out a drum roll on my stomach while I stretched out on my bunk. I did an air guitar lick I wished he could see.

"Groovy! We can check with Supply Sergeant Shultz. That sucker can get anything if you're willing to pay his price. He runs a real con game down at supply. He said he could replace my harp, but it would cost me fifty bucks. Fuck him! I'll have my mom send one for five dollars," Mike said.

He continued telling me about the supply sergeant. "You should see him, he looks like a giant, fatted frog sitting behind his messy desk. I'm surprised he's never been called out on inspection. His head is bigger than a medicine ball but not as cute. The dude shaves once a month if he remembers. I figure he learned his trade back in the Bronx where he comes from, where everything is corrupt so they say. Always a hot-boxed, gnawed on cigar that looks like a dog turd hanging from his drooling mouth. What a tool. A tool complete with drool," Mike scoffed.

"Can't wait to meet the man. I'll have to think about gettin' that drum. I don't want the Brass changing my MOS to drummer boy after they hear me play like those poor kids in the Civil War leading the attack. Besides, I might drive everyone nuts around here," I said.

"Too late, Yank. We're already there. Drummer boy leading the attack? Not likely. Over here battles aren't fought that way. Skirmishes are what the grunts call them, firefights. Sometimes they only last for a few minutes. You'll be lucky to get a photo of the enemy. They're sneaky little shits that hit and run, especially at night. They're like mosquitos. Damned hard to get a decent photo of them while they're alive. I've got plenty of shots of the dead ones. All I've been able to get pics of is our guys pouring rounds into the heavy jungle cover, maybe some shots of smoke from artillery and mortar rounds. Scary shit, dude, but that's why we're here. Here in heaven. My day's coming. I'll catch a break and get the shot of a lifetime, it's my fucking destiny, man." There was seriousness in Mike's levity, his way of dealing with his job and with Vietnam.

"I'll try to like heaven while I'm here, Mike. You make it sound fun, and I hope I get my own front cover shot too. Got to be out there somewhere," I said.

"How about I show you around?" he said springing from his bunk.

"Hell yeah," I responded jumping down to the concrete floor Mike helped pour four months earlier.

"I'll take you to the two most important places on the base; the supply barracks and the enlisted men's club. You'll get everything you need at these two spots including your camera gear and alcohol. I hope you like San Miguel, that's about all they have most of the time."

We dodged Jeeps, trucks, and soldiers on our way through the dense mid-day heat exchanging stories of our previous lives back in the States. He was the yearbook photographer in high school, just like I was, and had built a darkroom in a basement bathroom. He told me how much he liked to hunt and fish with his dad and uncles. He had already made plans for a family whitetail hunt in the Oregon mountains the next fall after he rotated. He was going to get married to his high school sweetheart, Linda, when he got home in six months. Every soldier in 'Nam made plans to do the same things they took for granted in their past lives, myself included.

We ended up at the EM Club, enlisted men's club, for a few beers after an hour tour of the compound. San Miguel it was, and there was plenty of it. The club was a spartan sized room intended for temporary use until a larger one was complete in December. It was air conditioned and the beer was cold. I was beginning to like heaven.

The empty cans began to pile up in a handsome pyramid on our table. We were copping a good buzz, telling bad jokes, and laughing hysterically at them.

I had my back to the entrance, but Mike had a good view of the doorway. I heard it open and two soldiers walked in with the late afternoon sun spilling across the floor. Mike squinted and recognized who they were. His round smile straightened as soon as the door closed behind them. He whispered as though he was in church, "Lurps."

I didn't know what he was talking about. "What's that?"

"LLRP's-Long Range Recon Patrol, man. Probably...Yup, 101st Special Forces, but one of them is wearing a Green Beret," he said in an even smaller voice when he saw their tiger striped fatigues and their green and brown faces. "Don't look, man, we don't want to piss 'em off. They're the baddest of the bad.   Charlie calls them "Men with painted faces" because they stripe their faces with camo paint. Look, but don't stare. Rumor has it Charlie and the NVA put a bounty on them, a thousand bucks if they capture one. I pity Charlie if they get caught by the Lurps," Mike whispered.

Mike strayed his eyes back to the men without turning his head. "They usually go out in six-man teams always in the shit. Most of the time they go on patrol in the boonies for a week. Wherever the most shit is happening, they've been there."

The two LLRPs had just returned from a four day mission. I sneaked a fast peek to see what a fighting machine looked like. They were haggard and worn out, their shadowy faces nearly hidden below soiled headgear.   One was wearing a tiger stripe boonie, the other wore a green beret. All I could say was, "They look like death, man."

Mike rolled his eyes cautiously to the opposite end of the bar, "Man, that one keeps looking at you, the one with the green beret. Holy shit! I told you not to stare."

"I didn't, Mike, I swear," I said squeezing my words in a whisper.

The Lurp continued to stare, more constant and deliberate.

"What the hell did I do? Okay, I have to look back. Hold your ass brother." I turned toward the men.

"What the fuck!" the red-haired one said. "What the hell are you doing here?" This time with a hostile slam of his beer on the table. "I'm gonna' put some hurt on you, you thief."

Breshears put his head in hands in disgust, "Jeezas! Get ready, Yank, you better fall as fast as you can when he hits you."

I studied the man in the painted face while he walked toward our table. He removed his beret. I couldn't believe my eyes as he got closer. I screeched, "I'm gonna' kick your fuckin' ass, tough guy!"

Mike Breshears melted in his chair. He tried to intercede when I rose to confront the Lurp before he reached our table. We grabbed each other in a fierce bear hug, and began wrestling. Each of us grunted and strained to take the other one to the floor. I squeezed the Lurp to my chest, "Fitz, you frickin' bastard. What the hell you doin' here, man? Holy shit, man!"

It was Mike Fitzpatrick, one of my best friends.

"Don't you ask me shit, little brother. I'll do the talkin'. Now, what in hell are you doin' in that uniform? You ain't supposed to be here!" Fitz got a better look at me, holding my shoulders while pushing me away at arm's length. He saw my nametag, "Main? Who the hell..."

I stopped him immediately before he could say another word. I grabbed his arms tightly, and gave him the evil eye, "Don't say it. I'll explain it all in a bit, as soon as I can get alone with you."

He studied my appearance, much like Stosh Kuznicki did back in Detroit. Carefully going over my green fatigues, looking at me like I was a ghost. He said, "It better be good. I can only imagine knowing how good you are at dishing out bullshit."

We laughed and hugged. He picked me up and swung me around with my feet dangling off the floor. "Holy shit, little brother. I can't believe yer' here."

"Come on over to our table, I want to introduce you to my buddy. He's a Mike, too," I said.

Fitz brought his Lurp partner, Brian Rutledge, over to our table. Breshears still hadn't settled down yet, still struck with fear of having to duke it out with a couple of killers.

"You had me going, Yank," He said smiling and taking in the sight of the two Lurps without worry. "If you're going to pull this shit on me anymore, you better give me a warning next time."

Fitz and Brian Rutledge had just returned from a mission near Dak Pek, Kontum Province in the central highlands. They had captured an NVA lieutenant, and brought him back to MACV HQ at Long Binh for interrogation. Both of them were stationed in Pleiku. Fitz had joined a five-man LRRP team to take them back in the bush where he and his unit had discovered a concentration of NVA soldiers a week earlier. They had leap frogged to several bases to get to Dak Pek where they were dropped by a HU-1H Huey out in the jungle. Their mission was complete so we set in for a grand drinking session.

Fitz asked what my MOS was. He wasn't surprised. I wasn't surprised with his either.

Kicking ass came as easily to him as words and photos came to me.

"I thought it was gonna' be 'nighttime garden specialist' or something to that effect," Fitz laughed.

Breshears and Rutledge, not knowing what the hell we were talking about, wondered why we were laughing so vigorously. Fitz told the story of our late night garden adventure back in July. All of us had a knee-slapping laugh.

The ten-cent San Miguel's kept coming, along with the raucous laughter, until Fitz and me reached the inevitable. We sat facing each other, our smiles faded and our eyes finally met to deal with the memory of Charlie Fitzpatrick. A stream of tears came to us both while we held our fists against one another.

"You heard, ay?" Fitz said brushing his sleeve against his cheeks.

"Yeah, I did. Mom told me."

Fitz raised his can. We brought ours to his. He bellowed, "To Charles Dane Fitzpatrick, Wolfhounds."

That was all that was said.

CHAPTER TWENTY-SEVEN

Breshears and Rutledge stayed inside the EM club adding to what was now an impressive castle of empty cans that took up the entire space on two tabletops. Fitz and I went outside. We propped ourselves against the sandbags at the entrance. I began telling him the history of how I got to where I was. He promised he would never reveal my story to anyone in 'Nam, or back home because there was too much at risk for me. When I was finished and returned to the part where Rand and Uncle Boogie were murdered and what I did in retaliation, I must have shown a tinge of remorse. He stopped me.

"You did what you had to do. You were trying to survive. Don't think you did something wrong. The jungle you were in was no different than here. Those dogs needed to pay for what they did. Who else were they going to kill further down the road? An eye for an eye, I say, brother. I'm proud of you. Proud you made it through Fort Gordon too. I was there, and it wasn't easy. You had to improvise and overcome, that's what a soldier has to do. You're in the wrong outfit, man, we could use your sand in the one-o-one. Right on, little brother."

I felt renewed, justified by Fitz's rationalization of the ordeal. He had a good laugh when I told him about my meeting with the base commander at Fort Gordon.

"Only you could fall in a pond a' shit, and come out smelling like a rose. What did he say? Brilliant, troop?"

"No, he said, 'brilliant, son.' I wanted to hug him when he changed my MOS. After all, he regarded me as his Yankee son," I replied.

Breshears and Rutledge, arms over shoulders, staggered into the evening swelter, singing terribly off-key to the chorus of, "All You Need Is Love," but their "da-ta-ta-ta-ta-da's" were pretty good. It was time to end our soiree and head back to our quarters. Fitz and I gave each other another bear hug saying goodbye this time. He and Brian Rutledge wandered off in the night to who knows where.

Mike Breshears and I made our way back to our hooch laughing and singing more Beatles' tunes. Somewhere along the way, before we reached our bunks, I gave Mike a new name Frodo, the intrepid hero from The Lord Of The Rings, because he stood toe-to-toe and drank beer for beer with the bad ass Lurp. I would be the only one in the 221st who called him Frodo.

Vietnam at night was a time to be scared. That was Charlie's time to play and pay a visit, and he did. He often didn't stay long, just enough time to screw with us, interrupt our sleep with a few rounds of mortars, and light ammo fire from AK 47's. Sometimes they lobbed in more than that in the form of 82mm mortars and B-40 rockets that devastated the base. I pitied the grunts who were in camps out in the bush, the 'shit' as it was called. They had it worse.

That night was sleepless despite the dozens of San Miguel's Mike and I killed bullshitting at the Enlisted Men's Club with Fitz and Rutledge. Charlie dropped a few mortars inside the base after midnight reminding us he was out there. All of us were jarred from sleep. We jumped into action and waited for more to come.

This time the short attack was in response to a surprise money Conversion Day change. GI's had to convert their real American money into MPC's, Military Payment Certificates, as soon as they arrived in Vietnam. The US Government changed the design of the certificates often to throw off the black marketers in Saigon who were known to make counterfeit MPC's. The old MPC's would have to be exchanged for new ones quickly because the old currency would be useless. The local VC was pissed because they were sitting on a horde of old MPC's they didn't have time to convert before the change.

After the brief attack, we flopped ourselves back into our bunks. Mike said not to worry unless we heard sirens and call to arms. Not very comforting, but that was how it was.

Roll call was at six AM. NCO Anderson woke us in a much less frantic hail than what was the standard back at Fort Gordon. We hurried to get dressed just the same to make formation at the head of our barracks for the daily roll call. Our platoon leader, Aaron Brooks, inspected our group making sure everyone was there. A Lieutenant walked along the platoons checking our status. E-5 Brooks responded, "First squad all present." Before we dispersed, Anderson called out assignments for the day.

Some guys had barracks cleaning, others had yard pickup duty. Everyone had an assignment. Anderson's voice rang, "Breshears and Main?"

"Yes, sir," we responded.

"Garbage duty."

We were dismissed. Mike and I walked on to the military police mess hall where the 221st ate their meals. I kicked at the gravel.

"Garbage duty? We're famous photographers, not garbage jockeys, dude. How ignoble. What a waste of our wonderful talents. Shouldn't we be getting shooting assignments?" I said.

"That'll come, for sure. But, oh no, man, garbage detail is the best job we can get. We can piss away the whole day doing it. Just driving around in a deuce and a half picking up shit, and taking it to the dump. We'll stop at the PX to get a case of beer, and hang out at the dump all day. Frickin' groovy, man. Don't worry, the assignments will come. I'll ask Lieutenant Patterson if I can bring you on the next one," Mike said.

Mike was a light eater, a piece of cold toast and some fruit was plenty for him for breakfast. I packed my tray with an assortment of things, anything but scrambled eggs that came out of box and had green things in it. Mike looked up as Howard 'Pony' Shetland stood in line with his meal tray.

"Oh shit, I hope he doesn't join us. I know he will when he sees me," Mike said dismayed and irritated. "If he does, get ready to meet the biggest asshole in the 221st, Pony Shetland. I hope you don't vomit after talking to him."

Mike and Howard Shetland were together in photo school at Fort Monmouth, New Jersey. Shetland was always pulling ignorant pranks on his mates, like loosening saltshaker tops at the mess table so a guy using one would ruin his meal. A group of the guys went off base for a few beers one night, and Shetland started a bar fight with some locals. On the way home in a taxi Shetland held his flaming lighter to Mike's hand while Mike was dozing off. Shetland was either a guy who didn't get enough of his mother's tit or simply had a death wish.

Mike went on to say, "We left Washington State together with the 221st on a troop ship to Vietnam. Shetland told me he intended to come home with a chest full of medals after his time in country was up, and he didn't care who got in the way. He was gung ho as they came, he should have been in infantry with all of his plans for valor and heroism."

Shetland took a seat next to Mike, as we anticipated. "Hey, Dickhead, what ya got this morning?" he said jabbing Mike in the ribs with his elbow. Mike flinched from the less than gentle jolt.

"Pony, I wish you wouldn't do that, man." Mike tossed his spoon on the table and wiped his mouth with a napkin. Shetland's presence was enough for him to lose his appetite.

"Who's this dude?" Shetland asked after sticking his finger through Mike's uneaten toast then rubbing his buttered finger on Mike's cheek.

"This is Yank Main, a new guy just in."

"Cherry, hey? Think he'll make it?" Shetland said.

The guys in the 221st never called a new replacement, "Cherry," that was infantry jargon. Shetland wanted to act and sound like a ground pounder. He gave me a once over and said, "I bet he hides when the first mortar hits. What the hell kinda name is, 'Yank'?"

I gave Pony Shetland an inquisitive look of distrust and annoyance. He was short but squarely built like a box of saltine crackers with dark brown hair.   His hands were small like those of a pubescent teen. I didn't want to remind him of the old adage, but I couldn't wait to take a stab at him, "What the hell kind of name is Pony? No, I don't think so. I can handle it."

"We'll see. I look forward to it, man. I ain't afraid a dropping the Graflex for an M-16. I'd just as soon do that anyway," Shetland said while he used his fork for a fake riffle aimed at me. "Ask Breshears why they call me Pony."

By now Mike had as much as he could stand of Pony Shetland, the guy was a real piece of work. "Nah, you go ahead and tell him, it's your story."

"Okay," he said.   Shetland reached for his crotch and grabbed a hand full, "Cause I'm hung like a small pony. That's why." Shetland laughed while he yo-yoed his package.

I couldn't resist. "Is that so? I thought it was cause your last name is Shetland like the little pony kids like to ride at the circus."

Pony Shetland held his fork tightly in his fist. Before he could retaliate we got up and left the mess hall to get our deuce and a half from supply. I gave a quick look at Shetland. He was throwing daggers at me through a skin-tightened glare.

"Way to go, Yank. I hate that asshole," Mike said chuckling.

CHAPTER TWENTY-EIGHT

Heavy headed from the beers we drank the night before we decided to forego the case of beer we planned on bring along for our day's duty. Instead we opted for a gallon jug of water. We tooled around the base in the clumsy deuce and a half, picking up trash, and talking about his past assignments. We passed two old papa san's who were hired to take care of shit burning detail. The trays consisted of fifty-five gallon barrels cut in half to be used as human waste containers in the shit houses. Every day the old men collected the half barrels and doused them in diesel fuel before setting them on fire. The stench of the black smoke was nauseating. Mike stomped on the throttle to whisk us further down the road away from the blazing shit. The 221st were far too classy to be required to burn shit like other outfits had to do by themselves.

Mike had been in a few dicey spots up country, but the "money shot" still eluded him. He was worried about being able to take a decent series of photos with the archaic, clumsy equipment we had to use in the field.

Rumor had it around base that the army's photo equipment was picked out by a naive, do-gooder wife of a higher up in the 221st. She decided she was going to outfit the photographers with what she felt was the "right" equipment. So on her fanciful and whimsical state-side shopping spree she took the advice of some purest camera store dumb ass who convinced her the standard issue still cameras should be Graflex XL's. They captured good photos and worked well for "grip and grins," when someone was receiving an award or static scenery and building photos. But they were slow to operate, big, heavy, and bulky with only ten shots per roll of Kodacolor film. If the money shot needed an eleventh frame you were just plain out of luck. Thank God she wasn't selecting the weapons the grunts used. At least they had plenty of room for extra shots in their M-16s, and the magazines could be changed out quickly. When the international news teams showed up the photographers were using modern, motorized Nikons with a fine selection of auxiliary lenses. It was as though we were showing up with knives for a gunfight compared to them.

Mike had reached the halfway point with six months left in his tour, but he wasn't going to shy away from any photo assignment, no matter where it took him or what he had to use for a camera. He had learned how to get the most out his Graflex despite its shortcomings. He didn't get excited about "grip and grin" photo shoots, this was too tame for him because any army photographer could do them. He preferred going out in the shit where he was always searching for the chance to get the one photo that would capture the throes of battle even if it brought him in harm's way. He wasn't gung ho crazy-dinky dow, like Pony

Shetland, he was just a damned good army photographer.

We had endured the swelter of the Vietnam heat, but our head-throbbing hangovers stuck with us throughout the long day. By the time we returned the truck to the motor pool we were revived, and a cold beer was in order. Down the road from our barracks a few industrious guys had constructed a tent out of a billowing parachute with a canvas awning stretched over its entrance. Inside was a fifty-five gallon drum filled with ice and endless cans of beer. Just what we thought we needed. We joined the twenty or so men who were way ahead of us in beer consumption. We had to play catch up if we were going to be at their level of comfortable intoxication.

"I'll buy if you fly," Mike said taking a seat on rickety lawn chair.

I went to the barrel and searched for a couple beers in the ice-cold water. I thought I would faint when I dragged my hand through the ice in search of a couple beers. The chill was a shock to my overheated body, but I managed to pull out two Budweisers. I folded my ass on the ground next to Mike. Each of us crunched our church keys into the cans and took long gulps that sounded out, "Good, good, good, good." Mike grimaced looking at me. I returned a strained grimace. We both grabbed our faces as though we had been electrocuted. An instantaneous brain freeze crippled us and put us out of commission for a painfully brief moment.

"Wasn't that fun," I said massaging my temples.

"Wow! We better have another," Mike said shaking the freeze away.

"Hey, I'll get you guys beers. Stay right there," a familiar voice spoke from behind us. It was Pony Shetland.

Mike spoke, "No, no, I'll get 'em. Don't bother."

"Aw, come on, it's the least I can do for my fellow brothers. Sorry about this morning, Mike, I was just horsing around. No harm done. Okay?" Shetland extended his hand for me to shake. I complied with a firm grip on his hand. "Pretty strong grip there, Yank," He said.

"Yeah, I've been working out on garbage detail all day."

"I'll be right back. Buds?" he asked.

"Sure," Mike replied. Pony walked over to the beer barrel. "See? The guy's an enigma, ya' never know what to expect out of him. Maybe there's a bit of hope for him after all."

Pony returned in short order, handing us two chilled Buds. "What a ya' say we have a toast? To the men in the 221st."

Pony opened his. When we opened ours, beer spewed in our faces in a robust gush, drenching us from head to heel. Pony scampered out of the tent bent over laughing like a drunken hyena.

"Forget what I just said, there's no hope for that prick," Mike said sloshing the beer from his face with the palms of his hands.

It took a while for the beer to dry, mixing with our sweat in a sticky glaze on our faces. "The hell with it," I said. We made a few more trips to the beer cache, and proceeded to catch a buzz.

Later Lieutenant Allen Patterson, a lightly built California guy in his late twenties, joined us. He was fun to be around, even though we weren't allowed to mix with our superiors. Patterson was relaxed and easy going. He liked rock and roll music, like we did, and never wavered from being truthful with us.

Mike introduced me. I didn't know if I was supposed to salute or offer my hand for a shake. I rose to my feet and saluted to be sure.

"Relax, Yank. No need for spit and polish with me," he said extending his hand for me to shake.

Patterson fetched a chair to join us. "I just talked with HQ. We might be heading out of here in the next few days up to Kontum Province. There's been some action near Dak To Airbase. The NVA has been gathering in the hills nearby, and it looks like we're going to do something about it. The 173rd, and the 3rd of the 8th is getting ready to engage, and we're going to cover it." He turned to me, "You think you're ready for an assignment?"

"Hell, yes I am, sir."

Mike asked, "I'd like to take Yank with us, can we use three still shooters on my team?"

Most photo teams had two still shooters and a "mopic," a motion picture photographer, inserted with an infantry detachment when HQ felt an engagement should have photo coverage. By all reports there was going to be a significant engagement with the NVA up country in the Central Highlands near Dak To. "Yes, I need you to get his feet wet the right way, Mike. We'll be sending more than one packet up there, anyway."

I made a silent fist pound and thanked Lieutenant Patterson.

"We'll see if you still want to thank me after it's all over." Patterson replied as he was leaving.

"Fuckin' ay!" I squealed joyously, excited to get my first shot in the field. "I can't wait, dude."

Mike wisely avoided showing any reaction. "Stay cool, Yank. This won't be any Sunday walk-in-the park photo shoot of flowers and happy kids' faces. We're going into the shit, brother."

I reduced my exuberance to a satisfied smile. "Sorry, Frodo. I'm just excited to go out on my first assignment."

"I was too on my first one," he said. "How about another brew before we hit the showers?"

"I'll buy, if you'll fly," I said.

We toted the beers through the early evening heat on our way to shower off the day's grime and dried beer that was making our eyelids stick together.

The water was cold and sobering when it cascaded over my face. Suddenly, debris began landing on the tin roof in a loud clatter. Mike and I grabbed towels and bolted through the door to get prepared for the attack. When we got outside, there stood Pony Shetland with a fist full of gravel in each hand. He had pulled another of his goofy pranks, throwing gravel and anything he could toss on the shower's metal roof making it sound like we were under attack.

"Got ya's again, suckers!"

Pony Shetland walked away slowly not laughing or celebrating the pratfall we reacted to as though he was disappointed by failing to get more of a fevered reaction from us.

We returned to the shower room to get dressed. Mike muttered, "The guy just doesn't get it. I'm worried what he's going to do next."

CHAPTER TWENTY-NINE

It was now November 6th, five days in country, and still no assignment. It was as though the army had hired me for a job that I didn't have to do. A job with no tools, except a rake and a shovel and some arm-strong garbage lifting. We didn't hear any more about going up to Dak To or the NVA build up, but it was happening just the same. Victor Charles was active throughout the country, more than usual. It was puzzling to the brass down in MACV Headquarter. "What does Charlie have in mind with this activity away from the larger cities?" more than one General questioned. The enemy was planning something.

At last my first assignment came. Mike and I were getting bored with drinking beer and trivial base duties. We were making our bunks when Lieutenant Patterson summoned us for a morning trip to Pleiku, Kontum Province. We were to hook up for a "sneak and peek" to document a LRRP squad mission with a group of Montagnards, or Degars as they were known. The Montagnards were indigenous to the mountainous areas of the Central Highlands. They were fierce little warriors who hated the VC and became our allies fighting against the NVA and VC.   Being skillful trackers and having a long history of strife with the general Vietnamese population and government, "Yards" were a tremendous asset to the US military when they joined LRRP and Special Forces to fight against our common enemy.

Our team was comprised of Mike Breshears and me using Graflex XL still cameras and Lieutenant Allen Patterson would be shooting motion picture footage with an Ariflex 16mm camera.   I was replacing Pony Shetland who couldn't go because of a bad case of morning drip. He had been hooking up with the bargain basement ladies of the night down in Saigon. He was always bragging he was able to get laid for a few piastras less than the going rate. I guess he got what he paid for.   There would have been another mopic shooter, but going out with the Lurps necessitated a smaller squad.   I was surprised to find myself included until Patterson explained. "The combat photo teams are all out on assignment up north in the I Corps region, so we were called in to cover for them. I don't know who you two know, but you both were requested by name."

I had a good idea who was doing the requesting.

When we checked out our camera equipment from supply we were each issued Colt 1911 .45 caliber pistols, relics from the Second World War. Mike didn't care to holster the pistol because it was extra weight. "I guess they give us these in case we have to commit suicide." I was uncomfortably stunned by his comment.

The photo gear was boxed and loaded onto Jeeps. We were transported to a chopper pad inside Long Binh base. From there we would take a UH-1 Huey and leap frog north, stopping at Tanh Linh, Tuy Hoa, Loc Thien and finally Plei Me to meet our Lurp commando counterparts.

The long flight was tiring, and my ass was hurting from the uncomfortable seat. My head began to ache with the constant, quick throbbing drone and blathering wind the chopper's blades brought inside the cabin. There wasn't much talking between us after we were briefed by Lieutenant Patterson on the first stretch of the flight. By mid-morning we could see the triangular shaped Special Forces base coming into view as we crested a mountaintop. Inside a separate barracks housed a team of Montagnard Special Forces. The base was carved out of a thick, overgrown jungle at the foothills of the high country inhabited by Montagnards. The red clay earth contrasted sharply to the verdant hills that surrounded the heavily fortified base.

We landed on a helipad outside the base perimeter. To our right was a clutch of burned out Montagnard family longhouses flanking the helipad's north side. The base had endured a vicious, weeklong enemy siege on October 19, 1965. Several thousand VC had managed to bring their attack to the barbed wire perimeter before being repelled by the 5th Special Forces Group and Montagnard fighters who were defending the base. When the 1st Air Cavalry interceded the battle was over. Mortar and artillery craters still pocked the landscaped near the base.

The ever-present swelter of humidity and tropical heat became stifling when we left the whipping blades of the UH-1 behind at the landing zone. We headed for the base headquarters to meet our Special Forces team.

Brian Rutledge was the first person we met inside the planning room. He and Mike had a laugh remembering their drunken revival a couple days earlier back in Long Binh. He would lead the squad and had requested Mike and I join his unit. Apparently after drinking with Mike, and getting a good recommendation from Fitz about me, he felt we could hack it. It wasn't going to be easy, though, we would have to hump our gear into the highlands to check out an NVA concentration a Montagnard patrol had discovered earlier that week. Our job would be to document the buildup for an action MACV could disseminate and plan recourse for. The Lurps and Montagnards were not to engage the enemy. They were going to lead us to them so we could carry out our assignment, then get us the hell out as fast as we could.

Ten of us returned to the helipad where the UH-1 had been refueled and was waiting to carry us into the mountains. The six-man Lurp team was part of the 5th Special Forces who had trained at the Recondo School in Nha Trang. They were battle hardened ass kickers who carried the aloof appearance of outer space in their eyes.

The Lurps traveled light with Dave Mathias and Vic Tomes toting M-60 machine guns. A black Lurp, by the name of Conrad, was cradling an M-79 Blooper on his lap. Donny Helms, a short but muscular E-5 with large, veined forearms was packing a Prick 25 radio. Tom Fellows, who the others called Tom Tom, was armed with an M-16, so was Brian Rutledge. All of them were dressed in tiger stripe fatigues and boonie hats. Their faces blotched in green and brown camo paint. Each of us carried a rucksack.

The Lurps were quiet as strangers who had never met before when we unpacked our camera equipment and boarded the Huey. When the Huey lifted, Rutledge leaned across the aisle and shouted over the noisy take off. "When we get there, you boys do as I say, and stay close and goddamned quiet, you understand?" We nodded. My eyes began to widen at his ominous warning. This was it! We were going to enter the "shit."

The Huey whirled at treetop level above the mountains for a twenty minute flight where a Montagnard team was waiting for us at a machete cleared LZ deep into the triple canopied forests west of Pleiku City. We weren't far from the Cambodian border. This was Montagnard country. When the Huey landed we deployed into the waist high brush in a hurry. Four Montagnards, Y Bham Anuol, Nay Tuett, Y Dhong Trongan, and Y Tlur Uban, the leader and military interpreter, led us into the thicker cover of bamboo and lianas shrubs growing below thap lu'u and sky-high hopea trees. The Huey lifted away quickly, instantly out of sight with only its chop-chop sound fading away through the sunless, darkened canopy of trees where only scattered shards of sunlight streaked to the forest floor.

We were dripping with sweat. When Y Tlur Uban gathered us in a semi-circle for a brief overview of instructions and warnings, we raised our cameras taking his photo where he was crouched on dead leaves, fallen branches, and twigs that snapped under the weight of his knee. He was carrying a crossbow for his weapon. The other Montagnards carried M-16s. He nudged his finger over his lips in a "shush" pose. "You hear that?" he said pointing to the twigs beneath his knee, "You not make that sound. Bookoo noise. VC hear, go bang, bang, ca ca dau, you dead!" He went on to tell us there were one hundred-forty species of poisonous snakes in Vietnam, along with hungry, aggressive tigers, and boa constrictors searching for a meal. He warned us to be careful where we reached for trees and branches when we climbed along the steep mountain trail where there could be a snake. One snake in particular, the two-step viper, was especially wicked. If you were bit you had two steps before you died as the story went. I hated snakes and would make sure I knew where my hands were going at all times—gripping my camera.

Uban was the only Montagnard with us who spoke English, heavily broken as it was. He and his men were thin, but tightly wound in small frames. Their skin was a dark, mottled color. They did not have the epicanthic skin folds above their eyes, like the mainstream Vietnamese I had seen, but were of the same physical size. After our brief meeting we began to hump through the tangled mountain forest trail heading for the area Uban had seen the enemy. The Montagnards led the way with Rutledge running point in our group. Dave Mathias followed at the end with his M-60. Our photo team was placed smack dab in the middle of the Lurps for safety reasons.

It was a slow, cautious, uphill climb with the "Yards" stopping frequently to listen to the mountain. We continued at this pace for the rest of the afternoon until Uban halted us for a rest near a grove of young bamboo saplings. We drank sparingly from our canteens. Some of the Lurps edged carefully away from the trail to take a piss.

The Montagnards crouched low and listened for any unusual sound, but the jungle forest was as quiet as a Sunday night church. This bothered Uban. Absent was the sound of birds and other fauna that was typically present. Uban motioned for us to stay put when he knocked an arrow bolt in his crossbow. He went off on his own in a deep knee bend crawl further up the trail. We dared not talk, smoke, spit, or otherwise make any noise until he returned.

Rutledge edged over to Patterson, Mike, and I. "If we find them we'll get you close enough to get your photos, but do it quickly. It's not like they're gonna' stand and pose for you."

"Can you get us in a position where we can get different angles of their camp if that's what we find? We need to doc' as much of them as possible," Patterson said.

"Depends on how many and the cover they're set up in," Rutledge replied. "We'll know here as soon as Uban returns. That is if he finds anything."

Uban had been gone for an hour. Mike and I took a few photos of Rutledge and his crew while we waited on the narrow trail. Patterson shot movie footage of us taking their photos. Uban returned to tell us he found a small group of three VCs set up in what he thought was a perimeter camp near a grove of bamboo and ancient hopea trees. He felt they were there to notify a larger group further up the trail if they encountered guys like us. "We go now. You see."

I took a deep breath and checked my camera settings. The triple canopy foliage allowed little quality of light to make a decent exposure. We set out for the hidden camp in the same procession as before.

The sounds of the rain forest returned. Songbirds, chirping bugs, and animals surrounded us. A nervous grey-shanked douc monkey leaped from tree to tree to evade us. We continued in a crouched crawl until Uban stopped and motioned with his tilted face in a sniffing gesture. "Smell that?" We detected the smolder of a campfire.

We proceeded further up the trail. We could hear laughing and fast up swinging voices speaking Vietnamese. It was the VC Uban had seen earlier. They were near a hollowed out log inside the small bamboo grove trying on bronze and copper bracelets they found inside the log. A small fire smoldered below a large, unattended steel wok nearby. Three AK-47's were stacked in a tripod near the fire. It must have been a hundred degrees in the stagnant forest, but I felt a chill shoot through me. We hugged the forest floor on our bellies. We dared not take a photo, we were too close and they might hear us.

Uban held up his fist telling us to wait while he and his men inched closer to the VC who were parading and laughing at the treasures they were wearing. There was something about the enemy wearing the bracelets that angered the Yards. Uban and his men crawled unnoticed beneath the ferns and low growing shrubs to within twenty feet of the VC. Uban loaded a bolt in his crossbow and took aim. The twang of the bow sounded. The short arrow ripped through the throat of one of the VC, lodging itself in a bamboo tree. The other two were caught dumbfounded, wondering what had happened, giving the Montagnards enough time to swiftly charge and kill them with their knives. It all happened with deadly, stealthy precision within a few seconds and barely a sound made.

Uban waved for us to join him and his men who were removing the bracelets from the dead VC and putting them back into the hollow log. The log was a sacred burial site for a Montagnard elder, a place where his remains and possessions were interred.

Our photo team documented the grisly scene for MACV and the after action report Rutledge felt he should make. We took photos of the angry looking Yards holding their knives and crossbow standing defiantly over the dead VC. The Lurps investigated the immediate area for more information. Mathias and Conrad went into the bamboo thicket and returned to tell us of a discovery they made. We entered the dense bamboo for a few yards when we came upon two enormous caldrons filled with enough fresh rice to feed a company of men.

The cache of rice was a dead giveaway to how many enemy was nearby, at least enough of them to require a food stash as large as the one we found. We were running out of light in the darkening, late afternoon mountaintop.

Uban led us further into the forest, beyond the small camp, until we found what we were looking for an hour away.

"Damn!" Rutledge whispered. We could clearly see the dozens of NVA troops and VC guerrillas from our elevated position overlooking several hooches on stilts and the sparse clearings they had made near them. They were well armed. Stacks of 82mm mortar rounds and other ordinance were thinly covered with camouflage netting.   There were rows of AK47 rifles propped against makeshift horizontal braces that resembled hitching posts. We began filming the large encampment immediately, Mike and I must have gone through a half of a dozen film backs, while Patterson burned through a one hundred foot reel of movie film.

Rutledge whispered to Patterson, "You get enough shots yet? Let's boogie. We've got to find a place to set up camp for the night."

Patterson lowered his Ariflex and motioned for the rest of us to end our filming. We got enough photos to show MACV what the enemy was planning. So far it was a successful photo mission, all we had to do now was get the hell out of Dodge without being discovered.

We didn't stop during our three-hour hump retreating back through the forest until the trees and shrubs were merely a grey outline facing us. Rutledge moved to what he thought was a safe distance off the trail to set up camp.   The Montagnards departed leaving us to fend for ourselves, but the Lurps were well experienced in nighttime missions. We had complete faith in their expertise in survival.

Vic Tomes and Tom Fellows began setting up trip wires attached to flares. Claymore mines were placed at the perimeter of our camp before complete darkness surrounded us. Tomes would pull first watch, Fellows would relieve him, followed by Conrad, Mathias, and Rutledge as the night wore on.

Rutledge brought our photo team to the center of the camp in a tight grouping. The rest of the Lurps made a circle around us with their feet facing us where they bedded on the forest floor. There would be no fire to heat water for the Lurp rations that were surprisingly tasty. We had C Rations in our rucksacks, but they were awful compared to what the Lurps carried with them. We also had flashlights to use in an emergency.

I couldn't sleep. The day's events had been just too overwhelming to dismiss by closing my eyes and falling asleep. The mountain air cooled as the night wore endlessly on. Everyone but Rutledge and I seemed to be sleeping. He was about ten feet away from me holding the claymore clicker, watching and listening for any disturbance. Conrad was the closest Lurp near me. His heavy breathing and occasional snoring had stopped. He was now making an unfamiliar sound, like he was trying to speak during a nightmare but could only make a muted "S" sound every so often. This went on for ten minutes. I began to listen closer to his indistinguishable murmur. The "S" word began to sound more like "Snake." He was lying motionless, like he was paralyzed. I reached for my flashlight, believing he was calling for help. When I clicked it on I directed the narrow beam on Conrad's body. Coiled on his chest, inches from his face, was the notorious Banded Krait—the dreaded two-step viper. Conrad had indeed been saying "Snake" all along. The viper had chosen Conrad's warm body to coil up on for the night.

Rutledge noticed the flashlight's beam immediately. He could see the snake, too. He whispered, "Do not make any sudden movements or he's dead, Yank."

"I won't," I said not taking my eyes from the snake. Conrad's eyes were as wide opened as a Mason jar lid.

"Don't move, Conrad," I said in my smallest voice.

He blinked, "No shit!"

I had to think fast for a solution. I was in the best position to do something for Conrad. I knew snakes reacted to warmth and coldness; they were most active when warm and lethargic when cold. I would gamble that the viper was cold and could not react with a bite if I quickly covered it with a towel. I slowly rose to my knees, holding the light on the snake. I called Rutledge over to take the flashlight so I could remove it with both hands.

"You better be quick about it, Yank. Both of you are in peril, dude," Rutledge said taking the flashlight from my hand.

I removed the towel from Rutledge's neck and spread it open in my hands. The snake remained motionless until I covered it with the warm towel. I could make out the shape of the viper's head beginning to move beneath the green towel. I brought my right hand behind its head and grabbed it in one swift motion. The snake writhed and coiled inside the towel. When I lifted it away from Conrad's chest its body hung three feet below the towel. Tears were spilling from Conrad's eyes down to his temples. His forehead was dripping wet. In one adrenaline fueled motion I tossed the snake far beyond our perimeter where I could hear its body thud on the ground. Conrad reached for me with his outstretched hand. I pulled him upright. I thought I would pass out during his suffocating hug.

During the process of removing the snake I hadn't noticed everyone had been watching the entire ordeal. We all wanted to cry out in cheerful hoorays of joy, but that would have been a dangerous and foolish thing to do deep in enemy territory.

CHAPTER THIRTY

When dawn had arrived with the jungle backlit from the sun rising, some of us were shivering beneath our ponchos we had put on after the snake's visit. The mountain air was damp and cool from a fine mist dripping from the canopy of broad leaves above us. The central highlands could be cold at night and hot as the hubs of hell during the day. We hiked down the hillside jungle to the LZ that was bursting with sunlight. Rutledge had Donny Helms called for an extraction, while we waited cloaked within the dense jungle cover near our LZ. Rutledge took the mic, there was a brief conversation I couldn't hear, but we could hear the UH-1's flop-flop approaching from the east. Rutledge tossed an M-18 smoke grenade that puffed green smoke to mark the LZ so the pilot could find us.

We boarded the Huey and flew off to the rising sun. Rutledge spoke to Patterson so he would know where we were heading, but Mike and I had no clue. When the chopper headed into the sunrise we knew we weren't going south toward Plei Me. A short time later we landed at Pleiku Air Base, commanded by the 9th Air Commando

Squadron, named APO San Francisco. Somehow our plans to return to Long Binh had been changed. We were going to be re-deployed, and wouldn't discover where until we landed.

On Thursday, November 9th, Mike and I were exhausted. Patterson took our exposed film so it could be airlifted ASAP back to MACV in Saigon for processing. He told us to go to the Press Corp tents, "Crash for as long as you want, as long as it's no more than an hour," he said. We found a couple vacant cots to sleep on. We were weary, enervated, and dulled in our senses. Neither of us gave a shit how uncomfortable the boney, thinly padded beds felt when we collapsed onto them.

"That was really something you did up there, Yank," Mike said. He was sprawled on his cot, his arms folded across his chest, his voice weak and shallow with fatigue. "I think you made a good impression on everyone, especially Conrad."

"Conrad," I sighed. I smiled tiredly like I had survived a bad dream that was real. "He almost crushed me. You should have seen the look on his face while the two-step was inches away from his chin. Holy shit! I can't believe I did that. I frickin' hate snakes, Frodo."

"I guess he did too. I wonder what Patterson is thinking? I'm sure he knows that you can cut it out in the field now." Mike said.

"I'd like to see the photos we took. I hope they turn out okay. It was so damned dark up there. When we get back let's go over to the lab and check it out, okay?" Mike was out like a batter hitting a pop fly to a golden glove shortstop. Moments later so was I.

We slept soundly for an hour when Patterson woke us. It felt like a blink in time.

"Time to go to work, fellas. The Big Guy is on a chopper less than twenty minutes away. Grab your gear, and load up for a grip and grin with General Westmoreland, the commander of the US forces in Vietnam."

Mike and I gave each other a surprised look. There was no time for us to clean up or change clothes. We loaded our film packs with fresh rolls of Kodacolor film, attached potato-masher Metz electronic flash units on our cameras, and sprinted off to the helipad to wait for Westmoreland's arrival.

Westmoreland's entourage circled the base and landed in an enormous, thunderous sounding C-47 Chinook helicopter. He came there to brief the 4th Infantry on Operation MacArthur that had gotten underway, November 2nd. The dust and debris rose in a storm cloud around us. We covered our cameras and waited for him to disembark. Aware of maintaining his glorified persona and title, he was first off the aircraft sprinting toward us as though he was leading the charge of a dozen aides and other brass following close behind. Patterson, Mike, and I recorded his arrival, staying in front of the group, taking more photos as he made his way to the command center.

We filed into a large convening room at HQ for Westmoreland's meeting with General Peers and Lieutenant Colonel Glen Belnap to discuss strategy. I was holding my camera against my eye to pose a shot of the general shaking hands when a strong hand gripped my shoulder from behind. "I see you've come a long way, Yank."

I turned to see who it was. I immediately guffawed. "Major General Richardson, sir. I'm so glad to see you again, sir. What brings you all the way over here, sir?" I said.

I briefly told him I was now with the 221st Photographic Company at Long Binh. He said he knew that already. I was humbled he had taken the time to check out where I ended up, as he had promised back at Fort Gordon.

"I'm getting a sneak and peek for my next job. I'm transferring soon to MACV in Sa-gown, to be with General Westmoreland," he said with his Texas twang.

"May I take your photo, sir?" I asked comfortably at ease in his familiar presence. Mike was standing near to us, camera in hand, his mouth gapped open.

"By all means," he replied. An American flag was propped close by. I maneuvered where I could include the flag in the background and snapped two photos. Mike took a shot of me taking the major general's photo.

"If you get down to Sa-gown, stop in at MACV, and we'll talk, Yank." I blushed in humility and turned to Mike who looked astonished. Before I could say goodbye, the major general returned to Westmoreland's group without saying anything else.

We finished our assignment. Once again Patterson took our film to be sent back to MACV for processing, but our day wasn't over yet.

"How the hell do you know the Major General so well, Yank? Christ, you guys talked like you were long lost friends. I'm impressed, once again, with how you get around," Mike said as we sauntered to the mess hall for some chow.

"If it wasn't for him, I'd be pounding the ground somewhere else toting an M-16 instead of this," I raised the camera. "He changed my MOS from 11B to 84B and 71Q back at Gordon after he read a story I wrote in the Rambler. He called me to his office. The dude had a beautiful Nikon F with a slew of lenses. I gave him a lesson on how to use it. That's how I got the 84B MOS. I wished the hell I had one here." I raised the bulky Graflex. "This piece a crap will never come back in my hands again."

"I know what you mean. I see these guys from the press flying in from the world with new Nikon's and Leica's strung around their necks. Lucky bastards. 71Q? Isn't that journalist?"

"Yes it is. I haven't been called to do any writing yet. Maybe that's coming? I really don't know," I said.

"Jesus, Yank. What else you got up your sleeve? You going to tell me you're a brain surgeon next?" he laughed.

"Would you believe I can embalm a body?" I said. I caught myself before I revealed any more of my past.

"I don't doubt you, Yank. Just don't be sizing me up just yet. I still haven't gotten the money shot."

"You know what they say?" I asked in jest.

"What do 'they' say, Yank?"

"When given lemons, make lemonade!" I gave Mike a shove that tilted him sideways and took his photo.

"Now isn't that proverbial?" He gave me a returned shove and took my photo. "You ass!"

We had barely finished our meals when Patterson came back to us. "Time to squeeze your cheeks and grab your gear, boys. We're on the road again."

"Come on, Lieutenant. We haven't even had time to dry off yet. Where to now?" I griped when I shouldn't have. I followed with an apology.

"We've got another assignment. No bitching is going to change our orders, let's move out. There's a chopper waiting for us. We're hooking up with the 4th Infantry at a fire support base near Dak To in Kontum Province. It's going to be a hell hole from what I hear."

"Lieutenant, we're getting low on film," Mike said.

"I'm way ahead of you. We're all restocked with plenty of film. We'll meet up with another photo team from the 221st at the fire support base."

"Who's joining us?" Mike asked hoping he wouldn't hear Pony Shetland's name.

Patterson knew of Mike's aversion to Shetland. "Yeah, I'm afraid he's on board, too. Get over it."

We returned to the barracks to fetch our rucksacks. Mike was quiet on the way there.

"We'll be fine, Frodo. Don't worry," I said trying to ease Mike's logical concern.

"I hope that S.O.B. doesn't do something foolish and dangerous. Remember what I said about how he plans on being a hero?"

"Yeah, I do. You don't think he'll..."

Mike stopped me mid-sentence. "We've gotta' watch our asses around him, Yank."

We boarded another UH-1 in the mild, early afternoon breeze. Large, billowy cumulus clouds drifted above us. A grizzled, nervous gunner, with an aging tattoo reading "Mom" inked on his upper arm, sat locked and loaded behind an M-60 machine gun. He stared at the jungle below us during our entire trip to base camp Dragon Mountain outside Dak To.

CHAPTER THIRTY-ONE

The pilot shouted, "Hold your asses," when we descended to base camp Dragon Mountain in a steep and swift drop, but we couldn't hear him over the chopper din. Mike was sitting in the doorway of the chopper fully dressed in his combat gear, his rucksack strapped on his back, his feet braced on a landing skid. He was a well-seasoned chopper passenger and knew the centrifugal force would keep him in place. I grabbed the tube bracing under our canvas seats for extra measure.

The base was heavily fortified with troops from the 173rd Airborne Brigade, and the 4th Infantry Division assembled for what was called Operation MacArthur that began November 2nd. They were packed up and ready to have another slugfest with the NVA who were determined to rid the Central Highlands of American forces.

The NVA had been infiltrating the surrounding highlands for months coming in from Laos and Cambodia along the Ho Chi Minh Trail. Search and destroy missions from the 4th Infantry had been engaging the NVA since the middle of summer. November had been particularly brutal with the enemy amassing four divisions in the jungle highlands nearby. The firebase had become a collection point for enormous caches of enemy artillery and weapons the 4th Infantry Division had confiscated from the jungle. Everywhere we looked there were stacks of rockets, artillery rounds, grenade launchers, and AK-47's heaped in piles all to be destroyed.

We knew immediately something wicked had been happening in an ongoing battle with the NVA. More awaited five miles away near the Laotian border. Most every soldier we encountered showed the drawn down face of despair when we mulled around the base to find our temporary quarters. The base was devoid of barracks, tents only, strung out in long rows throughout the base camp. We didn't know we were stepping into a nest of ambiguity where fear and uncertainty was in everyone's eyes. Eventually, the severity of the bad news got to us like it had gotten to the others. When we walked past the rows of tents, soldiers were scrambling about looking for writing material while others were sitting inside writing letters.

"What the hell's happening, Lieutenant? Is there some sort of written test going on we don't know about?" I asked.

Patterson halted at a pale looking Corporal with the 4th Infantry who was sitting on a sandbag outside his tent scribbling out his letter. "What's going on around here, Corporal? Why are so many of you nosed into writing letters?" He asked the forlorn soldier.

"Sir, we're all writing letters back home, because they say it could be our last chance to say goodbye," the Corporal replied. "There won't be time for it tomorrow."

"They" was always the dreaded harbinger of any bad news in Vietnam. Only gut instinct could disseminate its validity. All signs pointed to "they" being on target at Fire Base Dragon Mountain. The 221st was going to fly out to join the 3rd Battalion of the 8th Infantry Regiment who were already on the ground, engaged in a ferocious battle with elements of the NVA's 32 Division near Hill 724. The 173rd Airborne Regiment was headed to a different hill named 823, six clicks to the north.

When we reached our tent, Mike began writing two letters; one to his parents, the other to Linda, his wife to be. When he was finished, I wrote one of my own using his note pad. Mine was addressed to my parents, but I couldn't remember my street address as I never wrote home until now. I simply labeled it: Pa and Mom Cosette, General Delivery, Chandlerville, Michigan. I knew Evirgil Peacock, the town's postmaster, would get it to my parents. Mike put his letters in the outgoing mail. On second thoughts, I stuffed mine in my shirt pocket when we were called to the helipads for takeoff.

While we hiked to the staging area, Mike's name was called out. Pony Shetland was racing up from behind us, excited as a kid on a new bicycle now that he was cured of the clap and going out on a dangerous assignment. "Hey, boys, isn't this far out? I'm heading for the real shit this time, man. I'm going in with the 173rd." He edged up to Mike. "I can't wait. How you doin'?" Shetland gave Mike a sharp slap on his back.

Mike grimaced. "Not for shit, but I'm sure I can feel worse, now that you're here."

Shetland was going out with a separate photo team to be inserted with the 173rd at an LZ near a hill named 823. "Aw, come on. This is a big day, boys. The shit is hittin' the fan from all angles just a hop, skip, and a jump away. I can't wait. If them cocksuckers get too close, I'm doin' something about it. You watch me!" He looked my way. "You better stand tall, Cherry."

I stepped in front of Shetland and gave him a stiff forearm shove pushing him backward. "Why don't you just fuck off, dick head?" I screamed. If he wanted to duke it out I was ready. I placed my camera on the dirt and stood ready to fight. Patterson intervened.

"Cool your jets, Yank. Pony, shut your pie hole. We're not going to a USO rock concert. You better get your shit together, and get serious. We've got a job to do, and it's not going to be fun."

Shetland dropped behind us and continued to the choppers with his photo squad.

"What did I tell you, Yank? That sonovabitch thinks he's John Wayne with a camera."

"I can't stand him. I'm glad he's not with us today. If we make it out of here, I'm going to take him behind the barracks, and kick the shit out of him!"

"And, I'll be there with my camera to document it. Right on, Yank."

The whirling and whipping and thunderous bellowing of the amassed Hueys and Cobra gunship choppers churned the air into a boiling hurricane when our photo teams piled onboard. We were on the same UH-1 we came in on earlier that day. The same gunner, now more fidgety than before, rocked back and forth behind his M-60 tapping his knees and talking to himself. When we lifted away I could hear him praying, occasionally making the sign of the cross.

Rain was falling when the chopper pilot dropped near the forest floor for us to disembark. The ground below us had been obliterated by artillery. Shredded trees and brush made it impossible for the UH-1 to touch down so we prepared to jump to the ground ten feet below us. C Company was waiting for us when enemy gunfire erupted. Our M-60 gunner fired on the enemy, but the pilot had no choice but to fly us back to the fire support base. There was no way we could land or jump during the hailstorm of incoming small arms fire. We made two more trips back and forth before we could depart from the chopper at 4 pm, November 10.

The forest floor surrounding the LZ was an eerie, fleshless skeleton of what it had once been. The entire forest and ridgelines had been completely denuded by constant artillery and napalm strikes from the day before. The steady rain was glistening mirror-like on what foliage remained. The only way off the UH-1 was a dangerous leap from the landing skids down to the shredded jetsam of mashed trees and shrubs left by 105mm artillery strikes. Mike leaped first, then me, followed by Patterson, Maurice Cauchi, and Charles "Butch" Keneipp. When the chopper departed we raced for cover amidst the yak-yak-yak of AK-47's and M-16's, some of the rounds zinging around us.

The sun would be setting soon. Mike, Keneipp, and I raced away for a low spot that resembled a shallow grave but was unscathed by artillery. We ditched our rucksacks, covered our cameras in olive drab sacks, and hunkered in the ravine to wait for nightfall. If there was a hell, we were at its outskirts just a half of a mile away and seven hundred twenty-four meters high being the Devil's perch on Hill 724.

Darkness arrived like a door slamming shut in the sky. With it came the cold the Central Highlands was known for. We tried to lay motionless, but the chilly, wet mountain soil made us shiver. We clamped our jaws shut so our teeth wouldn't clatter. Nameless voices speaking English carried over the intermittent small arms gunfire in the dark calling out orders and positions. Some voices asked for more ammo. A Vietnamese voice sang out far to our right. The blooping sound of a M-79 mortar followed and crash-landed, stilling the voice forever. Suddenly, a similar whoop rocketed a flare high above us lighting the sky in a glowing, white light over the surround hills and ridges. Gunfire erupted again. Sheared off hopea and thap lu'u trees stood silhouetted like wrecked and splintered monoliths, lianas vines clung to them in unraveled, kinked cables stretching from tree to tree. When the tiny umbrella equipped flares landed, another series followed thumping and then erupting bringing its ephemeral light once again.

The flares and gunfire went on throughout most of the long night, silencing a few hours before daybreak. We didn't sleep. No one slept, friend or foe. We attempted to film the spectacular nighttime display despite the fear of bringing attention to our position.

Mike wiped his lens with his shirtsleeve. "It's just too damn dark, and my lens is fogged. These lenses are too slow to get a decent photo with these cameras anyway."

"What I'd give for a Nikon with a fast lens right now," I said.

We watched and waited for the morning sun to rise in what was the longest night of my life.

At last waves of light began bleaching away the fog around us like slowly turned pages of a book, each page brighter than the last. From our low position we wouldn't see the sun for hours, only the distant hilltops glistening white like frosting on cupcakes. The rifle fire and mortar explosions had ceased as though someone had unplugged them. My ears were ringing from the silence left behind. Mike and I shook from the cold and the fear of what was coming next, the order to advance. We didn't know to where, our assignment was to stay with the 3rd of the 8th no matter where they went. Their orders were to proceed to Hill 724.

CHAPTER THIRTY-TWO

Three days earlier Captain Taylor's Alpha Company had been slaughtered by the NVA at their base camp a half day's hump from our position. Captain Taylor was killed. Captain Terry Bell's D Company was choppered in behind Alpha for support, but it was too late to help Alpha Company. While Alpha was taking direct fire facing the NVA, D Company suffered casualties when the hail of gunfire blasted through Alpha Company striking D Company. Due to being in the rear, D Company was unable to return fire with Alpha in the way. Eventually, Bell's company repelled the enemy. Bell would not leave the dead behind when he was ordered to join Charlie Company to take Hill 724. He called for UH-1s to haul the KIA's away in cargo nets, a ghastly site of arms, legs, and faces held inside the bloody netting hanging below the choppers when they flew off. But it was the only choice he had to get them out.

Captain Falcone's Bravo Company was a half-mile away, clearing and constructing Firebase 1001 for artillery support on a sunny and pleasant morning of November 9th. The 105 artillery guns were now in place aimed at Hill 823, an anticipated battle site were the 173rd was dug in. General Peers, the commander of Operation MacArthur, had been on Hill 1001 earlier that morning to brief Bravo Company on tactical plans. Falcone waited for instructions to chopper out to D Company's location near the ambush site where Alpha had been hit. Bravo Company's job was to secure the area so C and D Companies would have a secured place to retreat should they be unable to take Hill 724. The call came on the morning of November 10th to head out. He called his lieutenants together for a plan briefing. By two o'clock they were on the ground at the ambush site.

On the morning of November 11th, Captain John Mirus, of C Company, merged with D Company giving them two hundred and eighty men between them. They were spread out in advancing columns throughout the forest. We could only see a smattering of small units near us. Struggling to crawl over fallen trees, gnarly waist high tree trunks, brush and vines, we made our way toward the hill a half-mile away. Mike and I took photos of the troops along the way.

Captain Falcone, Lieutenant Levie Isaacks, and the rest of Bravo Company 3rd of the 8th, were several hours behind us making an exhausting hump toward Hill 724. Crouched below the broad leaves of bang lang nuoc trees, their eyes locked on a platoon of NVA soldiers further ahead on their approach to Hill 724. The enemy was in plain sight, a shit pot full of them. They were easy pickings. B Company raised their weapons taking aim. E-4 Bob Walkowiak, a twenty-year-old radioman from Plymouth, Michigan, radio hailed "Saber," code name for LTC Glen Belnap, Battalion Commander of the 3/8th. Belknap was circling nearby orchestrating

Operation MacArthur inside a Cobra gunship. Captain Falcone took the mic. "We've got a platoon or more of NVA in front of us. Can we engage, sir?"

Belnap, unsure and hesitating in his decision, replied, "No, Captain. Let's wait to build a surprise attack. You got that?"

Falcone tossed the mic to Walkoviak. "I can't fucking believe him. We've got them right now, but he wants to wait for a surprise attack. How much more of an 'op' can we have to surprise them? Jesus Christ!"

Bravo Company held steady, as Belnap had ordered. The enemy drifted away beneath the canopy of trees. A perfect mid-morning sun burned down on the weary men of the 3rd of the 8th. Falcone's company spread out in columns and proceeded toward the base of Hill 724 where they would converge with us to secure the base of the hill.

Our orders came obtrusively when we followed the queue of other soldiers near us who were beginning to emerge from their foxholes where they spent the night.

There were hundreds of us. We spent most of the morning getting to the base of Hill 724. We found paths and trenches had been carved into the hill by the enemy. They had been on the hill for a long time before we arrived but had retreated to the forests during the air and artillery strikes launched from Ben Het fire support base days earlier. We began our steep climb, sometimes using foot holes dug along the well-used paths that led to the top of the hill. Rocks and boulders lay scorched by napalm flames. A fine layer of napalm crust covered the hill in a translucent, cellophane texture like that of a dragonfly's wings which crumbled beneath our boots.

Mike and I were sluiced in sweat from the midday heat, crawling over the sharp, fractured edges of rocks that had been uprooted by artillery fire, occasionally turning back to film C and D Company toiling along behind and in front of us. When we reached the crest of the hill at noon, there wasn't a living thing left in the aftermath of the bombings, only scattered artillery craters and shredded hopea trees strewn like a spilled box of giant toothpicks. Mike removed his rucksack and sweat soaked shirt. I opened the buttons on mine. A river of sweat was flowing down my back, running down my butt crack. We rested at the edge of a small mortar crater and guzzled from our canteens. We took photos of the exhausted soldiers pouring onto the hill like ants finding their nest. Some of C and D Company began digging in on the opposite side of the hill where LTC Belnap believed an attack would come from. He was dead wrong.

Precisely at one o'clock, hell reigned on our untenable position from above and below as though God was a deserter joining the NVA. A barrage of 82mm mortars and B-40 rockets exploded around us. NVA machine gun fire strafed our position killing and injuring many on the hilltop. Gravelly stones and human body parts erupted everywhere. I felt blood dripping down my cheeks, but I wasn't injured. It was someone else's blood. Charles Keneipp held his Graphlex to his face, taking photos of the hilltop carnage when a mortar landed close to him. His camera bore most of the brunt of the shrapnel saving his life.

But a few pieces of boiling metal struck his chin, cheek, and sheared off the top of his right thumb. Everyone was either scrambling to take cover in craters or were bellied down waiting to return gunfire along the ridgeline.

Lieutenant Patterson hovered near a shallow crater where a hopea tree had fallen over it. He screamed to us, "Take cover over here, now!"

We dove into the crater and covered our heads. Keneipp's face was bleeding badly. Mortars exploded everywhere around us, flinging shrapnel and stone in deadly bursts. Mike didn't want to stay put. He dusted off his camera and crawled out of the crater heading to the rim of the hill.

"Where in the hell are you going, Breshears? Get back here, pronto!" Patterson yelled.

Mike wasn't going to be denied his chance to record history. He disobeyed Patterson's direct order. "No, sir, I will not. I came here to photograph the battle, and that's what I'm going to do."

Patterson kicked at the dirt, "God damnit!"

Mike crawled toward the south edge of the hill where most of the action was happening. The enemy had been waiting, hidden in the forest for us to amass. Unknowingly, we had played into their plans. They began emerging from the forest below us to charge the hill at its weakest point. D Company was fortifying the north side, as Belnap had ordered, unable to offer any help. Patterson grabbed his camera and crawled from the crater. We followed. A few minutes later a mortar round exploded inside the crater catapulting the hopea tree into splinters above us. Had we stayed we would have been like the hopea tree, a vaporized remnant decaying in the sun.

Keneipp crawled behind a tree stump, blood was oozing from his wounds. A medic saw him and wrapped bandages around his face. On the other side of the hill, Maurice Cauchi was reloading his movie camera. He too was injured. His tape recorder was beside him recording the mayhem.

Mike was crawling over the edge of the hill to make his way down to a large crater that was occupied by six men from Charlie Company. They were firing M-60s and M-16s wildly toward the advancing NVA. It would take him an hour to make his way to the crater. An NVA sniper, hiding in a tree in the valley, fired repeatedly at Mike. The sniper's vantage point was not high enough for his rounds to strike Mike. His rounds nicked and pecked at the fallen tree above his head where he sought cover.

The battle had been raging for an hour before Captain Falcone's Bravo Company arrived in a storm of enemy gunfire directed at them. They buried themselves in foxholes and shallow grasses near the hill's perimeter while the NVA bombarded them with rockets, mortars, and machine gun fire. They were getting shot up like targets at a firing range. Lieutenant Levie Isaacks lay in the knee-high grass madly firing his CAR 15 rifle at the enemy. Despite three companies of the 3rd of the 8th, we were outnumbered by the NVA ten to one. We were getting slaughtered. Radioman Walkoviak was positioned near Isaacks when he received a call from Captain Falcone. Isaacks took the mic to report his squad was taking heavy fire. Falcone ordered Isaacks to leave their positions and run for Hill 724 to join C and D Companies.

Isaacks gave the order for his unit to make a mad dash for the hill amidst the never-ending NVA onslaught. Bravo Company disbanded in haste to make their way as best they could. Some of them made it to the crest of the hill while others were trapped below at the hill's base.

Mike, shirtless, was nearing the crater still taking sniper fire along the way. He was bleeding from the sharp stones that had sliced his chest and stomach. Only ten yards separated him from his "money shot" and the safety of the deep crater. It seemed like he was a mile away in his slow, agonizing crawl. He finally made it to the crater and began inching over the lip. He could see unexploded mortars buried half deep in the sides of the crater. He brought his camera to his face to take a photo of the men emptying their weapons on the enemy. There were several soldiers lying dead beside them, their bodies mangled and bullet ridden. Just as he made it over the crater's edge an artillery round landed in front of him. The blast killed everyone in the crater. Mike's body heaved in the air, his camera torn from his face. When the cloud of debris and smoke began to clear Mike's floundered body was lying amidst the debris, half way into the crater.

He was dead.

Lieutenant Patterson, not knowing what had become of Mike, crawled to the edge of the hill calling out to Mike. "Do you need more film?"

Soldiers cried out, "Doc, Doc!" Medics did their best to get to them, but there were too many for the overburdened medics to handle. I buried my face in the warm, red dirt of the mountain and wept.

The battle intensified around us, rockets and mortars exploding nearby, debris falling on us like angry hail stones shot from the sky, but there was nothing I could do but pray.

I wasn't the only one praying. The voices of the wounded came in muted gagging whimpers and desperate screams. Many of them calling out, "Momma, oh momma, help me!" Others pleaded sorrowfully, "Dear God, save me!" Neither God, nor mom came to save them. Their agonizing cries went on throughout the afternoon until some of the voices quit as death came to silence them forever.

God must have been looking in a different direction, because the battle continued without his intervention or pity. Levie Isaacks' men were pinned down at the base of the hill. Among them was Specialist John Collins from Pennsylvania sprawled in the grass near Isaacks, his legs mangled by shrapnel. Isaacks came to the fallen soldier with a medic. Blood was gushing profusely from Collins' legs. The medic applied tourniquets to stop the bleeding. Collins cried out, pleading to Isaacks, "Will you get me out of here, sir? Please take me home."

Isaacks promised, "You'll be the first one on a medevac, son. Just hang on."

Isaacks' situation was dire, the enemy still had them pinned to the ground. He saw a Prick 25 radio lying next to its dead operator a few, long yards away in the broad, open grass where there was no cover. Isaacks crawled to the radio. Enemy rounds were striking all around him, but none would hit him. It was as though he was shielded from death by a higher source, maybe

God had taken a peek at us. When he reached the radio he squawked the mic calling Captain Falcone. There was no answer, Falcone had been disemboweled by a mortar round. His last words were, "They've killed me!"

Isaacks called for "Saber," code name for LTC Belnap who was inside a Huey circling high above the battle. "Saber, Saber, come in."

Belnap answered, "This is Saber, go ahead,"

"Lieutenant Isaacks, Bravo Company here, sir. We need air support now, sir. We are getting overrun by NVA."

There was a pause before Belnap answered, "I'll have to get back to you, Lieutenant. I don't have any right now. It's all being directed on Hill 823 for the 173rd."

"There's no time, sir. We need artillery support immediately or we'll all die!" Isaacks desperately pleaded.

"I'll look around," was all Belnap said.

Lieutenant Isaacks dove into the shin-high grass frantically firing his CAR 15 at the enemy, some within twenty yards now. Behind Isaacks, an E-4 swung his M-16 in a hula-hoop circle above his head firing wildly, aiming at nothing, wasting his ammo. "Don't shoot me, goddamnit? Get down!" Isaacks screamed. Moments later the E-4 sprawled dead in the grass.

Isaacks continued firing from the damp grass. Out of nowhere, E-6 Rogers sprinted over to a position next to him. Rogers had received a "Dear

John" letter a few days before from his wife back in Chicago. The twenty-nine-year-old had taken it hard, acting aloof and depressed at the bad news. From a kneeling position, he fired at the enemy in a non-stop barrage. Isaacks yelled, "Get down, get down!" A moment after his warning, E-6 Rogers slumped across Isaacks' back, shot through the head by a sniper hiding in the trees.

Isaacks crawled back to the injured Collins. His tourniquets had mysteriously been loosened. He bled to death on the wavy grass. Isaacks continued toward the top of Hill 724, firing at the enemy, his ammo running low. When he reached the top of Hill 724, he thought of his options to save the men. The 3rd of the 8th were going to be overrun from below if something wasn't done immediately.

An enemy machine gunner, hidden in the jungle, had been chewing up our men throughout the course of the battle. He had killed many of our soldiers, while keeping Bravo and Charlie Companies at bay. Staff Sergeant Ortiz watched and listened from his place low in a crater. When he was sure he knew where the machine gunner was hidden he called out to Isaacks, "I know where he's at, Lieutenant, I can get him."

"Do it!" Isaacks yelled.

In a heroic action, Ortiz leaped from his position and charged the forest, ripping rounds at the enemy's position with his M-60 machine gun. His bandolier of ammunition sped through the red-hot chamber of his M-60 until he was out of bullets. Several soldiers nearby tossed their grenades to Ortiz. Enemy rounds zinged around his feet and past his head. When Ortiz tossed the grenades the enemy machine gun was silenced.

Scattered about the valley and hill, dead and wounded soldiers from both sides lay burning in the seething afternoon sun. The enemy continued their attack in a menacing onslaught. The 3rd of the 8th and the 221st were all going to die.

In a final attempt to get support, Isaacks took the Prick 25 and hailed a single engine spotter plane flying overhead.

"This is Lieutenant Isaacks. We are being overrun on Hill 724. We need fire support immediately!"

"What are your coordinates, Lieutenant? I've got a couple F-4 Phantoms in the area," the pilot replied.

Isaacks gave his coordinates. A few minutes later an F-4 jetted over the hilltops toward our position. His napalm strike burst in a hellfire explosion, scorching the rear side of the enemy's position. Isaacks hailed the spotter plane again. "Repeat! In twenty-five meters. Repeat, in twenty-five meters!"

Another F-4 screamed across the sky dropping a napalm bomb twenty-five meters closer to our position. We could feel the heat shoot past us like a blast furnace door had been opened. For the third time, Isaacks called for another drop. "Repeat! In twenty-five meters!" Again another F-4 dropped his napalm, but Isaacks still needed more support. "Repeat, repeat! In Twenty-five more, dammit!" He screamed at the mic.

The pilot responded, "No way, Lieutenant. You might be hit."

Isaacks pleaded, "If you don't drop again we will be killed anyway. In twenty-five meters, goddamnit!"

"You'll have to drop smoke, I repeat, you'll have to mark your spot with smoke!"

Isaacks pulled the pin on a smoke canister. A red fog of smoke fizzled in a long puff from the canister, rising in a cloud around him. In the moments following, Isaacks shuttered in fear, he couldn't see down the sloping hill where the enemy was getting closer. Would the enemy take advantage and charge? he thought.

An F-4 approached low to the hilltops and made one last drop of napalm. The jet was close enough for us to see the pilot's face. Billowing flames and smoke rose from the enemy's position below us in a fiery blaze of orange spreading across the valley and up the hill. We couldn't breathe. The exploding napalm robbed the hill of all oxygen. Intense heat surrounded us as we gasped for air.

The hill became agonizingly silent, even the slight breeze had been sucked up and stilled by the final blast. We prayed for the battle to be over.

CHAPTER THIRTY-THREE

It was after four o'clock when the last napalm bomb struck. The sun lowered on the western hills stretching long shadows around us. A harmless southern breeze swept the smoke away after the napalm's fireball quelled, carrying and dispersing the grayish cloud to the hills behind us. A frightening stillness overcame the hill. The gunfire had ceased, the radios were silent, and the men lay still as stone waiting for the enemy to resume their attack. Sporadic gunfire resumed, coming from below us, but only a whimper of what it was a few moments earlier. The rounds pecked at rocks and gravel in a feeble resumption from the enemy. They had been hit hard by the napalm strafes Levie Isaacks had called in saving us from certain slaughter.

Levie Isaacks rose from the ground and surveyed the pogrom below him. Wounded men cried out, helplessly unable to move. The bodies of the dead were heaped and contorted near small craters and large rocks where they had sought cover. In the distance, a peaceful valley shimmered in the late afternoon sun. Still holding his empty CAR 15, Isaacks spoke to himself.

"Thank God for the Air Force." He returned to his lying position behind a fallen tree and waited for the enemy to respond.

Evening began, bringing with it the cover of dense, sharp shadows decaying into a sweet-light ambience across the valley floor. The blanket of grayish hue from early nighttime filled in around us like a tide returning to a battered shore. A voice from atop the hill called out repeatedly, "Any of you who can walk or crawl come up to the top of the hill." Soldiers showing the enervation of the battle began emerging from makeshift foxholes, bomb craters, and uprooted trees. The more able helped some of the wounded to the crest of the hill. Out of the largest crater came a shirtless soldier limping toward us, his arms dangling unusable at his sides, his face unrecognizable by a slurry of dried blood and dirt caked in a macabre mask. His chest was peppered in black stains and shallow, red wounds. The soldier stumbled toward me as though he knew me and collapsed where I was sitting against a bolder. I studied his quiet face. His shoulders were wrapped in blood-soaked field dressings, his eyes shown the emptiness of emotion as though he had crossed over to the abyss of the dead where there was no quarter for him so they returned him to us. "Frodo? Is that you?" I asked still uncertain of his identity.

"Yes, it's me," Mike Breshears sobbed.

I wanted to pull him tightly to my chest, but he was badly injured and his breathing was shallow and weak. I placed my hand on his face, attempting to brush away the crust of blood and soil. I began to cry. His stream of tears left trails of moisture streaking into dark droplets of blood dripping from his chin.

"When the artillery round exploded inside the crater I thought you were dead, Frodo. Your body flew into the air," I wiped my eyes. "I thought you were dead, Frodo."

Mike leaned against me, as though I was a rock where he could find a moment of peace, his chest swelling and retreating on every breath. "I thought I was dead, Yank. When I woke up, everyone in the crater was dead from the blast, even Lieutenant Wade. Blood was running into my mouth and I couldn't breathe. I was drowning in my own blood. I thought my face had been blown off. When a medic came to me he removed my arms from my face. The blood was coming from my shoulders, pouring into my mouth. He wrapped these bandages on me and told me to stay put. I could see everything that happened after that. Men were being blown to bits right in front of me. I didn't move, I couldn't move. I felt like I was paralyzed."

The ground erupted with a burst of small arms rounds near us. We huddled together, helplessly hoping they wouldn't strike us. A rapid M-60 response followed. It became quiet again.

Darkness enveloped the hill in a cloaking shroud of inky blackness bringing the chilled, night air from the valley floor to the hilltop. A feeble rain began to fall, cooling the hill and the men until it ceased minutes later. The NVA had not left our perimeter. If they were going to make an uphill attack we would be in a nearly indefensible position.

Lieutenant Levie Isaacks called for the able men to retrieve any weapons and ammunition they could find scattered about the hillside. I searched the hilltop. Most of what we found was damaged and unusable. The men brought what was still of use to Isaacks. There were a few M-16s, M-60s, bandoliers of ammunition, a couple of M-79s, and a clutch of hand grenades. A Sergeant from C Company began passing the weapons out to those who could use them. Ironically, a hand grenade was given to Mike.

The evening wore on with the enemy resting in the forest below. Their shit had been kicked out of them with the napalm strikes, but there were still many more of them than us. We knew they could easily overrun us.

Instead, they halted their attack, only firing at us occasionally. We had several flares left and rocketed them overhead. The bright light illuminated the forest and valley surrounding us. The enemy could be seen approaching the southeast section of the hill. We opened up with a volley of small arms fire sending them back to the shelter of the forest.

A medevac chopper arrived to retrieve wounded. The hill was too steep to land on so the pilot hovered a hundred feet above us lowering a basket attached to a jungle penetrator cable. The men below placed a severely injured soldier inside the basket. Enemy gunfire peppered the chopper when it flew away with the basket still hanging below the chopper. A string of choppers came in ten minute intervals to retrieve more wounded. Each time they arrived the enemy opened up on them.

Isaacks hailed Fire Support Base 1001 on the Prick 25 radio. Minutes later, high above us, we heard illumination rounds erupt with a cascade of brightly burning flares drifting down around Hill 724.   Levie could see where the NVA were positioned. He made another call for air support on his radio.

Far in the distance the rumble of a slow flying propeller plane approached in the opaque sky circling above us as though it was anchored to a May pole on the ground.   A soldier cried out, "Spooky, Spooky!"   A moment later the sky brought down a terrifying red band of death, its dragon voice screaming, "Nuuunh, nuunh!" upon the enemy.   The hail of red whipped and sprayed at the enemy.   It was Puff the Magic Dragon dishing out a swath of hellfire and destruction on the forest below us.   Red phosphorous rounds flashed to the ground from the AC-47D gunship in a death ray beam of crimson light.   The iridescent bullets came every fifth round in a red-hot whipping and slashing, ripping loudly from its thirty caliber miniguns.

For a brief moment I felt pity for the NVA who were crying out in muted agony after Puff's wrath, but when I looked at Mike and the dead bodies strewn on the hill my feelings of pity eroded to nothing.

When daylight returned, we would retrieve our dead and wounded.

The battle for Hill 724 was over.

CHAPTER THIRTY-FOUR

The slant of morning rose behind us warming our bodies and revealing the poisonous carnage of the battle once again. The NVA had left during the night taking their dead and wounded. Below the steep hill slopes bodies were strewn beneath sheared off trees and near up rooted boulders. Napalm had seared the rubble in black char. Beyond our hill the green valleys lay peaceful, quiet, drenched in a cool cast of morning ambience as though nothing had happened. Some of us slept sparingly throughout the night despite the sullen cries of the injured and the choppers coming and going one at a time. Mike got some sleep lying between two dead soldiers whose dissipating body heat kept him warm.

The dead had begun to bloat in decay. Swarms of flies fed on the torn flesh of their faces, their bodies rigid in rigor mortis. The same flies found Mike and me landing on our faces and hands, feeding on Mike's dried blood. I offered a lazy swoop of my hand to brush them away but there was no artistry in my exhausted motion.

A graves registration detail was brought in to assess the number of dead who were being retrieved in black body bags and hauled up the mountain to be taken to Dak To airbase. A soldier Mike had taken a photo of the day before had been struck by a mortar. He was lying in two pieces in the belly of a crater with Lieutenant Wade lying lifeless near him. There weren't any wounds showing on the lieutenant's body. He was killed by the concussion of the blast. It was the same crater Mike had been in when he was injured. Lieutenant Isaacks found SP4 Ed Pippin still alive, sprawled in a vacant crater with his legs decimated by a rocket round. When Isaacks and a medic lifted him from the ground one of Pippin's legs came off in their hands. Pippen screamed and passed out when the last piece of sinew holding him together tore away from his torso.

Mike groaned when he awoke. He had refused to take a morphine shot a medic offered him the day before. By now all the morphine had been used. I wondered how he was able to sleep with the pain of his injuries. "How you doing, Frodo? You'll be out of here soon," I said. I helped him to his feet to move him from the pile of dead.

"There's something poking into my back, like a rock or something." He rolled to his side. I removed the hand grenade he'd been sleeping on. I placed it between us.

"What the hell were you going to do with this?"

Mike strained to move his arms. "That's what I was given in case they charged us during the night. I sure as hell wasn't able to throw it."

All of us had gone without food or water for a day and a half. What we had was rationed. A lieutenant came to us with an opened Lurp ration pouch. He gave us each a spoonful. When Mike swallowed he closed his eyes as though he was dreaming.

We needed a decent LZ so the choppers could come in to evacuate the rest of the wounded. Those of us who were not injured would be taken last. Mike was lifted away at eleven o'clock and was taken to field hospital in Dak To. I waited by his side when he crawled in the basket to be hoisted to the chopper hovering loudly above us. "Hang in there, Frodo. I'll see you back at Long Binh," I screamed. He tried to give me a thumbs up but couldn't.

Near the base of Hill 724, E-4 Bob Walkowiak tugged the pull cord of a chain saw until it started. He began cutting away at a mound of brush and limbs where the new LZ would be. Chips of wood hurled behind him while he sawed through the branches. Within the cluster of brush something moved below him. It was a badly wounded NVA officer. He was struggling to breathe, his chest showed a still oozing trickle of blood where an M-16 round had struck him. He had survived the napalm strikes but was going to die soon. Lieutenant Isaacks, Captain Wells, and Walkoviak dug him out of the tangle to question him but were stymied because they couldn't speak his language. The NVA officer was taken away in a medevac chopper but died during the flight to Dak To.

When the LZ was completed what was left of the 3rd of the 8th and the 221st Signal Company Pictorial boarded UH-1's late in the afternoon on November 12th. We went to Dak To. I sat in the doorway of the chopper, the same way Mike Breshears would have rode. I could see what Hill 724 looked like from above. What remained was a denuded skeleton of trees with shallow and deep holes strewn with broken M-16 and M-60 weapons demolished by artillery. The bodies of the dead had been removed, but they would remain forever in the minds of those who had survived the battle resurfacing in nightmares where the faces of the dead would return once again, over and over. The Spanish American novelist, George Santayana, once wrote, "Only the dead have seen the end of war."

When we were safely back at Dak To a meeting of Generals convened to assess the success of Operation MacArthur—the battles of Hill 724 and Hill 823. To the Generals success was measured by how many of the enemy were killed compared to how many we lost. They considered the operation a success as the NVA dead counted over a thousand. We lost eighty men on Hill 724. Before the end of the week, Hills 724 and 823 were abandoned. The NVA returned quietly to regain them without our resistance.

Two days later I was back at Long Binh with Lieutenant Patterson, Maurice Cauchi, and Charles Keneipp. The 221st Headquarters was sullen and depressed. The photo squad that had been sent to Hill 823 hadn't returned yet. We spent the morning in the lab looking over the still images we exposed during our mission. Patterson had retrieved Mike's broken camera along with Keneipp's and mine. Cauchi's and Patterson's movie film wasn't finished in process yet, so we began playing the tape Cauchi recorded on Hill 724. We sat in silence while the tape played out the sounds of the battle. Mixed within the explosions of artillery, rockets, mortars, and small arms fire, the voices of the wounded screamed out calling for medics and mothers. For some it was the last sounds their voices would make. We said nothing while we listened, each of us seeing the visions of men dying before us, wondering if there was something we could have done to prevent it. War's memories leave no chance for correction in its aftermath.

When the photo team from Hill 823 returned to Long Binh they were still haggard and exhausted from their similar experience. Lieutenant Patterson was called to Commander De Young's office. I followed Patterson out of the barracks. Pony Shetland was waiting outside looking as though he had fought the NVA alone. His eyes were swollen, his clothes caked in red clay, and he was limping. Patterson and he set out for the commander's office. I wondered what was happening and why he was being brought to De Young.

When Patterson returned to the barracks an hour later he was in a foul mood. He was cursing loudly and kicked a wastebasket on his way to his room. I let him settle for an hour before I knocked on his half opened door.

"Come in, Yank. Have a seat."

I sat on a stool near the door. "Mind if I ask what's going on, Lieutenant? What's up with Shetland being called to the man? What has he done now?"

"You won't believe it. That crazy sonovabitch decided he was going to be a hero on 823. He and two other soldiers were hiding in a foxhole. They weren't taking any fire, the NVA didn't even know they were there, but Shetland thought he was a hero, grabbed a guy's M-16, and started firing at the enemy exposing his position. Hell, if he'd just stayed there they could have ridden out the battle unharmed," Lieutenant Patterson said. "Instead, the NVA started opening up on them with machine guns and mortars. The two soldiers with him were killed, but that sorry prick never got as much as a scratch on him."

"Well what the hell happened to him? When I saw him he looked like he'd gone through hell," I asked.

"After the battle, some of the guys from the 173rd knew what he'd done so they fragged the fuck out him. He's lucky to be alive."

"What's going on with Shetland now?" I asked.

"De Young shipped him out to Saigon. He's no longer in our unit."

"Damn good thing. You know, Mike said Shetland might do something like that. Shetland told him he was going to make sure he went home a hero. What a sad sack a shit, Allen. Good riddance, I say."

We spoke no more of Pony Shetland. I stood to leave Patterson's room.

"There's something else that's come up. It's about you, Yank."

I turned and stopped in the doorway. "Oh come on, don't tell me I'm on the carpet too."

"In a manner of speaking you are," he said.

"I know, Allen, I did nothing on the hill, my camera was shattered." I said.

"It has nothing to do with 724. None of us could do any more than we did. I recommended you for a Distinguished Service Medal after our Lurp mission. You were outstanding, Yank. As far as I'm concerned you saved that Lurp's life. I recommended Breshears for a commendation for his actions on the hill even though he ignored my direct order to stay put in the crater. What he did showed a lot of guts. "

I leaned against the doorway and sighed a smile. "Thank you, Lieutenant. Mike deserves a medal. He put his ass on the line doing his job."

"Go over to the studio and get a headshot so we can send an article to your local newspaper about your achievement. Otherwise, we'll have to use your official mug shot from Basic."

That was going to be a problem. If the article reached *The Chandlerville News* I'd be sunk. Everyone back home would know I wasn't Richard Main. I told Patterson to use the headshot on my ID. I bolted away before he could ask any questions.

"Oh, there's something else I forgot to tell you," He said. He reached in his pocket for a folded sheet of paper. "You're being shipped out, too. There's a Major General Richardson who wants you down at MACV in Saigon for a new MOS position. You're leaving in the morning." He read the order, "Says you're a 71Q journalist now. Time to change hats, Yank."

I was astonished and pissed off. I didn't want to leave Mike and the 221st. "Do I have to go, Allen?"

"You better. It's not every day a soldier gets a request from a M.G. You must have impressed the guy somewhere along the way. Get your shit packed. I'll tell Mike when he gets back. We're going to miss you, dude. You'll be fine down there," he said.

I left the barracks and walked slowly through the homely light of the day toward the billowy parachute where a group of guys were drinking beer in the shade. I reached in the barrel to get a chilled beer. Maurice Cauchi was sitting alone at a table. I wondered how a Frenchman could be in our unit. He was older than us, forty something. His hair was receding, his face was pale and gaunt framing the defined features of his cheeks and jaw bones. I'd never spoken to him before. His head was still bandaged from his injury on Hill 724. I approached his table. "Bonjour, Maurice, Je suis, Yank Main. J'ai été sur la colline avec vous." (Hello, Maurice. My name is Yank Main. I was on the hill with you.)

Cauchi, caught off guard by my French, said, "Je sais que vous étiez. Vous avez écouté ma cassette, trop. Je ne savais pas que vous pourriez parler ma langue. (I know you were. You listened to my tape, too. I didn't know you could speak my language.)

"Je sais que certains Français, mais juste assez pour vous confondre. Let's speak English." I'd only confuse him with my poor French if we continued.

"Bon. English."

The heat of the day was at its peak. We sat at the table beneath the soothing shade of the parachute neither of us speaking. There was everything to talk about but nothing we could say.

By the time the sun sat beyond the hills Cauchi had left. I stayed at the table drinking beer until the sky darkened to night. Lieutenant Patterson heard that I was drunk, talking nonsense down at the parachute, and needed help getting back to the barracks. He came to fetch me. He held me upright, with his arm under my shoulder, leading me along the way. We had been through the gates of hell and back at Hill 724. He didn't care that I was crying and blabbering of its horror. He had seen it, too.

Perhaps it was best for me to move along I reckoned when I awoke in the morning. I tossed my duffel bag into the Jeep that would take me down to MACV, and Major General Richardson's assignment, whatever that was going to be.

Surely the worst was over now.

CHAPTER THIRTY-FIVE

Brookings, South Dakota

A not very pretty but downright inviting RN came to my room to empty my urine bag and check my blood pressure and pulse, the usual stuff that was routine attention for a dying man. When she said her name was Charlotte her voice purred. She was new on the floor, being expectantly careful, but lacking timorousness, while she checked my catheter for signs of infection. Father Rohn turned in his chair and asked if he should leave to give us privacy until her gleaning was complete. I knew he was becoming tired listening for hours to my unabridged story, but he continued to show a strong interest in what I was saying. "I suppose that's enough for a day, Father."

"No, I am intrigued by it all, Mr. Wild. Your life has been an incredible journey. I'll stay as long as you'd like me to," he said. He stood and stretched.

"I'd like you to come back tomorrow, Father. I'm exhausted and hungry," I said. I had been narrating for most of the day. Occasionally I'd doze off when he took a couple brief cell phone calls or had used the bathroom. He was patient and was there when I awoke. "Can you come back in the morning?" I asked.

"I suppose I should get back to Madison. I have a sermon to prepare for Sunday mass. What time can I return?"

"First thing in the morning. I don't sleep well so I should be awake."

Father Rohn departed in the late afternoon. From my second floor room I could see him slowly walk across the parking lot to his car. He didn't drive off immediately. I was sure he was trying to sort out my story and why I had contacted him. He would find out soon.

A wobbly wheel of the dinner cart chattered down the hallway stopping at my room. A young nurse's assistant, a candy striper as they were once called, entered to place my steel covered dinner on the over-bed table. A small, green note near the serving read "Low Sodium."

"Good afternoon, Mr. Wild. How are you feeling today? Let's see what we have here for you," the nursing assistant said. She lifted the lid off the plate. "Looks like turkey and steamed vegetables. Delicious!"

The bland looking portions were spartan in size at best, but it would be enough for my deficient appetite. There was a time I could have eaten twice as much and still be hungry. "Would you bring that brown hand bag to me, Miss?"

Her raised eyebrows showed suspicion when she lifted the bag off the floor and set it on my stomach. "Now, Mr. Wild, you wouldn't be fetching something from the bag that you aren't supposed to have are you?"

"Certainly not," I said, innocently. "Just some reading material and some Mrs. Dash." I pulled Mrs. Dash from her hiding place. "See?"

"Okay. Can I get you anything else?" she asked.

"Could you raise my bed so I can sit more upright and an empty cup? There's one in the bathroom. That will be all."

She raised the bed and brought the cup. On her way out she gave me a fallacious smile. When I heard the wobble of the dinner cart move further down the hallway I retrieved a bottle of Château Neuf-du-Pape and a corkscrew from the bag. The wine was a present from my publisher who had given it to me shortly after it was bottled in 2001. The fine burgundy wine would continue aging well if I had time but I didn't. A decent wine drank from a plastic cup was as sinful as boiling filet mignon, but I figured I could ask Father Rohn's forgiveness when he returned in the morning.

The turkey and wine didn't pair well so I concentrated on enjoying the single serving of wine. The first sip brought out the smell and taste of currant, pepper, and blackberries accented by hints of recycled Coke and Pepsi bottles leeching from the cup. I re-corked the wine and put it back into the bag. I planned on sharing the rest with the priest.

I slept well through most of the night only waking occasional to check for the early hint of a sunrise. Perhaps it was because I had a good cleansing of my mind telling Father Rohn my saga which was more like a confession. There is no greater pillow as a clear conscience someone once said. I looked forward to his arrival. He must have also because he came into my room at eight a.m., Saturday morning.

"Good morning, Mr. Wild. I hope I'm not too early," he said. He stood in the doorway waiting for a nurse to finish checking my blood pressure. He was dressed in civilian clothes.

"Not at all, I've been looking forward to your return. Have a seat."

The priest sat in the same vinyl chair as he did the day before. "How are you feeling today? You seem to have more color in your face."

"I slept some. How about you? I gave you a lot to think about yesterday, Father."

"Well, I didn't sleep very well. All you talked about had me up most of the night. I have some questions. I know you asked me not to say or ask anything while you talked. Maybe today you'll allow me to ask about things?"

"I know it must have been difficult, but bear with me. There will be a time when you'll see where all of this is going," I said.

"Yesterday you left off where you were reassigned to Saigon. What happened to Mike Breshears and the others who were on Hill 724 with you? Did you ever see Mike again? What about Mike Fitzpatrick? Did you see him again? Did you ever make it back to Chandlerville? Did you look for your son, Kristof? How did you become C.J. Wild? I'm sorry, Mr. Wild, your story begs for so many answers. Your family, did you see them again, or Henry Boudreaux?"

"We should begin with my new assignment with MACV, down in Saigon. I'll get to Frodo, Fitz and C.J. Wild soon. There's much to be told about these guys. I will tell you everything in time."

****
December 1967 Through June 1968

Major General Richardson sent his personal aide to bring me down to Saigon as expected. We rode in a canvas covered Jeep back to MACV headquarters near Ton Son Nhut Air Base. The driver delivered me directly to Richardson's office. When we met he told me I would be traveling all over the country to write and film for *The Stars and Stripes* newspaper. I was going to be a one-man roving reporter producing uplifting stories to build morale amongst the troops.

"The same kind of thing you wrote about back at Fort Gordon, son." he said.

I told him I didn't have a camera, film, anything to begin my job. That's when he gave me the Nikon system he had back at Fort Gordon. "I just can't get the hang of the damn thing. I'm sure you'll use it well, Yank."

My first assignment was to cover a medic team in the field. "We need to show mom and dad back home their kids are in good hands over here," he said.

I told him I knew a medic, Spark Fallon, who was somewhere in country. I might as well start with someone I knew. The major general said he had the means to find out where Fallon was, and I would go immediately to where he was deployed.

Fallon was with the 500th Med in the I Corp region of Vietnam near the seacoast town of Chu Lai. I flew in on a chopper and was taken directly to Fallon's unit. I got there too late to see Spark. He and his unit had just returned from a skirmish they encountered outside of Chu Lai. He was with a convoy of eight deuce-and-a-half's heading out of town when the VC attacked them. One of the guys took a round in the thigh. Spark rushed into the field to give aid, but in doing so he blew out a testicle. Damnedest thing. There was a Korean R.O.C.K. unit nearby who came to their rescue. Fallon was taken to a field hospital in Chu Lai. It was probably a good thing I didn't see Spark Fallon; I would have had to tell him how I got there.

I put a story together about how well Korean and US forces worked cohesively to defeat the communist enemy. I took photos of a team of ROCKs standing in with Fallon's medical unit. When I returned to Saigon the story ran in *The Stars and Stripes* with my by-line and photo credits.

For the next month I floated around Saigon doing short pieces with photo layouts of friendly intermingling of our troops with the indigenous tribes receiving American aid. Total bullshit stuff. GI's handing out candy bars and medical teams vaccinating children before a follow up unit would drop in and burn some of the villages to the ground for aiding the Viet Cong.   Some humanitarian aid missions were covert assignments to discover enemy presence as I later found out. My stories and photos were more of a cover up before the shit hit the fan for some of the villages.   The theme was "Winning Hearts and Minds."

I got a call from Lieutenant Patterson on a late November afternoon. I was at MACV headquarters going over some photos I took of a grip and grin award.   Patterson said Mike Breshears was stranded in Saigon waiting outside the replacement center at Tan Son Nhut still dressed in his hospital gown and robe.   He had spent two weeks recovering in a Na Trang hospital. When he was released he was dropped off at the center like he was an indigent hitchhiker trying to get home.

"Can you go down and find him, and bring him to the 221st?"

I was privy to a Jeep anytime I needed one, so I requisitioned a canvas topped Jeep from dispatch and set out to find him.

When I rolled up to the main entrance I found Mike sitting on the edge of a concrete barrier looking like a displaced refugee in need of clothes. He was shocked when I stopped and chirped the horn.

"What the hell you doing here, Yank?   You steal that Jeep? Holy hell!"

"Get in, Frodo, you bolo bastard. You've been on vacation long enough." Mike stepped into the

Jeep slowly, still tender from his injuries. I tromped the pedal, and we were off to Long Binh. We had a lot to talk about.

We skirted around the Saigon traffic as though we were in a cross-country race. "Slow down, Yank, I've spent enough time in the hospital."

After I slowed the Jeep he began telling me what happened after he was airlifted to the hospital. "I was taken to Dak To where I spent a day laying on a field cot, with dozens of other wounded men. When I finally got to Na Trang I hadn't taken a piss for two days. Finally, a surgeon came and pointed to me, and said I was next. I told him to take someone who needed help more than me," Mike said, laughing. "You know what he said? 'Holy Christ! We got another John Wayne do gooder here. Take him into surgery.'"

"What the hell, Frodo? You're not Audie Murphy, are you? Ah hell, I'm just excited you're back, brother."

I stopped the Jeep on Highway 1 to let an old man who was guiding an ox pulled cart across the road. There was a child riding on the cart. She accidentally dropped her stuffed animal. I jumped from the Jeep to give it back to her, but the old man wouldn't stop. The small child cried at the loss of her companion. I remembered my promise to my sister, Claire, how I swore I would get her a new Tuhta. I put the new Tuhta in my camera bag and continued down Highway 1.

"What are you going to do with that, Yank?"

"It's for my little sister, Claire. I promised her I would replace her favorite animal she lost last summer."

"Huh."

"I suppose you haven't been brought up to speed yet?" I changed the subject.

"Patterson told me about Pony Shetland, but I wasn't surprised. I want to know how the hell you ended up down here," he said.

I told him how Major General Richardson called me to join him at MACV. "It's been a joy ride compared to what we were doing in the 221st." I slapped the steering wheel. "See? I can get one of these anytime I need one."

"Lucky bastard!" He was excited about my new MOS and position at MACV. "Total gravy gig, dude."

I told Mike about my Army Commendation Medal for "heroic action, outstanding achievement, and meritorious service," resulting from the snake ordeal with the Lurps. He was happy for me and thought I deserved the award.

When we arrived at the 221st, Lieutenant Patterson took Mike to a private room at HQ. There were two medals lying on a plain tabletop; a Bronze Star, with "V" meaning valor, and a Silver Star. "Take your pick, Mike," Patterson said. Mike chose the Bronze Star, telling Patterson to give the Silver Star to Sergeant Jim Harmon, who he said deserved it more than him for his bravery on Hill 823 on November 11, 1967. Besides, Harmon was going to be a lifer, and it would help further his career in the Army.

I hung out with Mike and the 221st down at the parachute bar for the rest of the afternoon. We laughed at bad jokes while getting a good San Miguel buzz. The conversation, as expected, turned to the memory of Hill 724. All of us who were there fought back tears, and the reunion was over. I got back in the Jeep to return to Saigon. I told Mike I'd keep in touch, but I never saw or spoke to him again until after we both rotated back to the world.

The Lunar New Year, Tet, arrived in January 1968; the year of the monkey. With it came Victor Charles and the NVA were ready to unveil their big surprise they'd been working on for the past several months. General Westmoreland and his staff knew something tumultuous and grandiose in scale was going to happen with all the enemy activity going on in the jungles and highlands. The Ho Chi Min Trail was the enemy's main route bringing thousands of enemy into Vietnam from Laos and Cambodia. The entire country had been infiltrated from Quang Tri, near the DMZ, down below the Mekong Delta in the south. NVA General Giap's plan of deception was to dilute US forces by drawing us out of the urban areas and into border battles like Hills 724 and 823, precursors of what was in store.

I was in Saigon when the Tet Offensive erupted in the I Corp and II Corp regions in the north then throughout the entire country by morning, January 30, 1968. Eighty thousand dedicated enemy fighters brought hell to a hundred different towns in South Vietnam including Saigon. We nearly lost our embassy when it was attacked.

I scrambled about the city like a one legged man in an ass kicking contest shooting photos of the action in the streets and alleys. The city of Hue was devastated in a battle that lasted a month. Marines at Khe Sanh were under constant siege for more than two months. The enemy pounded them with non-stop artillery barrages all the while. The enemy must have felt Marines burned more slowly than their Army counterparts.

But in the end our forces prevailed, and life in 'Nam resumed to its previous way of miserable loneliness for home.

Mike Breshears left 'Nam in April 1968. Everything he had planned and anticipated during his tour in Vietnam came to be. He returned home and married his high school sweetheart, Linda. He went back to work as a longshoreman on a Columbia River dock. He got to go deer hunting with his father and uncles that autumn. While climbing a tree to scout his hunting spot a limb he was standing on broke, and he fell twenty feet fracturing his neck. He lay on the forest floor for twenty-four hours before his father found him. He was paralyzed from his neck down. He would spend the rest of his life bound to a wheel chair. Shortly after, Linda divorced him. He found a soul mate in a VA hospital in Oregon, Irenej who has remained by his side for all of these years.

On June 3rd, 1968, I was sent up country to Pleiku to do a story on a 101st Airborne unit. Their morale was low from months of "sneak and peeks," and "search and destroy" missions in Kontum Provence, a place I was all too familiar with after experiencing "The Hill" back in November.

Mike Fitzpatrick was with the 101st so I got the skinny on where he was. I would focus my assignment on his unit. My job was to do a "happy" story on the 101st to build their morale, an impossible assignment. I knew the only way to build their morale was to see orders issued for their return home, but the Army knew that already.

Once again, I got there too late. Mike was a squad leader out in the field on May 31st. He had only three days left before he was going home. He could have safely stayed back at the field base for his last few days, but he chose to go out with his men instead. He didn't want them to go out with a new guy who didn't have experience. His unit came under fire while they were ascending a mountainside. Mike led his troops through the battle, taking out the enemy with an M-16 and grenades. A sniper with an AK-47, hiding in a hopea tree, took aim at Mike and shot him. The bullet ripped through his jaw and shoulder. When I met with his company commander, he showed me a photo of Mike's injuries. His face was blown apart and resembled a strewn together pizza. He should have died in the field that day. A medic saved his life by giving him an emergency tracheotomy while he lay on the forest floor. The medic had a soldier fire a couple rounds from his M-60, using the red-hot cartridges to cauterize the neck incision. He used a hollow bamboo shoot for a trach tube and another as a needle to transfuse blood from a donating soldier lying above him.

Fitz spent two months on a hospital ship in the South China Sea, went on to a hospital in Okinawa, and then to another military hospital in Chicago. A year later he was released. He survived, but his injuries would plague him for the rest of his life.

Mike Fitzpatrick received a Bronze Star with "V," for his heroic actions in the field that day. When he returned to civilian life, the war had left a bitter memory and new bad memories to follow. The day he returned home he was spit on and pelted with eggs wearing his Green Beret uniform when he stepped off the train in Royal Oak, Michigan. The following day he smelted his medal to make a hash pipe.

CHAPTER THIRTY-SIX

Father Rohn turned in the chair and removed his glasses. The midmorning sunlight was brightly flooding the room through the window behind him. I asked him to close the curtain so I could see him better. "Could you bring that small bag to me too?" The bag held the wine bottle. I took the wine from the bag. "There should be a couple of glasses in the bathroom. I opened this last night but saved most of it for our discussion today. Let's have a glass of wine."

He poured each of us a glass and returned to his chair. "Tragic fates for both of those men, Mr. Wild. I was hoping for a happier ending for them. Some events in life we have control over, but others we do not. If Mike Breshears didn't climb the tree or the limb had been stronger below his feet, and if Fitz had stayed back at the field base instead of going into the field with his men, how would their lives be now? What would your life have been if you hadn't met Hana, or left Chandlerville? Have you ever considered that?" he asked.

"Fate is not predictable, of course. I have considered how differently mine would have been had I not laid the cards out as I did. I don't like to consider regret, Father. It won't change anything in the past, but it can make your future regrettable," I replied.

"Where did you go when you finished your tour in Vietnam? Did you go back to Chandlerville? You must have been facing a delicate quandary, missing your parents, Claire, and your brothers with an enemy waiting to harm you when you returned. How did you manage the dilemma? What did you do?"

"Richard 'Yank' Main's Vietnam tour ended November 1, 1968, but the soldier still had about two years to serve. I left the country and was stationed again at Fort Gordon to instruct new Signal Corp trainees in combat photography and journalism. I was there for four months when I contracted strep throat. The disease worsened because of my rheumatic heart condition. I was hospitalized, and that's when the doctor's discovered I had a significant heart murmur. I was released from the military with an honorable discharge in February 1969, two days before my nineteenth birthday. I wanted to become Christophe Cosette again, but the rolling ball I was hiding inside had bounced out of my control and took a change of course."

"Tell me what happened, Mr. Wild."

****

February 1969

A cold rain was coming down in Savannah when I stepped from the cab in front of the Western Sizzlin' on Sunset Boulevard. I was wearing my dress greens even though I was a civilian now. I hadn't worn plain clothes in over two years. I was proud of my rank of E-5, my "orders of wearing"' pinned on my left chest and the Distinguished Service Medal positioned at the top. I went inside the restaurant to look for Delores, the hump chested waitress who graciously serviced Zeke Walls when we were in AIT. I saw her carrying a platter of food across the busy restaurant. I hoped she would remember me. When I approached her she gave me an uncertain look before her memory of me returned.

We spent the night at her house trailer outside of town. She treated me well and made French toast for breakfast. We didn't talk much. She asked me how "that"' fella was doing, meaning Zeke. I didn't know, but I guessed he was sent to Vietnam like most of us had been. I asked her if I could use her phone and told her I'd pay for the call.

"You're calling home, I bet."

"Yes," I said. She left me alone and went to shower.

When I dialed home my father answered the phone in a bright, healthy voice. "Cosette Funeral Home, this is Romeo Cosette."

I cleared my throat to let him know there was someone on the phone, but I didn't say anything for a long minute. "Pa" was all I could muster when I spoke.

"Chris" was all he could say during his pause.

"Yes, it's me, sir." I asked him where he'd like me to begin my story.

"Anywhere you'd like, son," he said.

I couldn't bring myself to tell him the truth of what I had done, or where I had been for the past few years. Instead I told him I had been traveling the country on trains. He asked me if I was a hobo. I told him I was just a traveler, going wherever a train would take me, a seed looking for suitable ground to grow in, but I hadn't found it yet.

He knew why I had left Chandlerville. After Hana died he and mom talked to her grandmother. She told them I was no longer in trouble with the Bundschuh. Wolf Krieger, the fuhrer of the family, had been arrested for the murder of his deckhand and was serving life in Jackson State Prison. Hana's grandmother told them Kristof was given up for adoption, and he was placed with a family somewhere in the Midwest. That was all she knew of my son's fate. I told pa I would look for him for as long as it took.

"I'd like to come back home for a while. What do you think, Pa?"

"You can't, son. The military is looking for you. Your draft notice came, but you weren't here to show up at Fort Wayne for your pre-induction physical. They consider you a draft dodger. Don't come home! You aren't a coward, are you?"

A weary silence stilled our conversation. He knew I was crushed, and frightened, but for different reasons. I felt betrayed by my country, but whose fault was it? Mine. "I'm not a coward, Pa."

"Do you need money, Chris? I can wire money to you. Tell me where you are, and I'll send money today."

"I'll be fine, Pa. I don't need any money. Just tell me how everyone is doing."

He said my brother Verdie was living near Detroit taking evening art classes at Wayne State University, and was working at a tool and die shop in Warren. Denis was going to Wayne State Mortuary School so he could take over the business. They would get together all the time for dinner and drinks. Denis had gotten married to an Italian girl from St. Clair Shores. They had a baby girl. Claire was in second grade and was a good student. Mom was still soldiering on, attending St. Paul masses regularly, and making meals large enough to feed a platoon of men.

Pa went on to say he had taken ill with cirrhosis of the liver, had quit drinking for a year at that point, and was feeling healthy. I could sense his demons had not left him completely when he said the pressure of burying his friends haunted him, still. His only relief in the past came from a bottle.

I knew he had a soft spot for guys in the military. He served in the Navy during the Second World War. He told me it was especially hard on him when he buried Charlie Fitzpatrick. He was interred at North Allis Cemetery on M-211. Pa said Sean wanted to have his body cremated and his ashes spread on the Rainy River, like we had promised.   Instead, his parents wanted to visit Charlie at a cemetery.

When Evirgil Peacock, the Post Master, died, Pa refused to bury him until his son, Tom, who was on the USS Oriskany in the South China Sea, could come home from the war to see his father before he was buried.

He went on to tell of another military funeral he had conducted two months earlier.   There was an article printed in *The Chandlerville News* with a picture of the soldier telling about his bravery in Vietnam.   The young soldier saved a fellow soldier by removing a poisonous snake from his chest during a night mission.   When the soldier came home two months after the story appeared, every bar he went into people bought him drinks for his heroism.   The young soldier got drunk one night and died behind the wheel of an old car he drove into the big, painted rock outside of Chandlerville.

"What was his name, Pa?"

"I didn't know much of him.   His parents had left town a long time ago.   He came back because Chandlerville was the only place he had lived before he went to Vietnam.   His name was Richard Main."

Fate, once again, ground me into the dirt. Dick Main's dirt was six feet deeper.   He couldn't resist the temptation of being a hometown hero, despite our agreement, our vow not to divulge the truth, all of the sacrifices I thought I made.

Now, I was once again a ghost without a history for over two years of my life.

When Delores finished her shower I took her to the bedroom again. She offered a feeble, short-lived resistance to my advances because she would have to shower again. She gave in when I tongued the remaining droplets of water from her body. We made love for an hour before she reported late for work.

When I left Delores I ditched my uniform and set out on the rails again. I was lost. I traveled the country like Uncle Boogie and Rand had done years earlier, like a seed blowing in the wind looking for a place to take hold. It took two years for that to happen.

It was early October when corn was being harvested in the vast fields of South Dakota when I got off a Grand Trunk in Brookings. I was weary and tired of being lost. While sitting in a tavern near the rail yard I overheard a conversation between two men. One of them said he was leaving his job as a reporter with the local paper, *The Brookings Register,* and they hadn't found a replacement for him. I introduced myself to the reporter and gave him a short resume. He replied, "That's wild, man. What's the chance of you hearing our conversation, and being a writer and photographer? Totally wild."

The next morning I met him at the paper and applied for the job and got it. I used the name, Yank Main. That job lasted for a year. I started submitting articles under the name, C.J. Wild, to a few national magazines. They were accepting them as fast as I submitted them. It wasn't long before I had a new job as a free-lance feature writer and photographer with *Field and Stream*.

CHAPTER THIRTY-SEVEN

The priest and I sipped wine until the bottle was empty. I waited for him to begin speaking, but he remained silent. Instead he lifted the curtains and gazed out the window. I had given him a boatload of material to sort out. I knew he was trying to put everything together in some sort of manner he could understand.

I broke the silence. "Now, Father. Tell me of your life, starting with your childhood. Was it a happy life?"

Father Rohn returned to his chair. "My life? I've had a good life, Mr. Wild. I grew up on a farm not far from here in Madison. My parents were German immigrants, and I was their only child. We spoke German as our first language because they couldn't speak English very well. The first school I attended was near a German Hutterite colony. The teachers taught me English, but our primary language was German. When I was older I loved to hunt and fish. In the fall months, after school, I'd go home and get my dog, Dune, a stocky female yellow Labrador, and go pheasant hunting. Back then you could hunt pheasants with stones, there were so many of them. My parents took me every spring to the headwaters of the Mississippi River in Minnesota to fish. We had a small cabin on the riverbank. Those were good times."

"I know you weren't raised Catholic. How is it you converted from Lutheran? I'm assuming your family was Lutheran," I inquired.

"Oddly enough, my parents were Catholic. You are right, however, most of this area is Lutheran."

"What inspired you to go into the priesthood, Father? I imagine it's not an easy life considering a priest has to give up, you know, the physical comforts of a woman and the idea of having a family to leave his living legacy to carry on his name. My sister, Claire, made the same decision as you. She became a nun. But her reasons were probably much different than yours."

"Claire was on my list of questions to ask you. So, she became a nun? How remarkable. I decided to become a priest when I was in my first year of college at Dakota State College in Madison."

"Was it something you thought about for a long time, or was it just as simple as an epiphany that struck you suddenly?" I asked.

"It happened suddenly." Father Rohn searched the bottom of his empty wine cup. "I'd like another glass of wine, but I see we're out. I have a bottle of altar wine in my car. How about I get it? I have the feeling we are both going to need another glass of wine to continue. I get this odd feeling there is something brewing in your story."

"Sure, I don't think it will make much difference to my health, considering my other ailments," I said.

Father Rohn returned with a bottle of Cote de Beaune, 2009. He liked the big, hearty essence of burgundy wine too. He said the parish's budget didn't allow for expensive wine to be used at mass, so he purchased wine he preferred with his own money. I asked him to continue.

"I must have been a lot like you, Mr. Wild. I found myself searching out the more exciting things in life. I loved to ride on the edge, was willing to take a challenge head on. My first year of college was full of party life and girls. Yes, I've known the pleasures of the flesh before I became a priest. College life was a non-stop party for me. I nearly flunked out because of my recalcitrance to authority, and willingness to "ride that edge." Do you believe in divine intervention, Mr. Wild?

"I believe we are but specks of matter in a vast scheme of things. When you contemplate the universe, its endless expansiveness, and the probability of us not being alone in our minute world, a person would have to be incredibly obtuse to think there isn't a chance of a greater presence out there. Something more grandiose than us." I explained.

"Let me tell you why I believe there is a God. One late, spring night a group of my college friends and me were looking for something exciting to do after we had outlasted the rest of the party we had in a vacant farmhouse outside of town. There are plenty of those old farms near Madison, abandoned and left to decay over many years. This particular farm had an old, rickety windmill in the yard that was huge, still working, spinning slowly despite its age. We wondered if a guy could grab on and ride through a complete cycle without falling off. Guess who tried it?" he said. "The blades were turning slowly enough to latch on. I timed getting on a blade as it was turning, but it stalled when I took hold. I climbed up to the hub of its blades, and the mill began to turn again in the wind that was picking up force. It was an exhilarating ride for a short time, until the wind began to increase, spinning the wheel out of control. I desperately hung on, trying to stay even with the ground, but it was impossible to keep in balance with the fast, spinning wheel. I fell to the ground, and landed on the frame of an old plow hidden in the tall weeds. The plow's hitch was tilted at an upward angle, and I was impaled by the hitch. My friends tried to pry me loose but couldn't. I was losing blood quickly, dying before their eyes. It took more than an hour for an ambulance to come. By then I was unconscious from the loss of blood. In my delirium I found myself in a grave, covered in dirt. I frantically scratched and dug at the dirt to free myself, but with every motion I sank further below the surface. I began to pray every prayer I knew. I made a promise to God. If he saved me I would devote my life to the church, help people, and be a good person. I believe I am here today because of his intervention. I kept my word by becoming a priest."

"I am proud of you, Father. It would have been easy to dismiss your promise after you survived the accident. I have heard similar stories as yours, but not always have desperate promises been kept. Sometimes the mind rationalizes these events, and allows promises to fade to a guilty memory. I've tried to be true to myself and keep promises I've made, like finding my son."

"You began telling me about Claire. Why did she choose the convent?" He asked.

"Claire's reasons were to save her sanity. She became a nun to escape her demons. She found solace in the Church. Remember when I said she was born with the gift of clairvoyance?" I asked.

"Yes, I remember. Do you believe she was a true clairvoyant, having the gift of seeing into the future?"

"Yes. She was plagued by her visions. Years later, my mother told me that it all came to a crescendo when she was fourteen-years-old. She saw a vision of her father dying. She and mom were grief stricken. She believed our father was going to die. Two days after her dream, Pope Paul VI died. Mom said it was a divine vision.

Claire's life was chronicled by her ongoing foretelling. It tore at her and hounded her through her early life until my mother convinced her it was a sign from God. Although her visions were often ambiguous, they nevertheless came to light in odd happenings. Like the time she predicted a bad man would make me fall in the water. The bad man was Homer Pace. And, her warning me about bad men who rode on steel, that could only have meant my encounter with Bruno and Clarence so many years ago. Rand Stokes and Uncle Boogie still haunt me to this day. They were good souls who were murdered. I don't regret my vengeance against Bruno and Clarence. I often wondered if Claire knew what I did.

I visited Claire many years later. She was studying to become a nun at Basilian Order of St. Josaphat, in Hamtramck, Michigan. When she came to meet me in the lobby she gave me a warm hug. She said, "You never forgot your promise to find a new Tuhta for me, Chris," before I could take the stuffed animal from my coat and give it to her."

Father Rohn smiled, as though he was reassured in his belief of God by my story of Claire's gift, believing more strongly in the mysterious ways of the Lord. "I have goose bumps. She truly has the gift that only come from one source, Mr. Wild."

"Perhaps, but how would we react to such a gift? Would we consider it a curse? I don't know if I could find solace behind the walls of a church. Anyway, while I was in Hamtramck, I went to Stosh's Polish Market to see him and repay the money I owed him. But I found the market burned to the ground. Nothing in that old neighborhood had survived urban blight. I don't know what happened to Stosh, I wish I did. I needed to thank him for all he had done to help me.

When I drove away from the intersection of Mulberry and Vine there were three travelers huddled below the Chinese elm tree in the vacant field where Rand and Uncle Boogie took their last breaths. The men were attending a small fire that was heating a coffee can filled with slumgullion. They invited me to join them and share their meal. I told them I had visited the camp many years earlier. The tree and the field were special to me.

Before I left, I gave them the fifty dollars I owed Stosh.   I knew Stosh would approve, so I considered my debt paid."

"What ever happened to Fritz, Sean, and Henry Boudreaux? Did you ever see them again?" he asked.

"Sadly, Fritz was placed in a convalescent home in Tower back in the early nineties when he could no longer care for himself. He was like so many of the Greatest Generation having lost all of his friends and family over time. On a cold spring day, while the ice on Tower Pond was breaking up, he put on his moose foot for the last time and walked out on the pond. He fell through the fragile ice and drowned. At that time I was on the road doing a story on spring trout fishing in Minnesota. I found out about his death a year later, but I think of him often.

Sean, on the other hand, got drafted while I was in Vietnam. His original orders would have sent him there, too, if not for him approaching an Army Chaplin who intervened. The Fitzpatrick family had already lost Charlie, so Sean shouldn't have been issued orders to go to 'Nam. Instead, he went to Germany. He met a young girl, fell in love, and got married. They came back to the States and had two children. But his marriage only lasted a few years. He remarried, got divorced again, remarried for a third time, and had two more children. He's living a good life having retired from the Walter and May Reuther UAW Center where he worked for thirty years. The UAW bought Lou Maxon's retreat, and turned it in to a multimillion-dollar union education facility, the biggest employer in Chandlerville.

Do you remember me telling you about the party I was at, back in the summer of '67? There was John Veihl, Charlie Fitzpatrick, and Dean Wilderdpin sitting with Spark Fallon, and me?" I asked.

"Yes. How did they fare in Vietnam?" he asked.

"Dean and John were killed in Vietnam too. So three of those friends paid the ultimate over there. Chandlerville has never been the same since their deaths."

"You have lost much in your life, Mr. Wild. I will have my congregation pray for their souls at Sunday mass." He made the sign of the cross.

I continued with my story. "Henry Boudreaux became a Green Beret after we parted ways at Fort Gordon. I looked up his family in the Gonzales phone book while I was in Baton Rouge in 1987. I called, and spoke to his mother. She told me he was sent to Vietnam and died in a battle near Dak To, November 11th, 1967, on a hill called, 823. I was crushed to emptiness. We were only a half-mile apart on the very same day when I was on Hill 724. Mrs. Boudreaux said Henry was awarded the Medal of Honor after he saved four soldiers from his platoon when he dove on a hand grenade that would have killed everyone around him. I knew Henry would do something like that, that was how he was. She said he wrote home often and always spoke about me. He told her if I was ever to come to Gonzales, and he wasn't there, she should make me a grand crawfish boil so I could see what I had missed when we didn't make it there after AIT. I couldn't bring myself to visit the Boudreauxes, or his fiancé, Dele. I was too devastated to witness their broken hearts.

The only times I revisited Chandlerville was for three funerals. The first was for my father who died in 1984. I got to the VA hospital in Allen Park before he died of cancer. Even as I held his hand when he took his last breath, I never told him I was a soldier in Vietnam. There wasn't enough time before he died. When my brother, Denis, handed mom a folded American flag at the end of the funeral I wept. I was proud of him for being a veteran. To this day I wished I had told him I was once a soldier. I believe he would have been proud of me.

After his funeral, I visited the graves of Charlie Fitzpatrick and John Veihl. Dean Wilderspin had been buried in a Flint cemetery. It took me a long afternoon to find his grave.

I went to the mouth of the Rainy River before I left town. I took the letter Charlie Fitzpatrick wrote to me, read it aloud, and burned it, letting its ashes fall into the river. That was the best I could do to keep the promise I made to Sean so many years earlier.

I never told mom I had been a soldier. My brother, Denis, knew how to get a hold of me but only if it was an emergency. I was at home in Brookings when he called, June of 1998. He said mom was dying, and her life would end within a couple days. I flew back to Detroit, rented a car, and sped for Chandlerville. I got a ticket for speeding outside of town. The state cop thought I was lying about getting to my mother's deathbed. I arrived an hour after she had died peacefully at home on a hospice bed set up in her favorite place in the library room surrounded by a collection of books she so often urged me to read. Eric Hanover sang, "Amazing Grace," at her funeral.

The third funeral was for my brother, Denis. It was October 20th, 1998, opening day of pheasant season. I came home a month before when I learned he was dying of cancer. He was frightened and desperate to stay alive because he loved his wife, Fran, and his children immensely, and worried about their wellbeing. She was the only woman he ever loved. They took a trip to Sainte-Anne-de-Beaupré Basilica in Quebec, Canada to pray in the cathedral and hope for a miracle. The miracle never came.

After that I was sure I lost my faith in God. Why shouldn't I have? Some of the most beautiful people I had ever known died without any Godly help or intervention. Some of those souls died horrible deaths. Where was God's mercy, Father? How could he let them die when there are so many that are not deserving of life. The killers, and rapists, and abuser of the living often are not punished. When Mike Breshears suffered his tragic accident after he returned home, how could God let that happen to him? He was a good soldier, and person, and paid his dues on Hill 724. I have struggled all my life with the idea that God has a plan for all of us, and he works in mysterious ways. The only mystery I see is how he allows all of the evil in the world to exist, turning his back on those who have so much to live for. I suppose I'll never understand, but I have hope because sometimes there are small miracles. Like me finding you, Father."

Father Rohn watched and listened respectfully all while I ranted. Probably because he was used to hearing this sort of discourse in a confessional, and needing to be strong and wise to logic that sometimes is blasphemous.

"You have lived through many loves in life, Mr. Wild. You have been blessed by those good souls who left their mark on you. Good marks." He rose from his chair and stood at my side. "Now, tell me the reason why you reached out to me personally. I feel I know you now that I've heard you tell me of your life for these past two days. Why me?"

It was time, he knew it, and so did I. I asked him to bring my night bag to my bed. I reached inside and drew out an old photo. "Come closer, Father. I'll show you why." When he stood near my bedside, I pulled him close, and dragged my fingers gently across his face. "Manouge, manouge... Do you remember, Kristof?" I whispered.

Father Kristof Rohn's face brightened from the ancient memory, catapulted from the depths of his mind to the present. He leaned closer when I held the tattered photo of a blond woman holding a young boy on her lap in a field of black-eyed Susans, the photo I had been carrying with me for nearly fifty years. He studied the photo carefully. Tears began to well in his eyes at the distant memory that now resurfaced from the day we met. He reached for my face to feel the split in my chin, and then his similar chin.

We wept over the reunion of father and child. I told him I promised long ago I would never give up looking for him. All he could say was, "I remember, Father. I remember," while he cried.

My son put his arms around me and held me as though I was a child again, a child who had gone most of his life searching for a miracle until he found one.

A man should never die alone, especially an old soldier. He promised he would stay with me until the time when my life would cease, and he did.

At rest.

Sergeant Bob Watkowiak

Lieutenant Levie Isaacks

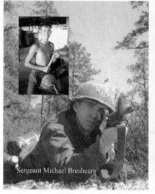

Sergeant Michael Breshears

Sergeant Michael Fitzpatrick

CHRISTOPHER CHAGNON
AUTHOR

Christopher Chagnon was born February 19, 1951, in Bad Axe, Michigan. He has written two best selling novels, The Dregs of Presque Isle and The Ghosts of Presque. The Soldiers of Presque Isle is book three of, *The Chandlerville Chronicles* trilogy. He is an award-winning short story writer and photographer living with Nannette, his wife of forty-five years, in Presque Isle County, near Onaway, Michigan. He manages time to hunt, fish, and play guitar or drums in a rock and roll band when he is not working on a new novel, short story or image.

35704194R00195

Made in the USA
Middletown, DE
12 October 2016